VENGEANCE OF A SLAVE

V.M. SANG

To my little sister
Cheryl Williams
Thanks for being you.

OTHER BOOKS BY V.M. SANG

Fantasy

The Wolves of Vimar Series
Book 1 The Wolf Pack
Book 2 The Never-Dying Man
Book 3 Wolf Moon

Elemental Worlds
The Stones of Earth and Air
The Stones of Fire and Water

Non-Fiction

Viv's Family Recipes

AD 70

T he Romans arrived across the river and lined up all the
men. They took every tenth one to be made an example
of, and then went into the woods and cut down trees.

Soldiers pushed Adelbehrt along with the rest of the popu-
lation to the field to watch. The commander of the Romans
told them they must see what happened to those who challenged the might of Rome, even though they were not in the
Empire. Rome must exact punishment for the raid on
Mogontiacum.

Adelbehrt understood little of what had happened, but he
knew a man named Julius Civilis had led a rebellion against
Rome, and the Roman Legions on the Rhenus went to put it
down. He knew some men took advantage while the soldiers
were away and launched their own attacks across the Rhenus,
and even laid siege to the town of Mogontiacum. He understood the legions coming back from the north relieved the
siege and now the Romans had come to punish them. What
he did not understand was why.

Adelbehrt tried to hold back the tears pricking his eyes.
His mother stood next to him, holding his hand while they
nailed the men to the crosses they had made from the trees

they had cut down. Women screamed when they saw what was happening to their menfolk. One woman tried to rush to her husband, but a Roman soldier hit her with the flat of his gladius. She fell to the ground crying.

The Romans held the chosen men apart from the rest of the village. A soldier took the first man and forced him onto the cross, which lay on the ground. The victim kicked and shouted, but the soldiers pinned him down. A man came over with nails and a hammer.

The man on the cross began to struggle again as he saw the approaching soldier. Another soldier held the man's arm still as the man with the hammer positioned the nail, then raised it. He brought it down hard onto the nail head. The sound of the nail ripping through flesh and bone assailed Adelbehrt's ears. The man screamed—a dreadful sound to the ears of the child. The man screamed again as the soldier drove another nail through his other wrist; then he passed out.

The soldiers nailed five men to crosses and the air filled with the metallic scent of blood. Adelbehrt did not know whether to hold his breath, close his eyes, or cover his ears. Screams of the men mingled with those of the women.

The sixth man's turn arrived. Adelbehrt heard his mother give a quiet sob. This was his father. When the soldiers laid him on the cross, his father did not struggle. He knew it would be futile. The soldier with the nails approached. Adelbehrt saw his father close his eyes and take a deep breath. When the nail pierced his flesh, his body tensed and he let out a soft moan, but he did not scream.

Adelbehrt felt his chest swell with pride. *My father is braver than the others. He didn't scream in spite of the pain.*

He looked up at his mother standing calmly and with dignity, knowing hysterics would not help her husband, nor her small family. Seeing the pain in her eyes, Adelbehrt's fists clenched at his side and his breathing quickened as he looked again at the soldiers, now raising the crosses to an upright position. These men had killed his father. His father had been innocent of the raids. He had not taken any part, but the Romans did not care. They just wanted to punish someone— to make someone a scapegoat—so others would learn not to attack the might of Rome.

The boy pushed back the tears forming in his eyes. He could hear his little sister crying as she hung onto their mother's leg, burying her face in her skirts, but she had only four summers, so she could be excused. His baby brother slept in his mother's arms, ignorant of what happened around him. *He'll never know his father,* the boy thought, looking up at the baby. He closed his eyes to force back the tears. He would never see his father again after today, either.

He forced himself to look at the crosses, searching for the one on which the Romans had nailed his father. He knew it would be the last chance he had of seeing him. He caught his father's eyes. In spite of the pain in them, his father gave a half smile and mouthed, "Look after your mother and sister."

Adelbehrt was six, and the eldest, so he had to show courage. A slight breeze ruffled his ash-blonde hair and he raised his hand to push it back out of his eyes. He didn't want to see the horrible death his father was undergoing, but something inside told him he owed it to him to watch and remember. A tear trickled down his cheek, and he brushed it away. He must stay strong. He was now the man of the family.

After the soldiers had lifted all the crosses, the people turned away to return to their homes. Some women tried to rush to their men, but the Romans beat them away. They would allow no one to try to rescue the men. They formed a circle around the crucifixes and stood with gladii drawn.

As the boy and his family walked sadly away from the field of death, a legionnaire approached his mother. She stopped and shook him off as he touched her arm.

"These are your children?" he asked in their language.

His mother looked at him, and her lip curled. "Of course."

The legionnaire reached out to Adelbehrt and touched his hair. The boy pulled back, not wanting this man, who had been complicit in his father's death, to touch him. He shivered as the strange man smiled at him. The boy thought he looked like a wolf.

The legionnaire spoke to his mother again. "I've never seen such pale hair. I see your little girl also has it. They'll make a fortune on the block."

Their mother looked at him in confusion. "What do you mean, 'on the block'?"

"Oh, we're taking a few of you as slaves. We always need more and it will teach you not to attack Rome in future."

"You're taking us as slaves?"

The man laughed. "Oh, not you. Just these two children. You're not valuable, but these …"

"No! You can't take my children," cried the boy's mother. "Take me, but leave my children alone. You've taken my husband and put him to death. Isn't that enough?" She grabbed onto Adelbehrt and his sister, nearly dropping the baby as she did so.

The legionnaire pushed her away and grabbed the children by their arms. The boy struggled, understanding this man intended to take him and his sister away from their mother. The legionnaire pushed them in front of him, toward where a group of crying children and screaming mothers stood.

His mother's composure broke, and she began to scream along with the others as she tried to wrest her two children from the officer. It was to no avail.

Seeing his mother crying broke Adelbehrt's resolve and he broke into sobs, struggling against the legionnaire. He was no match for the strong Roman soldier though, and the man pushed him towards where more soldiers held other prisoners.

No matter how much he struggled, he could not escape the firm grip of the soldier holding him. He turned and tried to bite. The man laughed and said something in Latin to him that he did not understand. His mother tried to come to him, having handed the baby to a neighbour, but a centurion knocked her to the ground.

Adelbehrt heard him speaking to her in their language. "Don't try that again or you'll regret it. Your tribe deserves all the punishment we mete out after your attack on us. Those children will bring a fortune with their light hair. Never seen hair like that. Almost white. They'll go mad for them in Rome."

He kicked out at the soldier, who then picked him up. Adelbehrt turned to bite his neck, but the man wore armour so he kicked at the man's hips. The soldier laughed and held the boy tighter.

Adelbehrt understood it would be unlikely they would escape and that, in all likelihood, he and his sister would be separated. Would some rich Roman buy them? What would happen to them when they were no longer pretty children?

The legionnaire carried the two children to where Adelbehrt saw a small group of others being guarded by more soldiers. This group consisted mainly of young boys and men over the age of ten, with a few of the prettier teenage girls. He could see no more small children in the group.

One of the girls, whom they knew quite well as she lived near to them, came and picked his sister up, soothing the sobbing child as best she could.

"Hush, hush," she whispered to the little girl. "I'll take care of you and your brother. I'm sure no one will hurt you."

"They killed my father," Adelbehrt sniffed and wiped his nose with his hand, smearing it over his face as he wiped his eyes.

"Yes, but they were punishing him for the attack on their city. You haven't done anything, so they won't hurt you."

"My father hadn't done anything either, yet they still killed him. Why are they taking us from our mother and little brother?"

"You're both very pretty children, you know. They haven't seen anyone with hair as light as yours, and they think you'll bring them a lot of money."

"Then we're to be slaves?"

"Yes, I'm afraid so. I am, too, and these others. They've taken all the boys of an age that might decide to take revenge, as well as a few of us girls."

His mother managed to break away and she rushed towards the little group of slaves, calling out his name. "Adelbehrt, Adelbehrt. Look after Avelina. Don't let anyone hurt her."

"I won't, Mamma. I'll take good care of her. Odila's here. She'll help us."

They crossed the river to the Roman fort of Mogontiacum. The soldiers lifted the children from the boat and a legionnaire gripped their arms, raising a bruise on Adelbehrt's biceps. He looked towards Avelina, who was sobbing and sucking her thumb. He tried to pull away to go to her, but the soldier holding him yanked him back.

Walls surrounded the fort, all built of stone. Adelbehrt looked wide-eyed at the defences. The village where he lived had been defended by a wooden palisade. The gate through which they entered Mogontiacum soared over them. Two towers stood at either side of the gate. Adelbehrt's eyes opened wide as they passed through the archway.

How did the men who came to raid here think they could get past these walls and gates?

Barracks stood to the left as they emerged from the gloom of the gate. A large building occupied the centre of a courtyard with another smaller one behind it. On the opposite side of the large building were more buildings.

The soldiers ushered the group of captives to a walled compound beyond the barracks and locked them in.

He understood he and his sister would probably be bought by different people, and wondered how he could fulfil his promise to his mother that he would look after her. Adelbehrt's eyes narrowed and he pressed his lips together. They had first crucified his father, a terrible death for the young boy to witness, then taken him from his family, home and friends. He thought he would also have his sister taken from him, so he subsumed his sorrow and fear by building his hatred of his captors.

Avelina had stopped crying and clung to Odila. He was glad of that, but wondered what would happen when she was not only taken from her mother, but from him too. Where would they take them to be sold? Here or elsewhere? Maybe even to Rome itself? What was his mother doing? Was there any chance there would be a rescue party? Could he make a break, somehow rescue his sister and get back across the river? All these questions spiralled through his head as he sat in the compound.

A legionnaire brought some food for them to eat and water to drink. He picked at the food, but drank some water. Odila tried to persuade Avelina to eat something, but the little girl still sobbed between the small mouthfuls the older girl managed to get into her mouth. Eventually, she fell asleep in Odila's arms while still eating. The day's events had all been too much for her. Adelbehrt himself began to feel tired, but before he went to sleep, he enumerated the reasons he hated the Romans:

They crucified my father; they took my family away from me; they took my home from me; they took my friends from me, and; they will take my sister from me.

The next day Adelbehrt woke wondering where he was. Then it all came flooding back. Tears again pricked at his eyelids, but he determined he would never again cry because of a Roman. One day, he would have revenge for all they had done to him. One day, he would be free again. He would also find his sister and free her too, should they be separated. Wherever the Romans took her, he would find her. After that, he would try to get back to his home across the Rhenus. He did not think about how he would carry out these plans; he would just take any chance he could when it came.

They sat in the compound all that day. The sun beat down on them, and all the slaves drank thirstily when the Romans brought water. The commander of the fort came and looked them over. He took a couple of the girls out and marched them over to the large building in the centre of the fort. Adelbehrt wondered what was going to happen to them. Were they going to be sold separately from the rest?

He thought about it for a while, then forgot about them as he tried to comfort his sister, who had begun crying again. "Don't cry, Avelina. Everything will be all right. Somehow we'll get away and go back to Mamma."

The little girl looked at him trustingly, and a half-smile appeared on her face. "Back to Mamma? I miss Mamma."

"Yes, so do I. It might not be soon, but one day we'll escape these horrid Romans."

"I don't like the Romans. They killed Papa."

"No, I don't like them either. We'll get away sometime, I promise you."

He did not know how or when he would be able to keep his promise to the little girl, but he determined to do so, whatever the cost. He smiled to see his words had comforted Avelina somewhat, that she had dried her eyes and sat more quietly.

Towards evening, the two girls whom the commander had taken returned to the compound. They entered the compound in tears. Adelbehrt wanted to ask them what had happened, but Odila kept him away from them. He wondered why, but she managed to distract him by talking about Avelina.

The little girl had once again started to cry, seeing the tears of the two older girls, so he did not find out what caused their upset. He did notice one of the young men, who had been courting one of the girls before they were taken prisoner, became very angry and some of his friends held him back as he tried to attack one of the Roman guards.

Two days passed. Avelina cried less, but called for their mother in the night, every night. She also began sucking her thumb again. She had almost stopped that childish habit before their capture. Adelbehrt also missed their mother, but he stuck to his resolve not to allow the Romans to make him cry. Even when the tears came to his eyes, he managed to prevent them from falling.

Each day, the commander took one or two girls and they always returned crying. Sometimes, one of the legates or centurions took a girl. They took Odila on the second day. When she came back, Adelbehrt asked her what happened, but she refused to talk of it. She seemed withdrawn after that, and sat in a corner with the other girls, not talking, but staring into space.

On the third day of their captivity, a civilian man came to the compound with the commander of the castrum. He looked the slaves over and called for Adelbehrt and Avelina to be brought to him. He asked a few questions in Latin, which Adelbehrt did not understand, but assumed they were about him and his sister. The man smiled and the two men walked away, talking.

The following morning, some men came and took all the slaves to the baths and stripped them. They washed them thoroughly and took their clothes away. What would happen now? That question soon had an answer.

The men who washed them took them to a building in the

market at the opposite side of the fort. They stood in a room, bare except for a table and chair under a window at one side. Guards stood by the only door, making escape impossible. A tall man entered and sat behind the table.

The man who looked them over the previous day came in. He ordered the men to take the girls out, with the exception of Avelina. Avelina cried out to Odila and tried to run to her, but one of the slaves who had bathed them, grabbed hold of her as she ran past. The Romans had taken seven girls from the village and, shortly afterwards, a slave brought two of the less pretty ones back into the room. Odila was not one of them.

Adelbehrt heard them saying the others had been bought by a brothel. He did not know what a brothel was, and the others deflected his questions when he asked. He decided, when he saw the looks of relief on the faces of the remaining two girls, that it could not be a good place. Something else to hate the Romans for. He mentally added 'taking Odila to a brothel' to his list of reasons to hate them.

The man in charge hung a board around the neck of each slave. Adelbehrt later learned that it gave information about the slave, including his likelihood of running away or committing suicide, as well as his name and where he came from.

They took the slaves out one at a time. He could hear people calling out something outside, but could not understand the words. When the slaves returned, the man who had taken them out, escorted them to the table by the window. People came into the room, handed over money to the dispassionate man sitting there, and then left with their purchase.

Eventually, their turn arrived. The slave merchant had left them until the last, and as they were led outside together, Adelbehrt realised they were being sold as a single lot. He could breathe once more. He could keep his promise to his mother to look after his sister.

Warm air embraced them and, as the sun shone on his

naked skin, Adelbehrt blushed at being nude in front of the bustling crowd filling the marketplace. He looked around and wondered at the large numbers of people still left, since all the slaves had been sold except the two of them.

The auctioneer picked Avelina up and another man did the same with Adelbehrt and held them so everyone could see the two children. The auctioneer spoke to the crowd and pointed at the children's blonde hair. A few *aahs* floated forward from the crowd, then people began to call out things. Adelbehrt decided the people were making bids for them.

They were a popular lot, if the number of bidders was anything to go by, but soon almost everyone dropped out, leaving just two men in the bidding war. Eventually, one of them held up his hand and turned away, thus indicating he, too, had dropped out. The man who had brought themout to the market place led them back into the room, and gave them plain tunics to put on.

Their purchaser walked to the table and handed over a purse of money, which the cashier counted carefully, nodded, and handed a paper to the new owner, who then came over, took each by a hand and led them out.

Adelbehrt looked at this mane He was tall, clean-shaven, with an aquiline nose and dark hair and even darker eyes. He did not look unkind, but was still the sort of man you would not want to annoy. He spoke to the children in a light tenor voice, but they did not understand him, so he called to a young man standing near the door and spoke a few words to him.

"This man says he's your master now and wants to know how old you are," the man interpreted.

"I have six summers and my sister four," answered Adelbehrt quietly, looking down at his feet.

The interpreter spoke to their new master in Latin and then interpreted the next few sentences.

"He's on his way back to Britannia and you're going to

accompany him there. You're to call him 'Dominus'. That means 'Master' or 'Sir'. You now have your first word of Latin. You'll soon learn to speak it though, so don't worry."

"I'm called Adelbehrt, and my sister is Avelina." Adelbehrt told him, not knowing his name had been on the scroll round his neck.

"Well, Adelbehrt, you'll be all right, just as long as you do as you're told and show proper deference to your master and mistress. Good luck." With that, he left them.

"What's going to happen now?" whispered Avelina.

'We're going to Britannia. We must call the man who has bought us 'Dominus' and do as he says."

Avelina began to cry. "Where's Britannia? You said we'd go back to Mamma. You said you'd escape and take us back."

"I don't know where Britannia is, but we *will* escape. Somehow, we'll get away, but I can't promise you it will be soon."

2

The children rode in a wagon, and their master rode a horse. A pretty, chestnut pony trotted behind, tied to the wagon. Adelbehrt found out the Dominus had bought it as a present for his son, just as he had bought the young boy and his sister for his wife and daughter. Realisation began to dawn on the boy that he and his sister were of no more worth to the Dominus than the pony.

A second wagon followed, driven by a slender slave accompanying the Dominus. Another slave, older, drove their wagon. Boxes of goods filled both.

The large wagon the children rode in bumped along the pebbly roads and the children were joggled this way and that, along with it. They sat between a large number of crates and amphorae, squashed in, as comfortably, as they could. The discomfort started Avelina crying again, and Adelbehrt comforted her as best he could, but he was only a little boy himself. Tears sprang to his eyes, but he quickly brushed them away. He would *not* cry. Not in front of the Romans.

Adelbehrt worried too because he could not understand the Dominus. His new master spoke Latin all the time. The boy sat in the wagon, frowning as the Dominus stopped the wagons and spoke to the slave driving theirs. The older slave got down, and the Dominus took his place on the driving seat. The slave approached the back Why the line break here? It's still the same sentence!of their wagon. He looked quite old to Adelbehrt, but he was in fact, only in his late thirties. He had short brown hair, brown eyes, and a smiling mouth.

"The Dominus told me to come and speak to you," he said in their language. "You can't understand Latin yet, and I can speak your language, so I'm to help you."

He smiled at the pair, and although Avelina stared at him with round eyes, Adelbehrt managed a weak smile in return.

"My name's Marcus," the man went on, "and I'm a slave, like you." He jumped onto the wagon between the crates and amphorae that filled much of its bed, and sat down. "I think the Dominus wants me to help you both to learn some Latin so you'll be able to understand what he wants of you, and also for when we get back to Londinium. You'll need to understand the Domina and the little Domina when we get there."

Adelbehrt looked at his sister, who once more sucked her thumb. "I'm worried about Avelina. She'd stopped sucking her thumb some time ago, but now she's started again. She's hardly talking, either. She used to be such a chatterbox before."

Marcus looked at the little girl and leaned forward to stroke her hair. She drew back and huddled against Adelbehrt, eyes wide with fear.

Marcus studied her for a few minutes. "I think she'll be alright eventually. It's a terrible thing for a little girl to be taken from her home at only four. That's how old you said she is? It can't have been much better for you, though, Adelbehrt. You're only—what?—six?"

Adelbehrt nodded in reply. "I miss my mother and baby brother." He looked down at the planks of the wagon. "And my father too, of course. But he's dead." Tears sprang to his eyes and he blinked them away before they could fall. He looked at Marcus, eyes gleaming with unshed tears. "I have to be strong to look after my sister, you see."

Marcus looked a nice man, Adelbehrt thought. Could he trust him though? After a few minutes, the boy decided he would trust him. After all, Marcus was a slave too, and he and Avelina would need all the support they could get against the Romans.

The wagon continued to bounce along the road, making for an uncomfortable ride. The other wagon followed, resulting in slow progress.

Inns or mail posts had grown up at regular intervals along the straight roads they travelled. The children slept with the slaves each night, Marcus and another man called Paulus. Paulus was everything Marcus was not. A taciturn man whom Adelbehrt thought did not like children very much. At least, he had as little to do with them as possible.

Marcus on the other hand continued to be friendly and talked a lot to them. He told them the Dominus was a merchant who lived in one of the cities of Britannia. He called the town Londinium and told Adelbehrt it was in the south of Britannia. The Dominus, he explained, had married a British woman whom he had met on one of his trips to Britannia, and he settled there with her. They had two children so far, a son of seven and a daughter of four. Marcus thought Avelina would be for the daughter.

She would learn how to wait on a young Roman lady, while Adelbehrt would probably be a house slave and learn how to wait tables, and be taught other duties. The Domina would most probably want to show her new slaves off to friends of the family.

"They will all be jealous that the Domina has a new slave," he told them.

"Why?" asked Adelbehrt, curious.

"You are very attractive children, you know," Marcus told him. "The Dominus was very pleased to be able to buy you. Your light hair is unusual. Then there's the fact that you are children, and the Domina will be able to train you herself. That's always a good thing. She can teach you how to do things in her own, preferred way."

Adelbehrt nodded, and Avelina continued to suck her thumb.

Marcus began to teach the children a little Latin as their journey across Gaul progressed. They would have to learn this new language as it was the only one spoken in the household, or in most of Londinium for that matter. Some of the local barbarians, he told them, spoke their own language, but it was not like Adelbehrt and Avelina's language.

As they travelled, he patiently pointed out things and gave the children the Latin word for them. He laughed at Adelbehrt's attempts at pronunciation, and made him repeat the words until he had them right. Avelina sat sucking her thumb during these lessons, watching with big round eyes, but she said nothing.

Adelbehrt struggled a bit with Latin, but he tried hard. He wanted to be able to understand what the Dominus and his wife wanted him to do. He had heard tales before the Romans took him prisoner of beatings if slaves did not do as they were told quickly enough, and he became afraid it might happen to him and his sister if they could not understand what the Domina asked them to do.

By the time they reached the coast, he had learned quite a few words, although he could not yet speak Latin beyond that.

Adelbehrt marvelled at the Roman roads, in spite of not wanting to think of anything good of his captors. The Romans built their roads straight as the crow flies and they paved the surfaces, unlike the roads where he came from.

When they left Mogantiacum, they travelled west and

continued in that direction until they came to the city of Durocortorum, in Gaul. They stayed there for a couple of nights for the Dominus to do some business, so Marcus told him. After that, they took a road in a northward direction. The wagons trundled on for just over three weeks, until they reached the northern coast of Gaul.

Adelbehrt stood looking over the crashing waves. He had never seen any stretch of water so huge. He could not see the other side. He had thought the Rhenus big, but he had never imagined a stretch of water so large the other side was invisible. Marcus called it the Oceanus Britannicus, and told him they were going to cross it.

This frightened him, but he kept his fears to himself, partly out of pride, but also because he did not want to transfer his fears to his sister. Her tears had dried up a bit towards the latter part of the journey through Gaul, but she was still not the happy, chatty little girl he had known in their home village. She had withdrawn into herself somewhat, Adelbehrt thought, and she still clung to him at night as he chanted his ritual.

"I hate the Romans. They crucified my father; they took my family away from me;they took my home from me; they took my friends from me; they put Odila in a brothel." Then he added, "They took my freedom from me." As he stood on a dock in the town of Gesoriacum early the next morning, waiting to get on the big boat taking them across this terrifying stretch of water, he realised if they did escape, a return to his own land would be nearly impossible. How could he cross this vast expanse of water again?

As he thought these thoughts, it began to drizzle, as if the sky itself lamented his plight. He almost cried again, but remembered his vow to himself that he would not allow the

Romans to make him cry ever again. He put his arm around Avelina.

"Don't be frightened." He spoke as much for his own benefit as that of the little girl. "The Romans cross this water all the time. I'm sure we'll be safe."

Avelina crept closer, as though she did not believe him, and he felt her shivering. The drizzle felt cool and their thin tunics did little to keep them warm. This was supposed to be summer, he realised, but the sun seemed to have forgotten. It was as cool as autumn.

They had to wait until the oxen that drew the wagons, the Dominus's horse and the little pony, had been taken aboard the ship before they boarded. A large merchant vessel was to take them across the stretch of water to Britannia.

To the children the sea looked massive. The Rhenus that they had lived beside, although a large river, did not prevent them from seeing the opposite bank. Here, the sea seemed to go on forever. Adelbehrt knew it did not do so because the Romans crossed it regularly to Britannia; nevertheless, the young lad felt it a daunting task to cross this vast sea.

In any event, the crossing turned out to be not as bad as he thought. The wind came from the south, and although it made it cold on the merchant ship, it blew them steadily towards the land over the sea. He stood in the stern of the ship, looking towards the land as they left it—the land he would probably never see again. The wind blew his hair back as it filled the sails, blowing them to a new life.

Adelbehrt suddenly felt an excitement course through him. Yes, he was a slave and, as such, had become the property of the man who had bought him, but Marcus had told him he was a good master, and did not often beat his slaves. True, he had taken more notice of the pony's welfare than that of the children on the journey so far, but Adelbehrt reasoned it had probably cost more than they had.

As the land disappeared, he felt the swell of the waves

driving the deck up and down. He smiled. He found the motion pleasant. The drizzle still fell, but he did not think of taking any shelter. He wanted to watch the sailors move about the ship and pull ropes to adjust the sails. They seemed to work as a unit, knowing exactly what to do. This life, he thought would be an exciting one. More than sailing on the Rhenus. Fishermen went out to catch fish back home, but this was much more exciting! The sailors had to overcome more dangers here and that idea thrilled rather than frightened him.

Avelina stood with him for much of the first part of the journey. To his surprise and delight, she started asking questions. He could not answer them of course, as she asked about the land they approached. He took her to the front of the ship ('the bow' he heard the sailors call it) so they could see the land when it appeared.

After a while, however, he became weary of standing. The drizzle had stopped and he sat down on a coil of rope next to Avelina, who shivered again. Marcus approached and sat beside the children.

"What's Britannia like?" Adelbehrt asked the older man.

"Depends where you mean, lad. Where we're to land, there are tall white cliffs. The town where we'll dock is called Dubris. It has a port at the mouth of a river. Then we'll pass through rolling green hills. You won't see many rivers in that part of the country, at least not like the ones you're used to. There are a few small ones—little more than streams really. About five or six days into the journey, though, we'll come to a large river called Thamesis."

"How far will we travel before we come to where the Dominus lives?"

"The Dominus lives with his family in Londinium and, in the summer, in a villa in the country. Londinium is on the banks of the Thamesis. He'll go there first, I expect, but he won't stay long this time."

Marcus smiled amiably at the boy. "As you've probably

gathered, he's a merchant and he'll want to trade some of his goods before leaving the city. Last year there was a storm and lightning struck one of the buildings. It caused a fire that destroyed, or badly damaged, many buildings and homes. Some of the goods he has will cheer up the people and, after that, the rebuilding, so he'll want to take advantage of that. People lost a lot of stuff that needs replacing."

Marcus stood and walked to the rail of the ship, where he turned and leaned back. "The Dominus' home wasn't burned, but he'll go to his villa in the country after he's finished his business. The family always stays there in the summer. It's common in Rome for the rich to go to their villas during the summer to escape the heat of the city. It isn't so important here in Britannia because the summers aren't so hot, but the Dominus likes to keep this status symbol, even here in Britannia. Anyway, there's the harvest to get in and it's pleasant in the countryside."

Adelbehrt chatted to Marcus, who taught him some new Latin words, until the Dominus called for him. The children continued to sit looking towards the horizon, waiting to catch a glimpse of their new home.

Adelbehrt occasionally wandered around the boat, getting in the way of the sailors, most of whom cursed him. He knew they were curses, although he couldn't understand them. Not all the sailors cursed though. One old man beckoned him over and let him help haul the ropes to raise more sails. Adelbehrt was thrilled doing this.

Eventually, after many hours aboard (Adelbehrt couldn't really tell how long), a dark line appeared on the horizon. Adelbehrt thought he saw clouds at first, but Marcus, who had come back to stand by them, told him it was the coastline of their new home.

Slowly it crept toward them, until they could make out details. First, they saw the white cliffs Marcus had described and next, the green of the lush grass growing on the top. They made out the shapes of the two Pharos, one on each hill on either side of the river on which Dubris stood.

As the weather had now cleared, and the sun had not yet set, they negotiated the entrance to the docks with ease and soon drew alongside the wharf. The Dominus disembarked first and oversaw the unloading of the cargo.

Adelbehrt did not know the contents of most of the boxes and crates, but suspected some might contain clothes for sale, as well as new ones from Rome for his wife and children, and goods to replace those people had lost in the fire in Londinium. It looked as though the slaves were considered cargo along with everything else, as they were the last to leave the ship.

So, this is Britannia. Wide-eyed, the boy looked around as he descended the gangplank.

The town was small, built around the docks on the river. A few ships lay in the harbour, but none as large as the merchant ship that had brought them here. A few people walked around and some stopped to stare at the ship tied up at the wharf.

Adelbehrt took his sister's hand as Marcus led them away from the ship towards what turned out to be an inn. Since the crossing took the best part of a day, the Dominus had decided to stay the night in Dubris before leaving the following morning.

They would take a road called Watling Street, Marcus told them. It went to Londinium and then across the country to the city of Deva in the north. The idea of building such a long road impressed Adelbehrt, even though he had no idea where Deva was. In the north of Britannia, Marcus told him when he asked, and that was a long way away.

The Dominus led them to a large inn in the small town. The elderly innkeeper knew him and greeted him warmly. The Dominus had a room to himself, of course, but the slaves, including the children, slept in the main room of the inn.

"I hate the Romans," murmured Adelbehrt before he fell

asleep, cuddling Avelina. "They crucified my father; they took my family away from me; they took my home from me; they took my friends from me;they put Odila in a brothel, and; they took my freedom from m*e.*" This time he added, "They took my homeland away from me."

With that, the boy fell asleep.

The next morning, the Dominus decided they must make an early start. After breaking their fast on some bread and a bit of cheese, the children climbed onto one of the wagons with the goods the Dominus had brought with him to trade, and the little group of travellers set off along the road towards Londinium.

The road ran absolutely straight, just like those in Gaul. It had been an ancient trackway used for millennia by the native Britons, but when the Romans came, they paved it for their own use. Adelbehrt could not help but marvel at how the Romans had built the roads. He thought it a great improvement on the tracks in the land of his birth; they became muddy in times of rain and sometimes almost impassable, even though they had been constructed with oak timber.

The Dominus led them through a rolling countryside full of lush green, forested hills. Occasionally, small farms and villages appeared along the road. In one area, Marcus told him, they made iron. The men chopped down the trees and used the resulting logs to heat kilns, where they then smelted iron ore.

"Britannia is the most important iron producing country in the empire, you know," he told Adelbehrt.

The travellers continued to follow the road, stopping at inns along the way, as far as the town of Durovernum. Here they stayed for a few days. The Dominus wanted to trade some of his goods in this town, which was larger than the other settlements they had passed. The children grew tired with all of the travelling, and Avelina had started to become fractious. She had learned a bit of Latin as they had progressed and she made use of the words she had learned to complain to Marcus that she wanted to stop travelling and go home.

"Avelina, you won't be able to go home." Marcus knelt down beside the little girl. "You now belong to the Dominus. You will live in his home and wait on his daughter."

"I want to go home to Mama." She broke down in tears and turned to Adelbehrt. "You told me we'd go back to Mama. That we'll escape and go home."

Marcus gently dried her eyes and spoke quietly. "Avelina, my dear, you are a gift for the Dominus' daughter. She's about your age and you'll be a companion to her. You'll like her, I'm sure. She'll teach you some new games that Roman children play."

Avelina stopped sniffling as she looked up at Marcus. "Will she like me?" she asked shyly, speaking in her own tongue.

"Of course she will. You're a very nice little girl. However, you must speak Latin. The Dominus' daughter doesn't understand your language."

"Yes, I … try," the young child stumbled in her new language.

After a couple of days, the Dominus declared he had done all the business he had wanted to in Durovernum, and they set off once again towards Londinium. It was with some trepidation on the part of Adelbehrt, as he knew they were getting close to what would be their eventual home, probably for the rest of their lives, unless they were sold again, of course. That was always a possibility.

Londinium—it had only been founded twenty-seven years previously, but already it had become an important town. The Romans built the only bridge across the river, which the merchant and his wagons were presently crossing.

Marcus pointed out to Adelbehrt the building work on the riverbank. "They're building wharves and jetties there." He spoke in Latin to them more and more, so they would be forced to learn quickly.

"Wharves, jetties?" queried Adelbehrt, scanning the riverbank.

"Places for ships to moor and for them to unload their cargo."

The boy nodded. "They'll be able to bring the Dominus' goods right into the town then, so there will be no need for the long trip from Dubris over the land."

"Quite right." The older man smiled kindly. "Well done, lad."

Adelbehrt felt quite proud at the praise from the man who had taken such an interest in them since their purchase by the Dominus.

He watched carefully to see where they went. To the left,

Adelbehrt could see a large stone building. He enquired what it was.

"That's the governor's palace," Marcus told him, "He has only been governor since last year. His name is Bolanus, I believe. We don't really need to know such things as slaves though. Politics is no concern of ours. We just do as our masters ask, no questions."

Adelbehrt frowned at this. Obey *without* question? What if the Dominus asked him to do something wrong? Must he obey even then? What would happen if he obeyed and got into trouble for it? Like stealing something, for example. Would his innocence be accepted if his master had commanded it?

They proceeded through the town until they reached a large stone house fronting the street. Adelbehrt looked around and noticed that many stone houses comprised this street. It surprised him, He had not seen so many stone houses in his life.

The building to which the Dominus turned had a portico in the centre of the wall, with a covered roof supported by two columns. On either side of the entrance, he noticed two windows. Then the Dominus dismounted his horse, handed the reins to Paulus, and walked towards the portico.

Adelbehrt saw a passageway on the left of the building, leading round the back. The wagons trundled towards this passageway.

"Servants and slaves are not allowed to use the portico," Marcus murmured as they travelled along the passageway towards a yard at the back.

Here, slaves released the oxen from their traces. More slaves took the amphorae of wine and olive oil that had accompanied the children for their entire journey and put them into storage sheds at the side of the yard, and then proceeded to unload the other goods.

Marcus lifted Avelina from the wagon and Adelbehrt jumped down.

"Where do we go now?" asked the boy, his curiosity overcoming any sense of anxiety at being in a new place. He stared around the courtyard.

"We go inside. Come on. Follow me." Marcus led them to the side of the house and in through a door. They entered a large paved open space. It had a large pool with a fountain in the centre, surrounded by pillars. The fountain was not flowing now as the family had gone to the country. Plants and small bushes grew in pots scattered around the area, and the boy saw stone benches for people to sit. Marcus told them this area, the open courtyard within the house, was called the peristylium.

Rooms opened out onto the peristylium. Some, Marcus explained, were bedrooms, but two were dining rooms and one a kitchen.

"What are we going to eat?" Avelina asked, speaking in her own language. She peered towards the kitchen. "There's no one in the kitchen to cook."

"Don't worry, little one," replied the older slave. "There are plenty of shops in the town where we can buy something to eat. I'll take you later and we can get food."

"But you're a slave, Marcus," Adelbehrt pointed out. "How can *you* buy food? What can you use for money? And how can you just go out by yourself?"

Marcus laughed heartily. "Oh, slaves can have money. Visitors to the house often give us tips if we please them. Many slaves save up their money in order to buy their freedom, but it takes a great many years to do so. Others spend it on themselves, and some even manage to save enough to buy slaves of their own."

"That seems odd. Slaves owning slaves," the boy mused aloud, frowning. "Don't slaves feel bad about others losing their freedom to serve them?"

"Some folk are born into slavery and know nothing else. Both my parents were slaves, you know. They came from near where you were captured; that's how I know something of your language. I was born here and as I'm the son of slaves, I too am a slave. I have nowhere else to go except here." The man paused and smiled at Adelbehrt. "The Dominus is a good master. He seldom beats us and we're fed well too. Not all slaves are. Many slaves are treated worse than animals, and are beaten mercilessly for the slightest error. Here, in this house, we're better off than many free men. Look around when you're out in the town and you'll see what I mean."

As Marcus said this, the Dominus strolled through a passageway that led from the peristylium to the rest of the house. "There you are, Marcus. I need you to come and help me with these blasted accounts. We sold quite a lot of stuff in Durovernum and I need to get the money sorted out quickly."

Adelbehrt's eyebrows rose when he heard this—at what he thought the Dominus had said. He was unsure he understood correctly. Surely, a man of the Dominus' standing, a rich merchant at that, would not want a mere slave seeing to his financial affairs? Adelbehrt decided to ask Marcus later.

"Get Paulus to look after the children for a while until it's time for the evening meal," the Dominus told Marcus. "He can get them settled in a bedroom."

The man walked out of the garden and back to the section of the dwelling the children had not yet seen. Marcus hurried to find Paulus.

Paulus came across the peristylium, somewhat reluctantly. He had not been very communicative on the journey. Adelbehrt always felt uncomfortable around the man. He was a tall fellow with unruly brown hair and light-blue eyes. His skin was pockmarked from a childhood illness and a large nose seemed to take up half his face.

Being in his early thirties, he was younger by some years than Marcus, but to Adelbehrt they were both quite old. The boy didn't much like him, although he had no reason for this feeling. He decided he should try to engage in some kind of communication with him as they were both slaves in the same household.

Paulus spoke gruffly to the children. "I've to show you where you'll sleep while we're here." He grunted. "I suppose this room will do. No one else is using it." He pointed to the room to the right of the entrance. "Of course, when we move back here in the winter, the Domina will probably give you other rooms. That's up to her."

"I ask Marcus why slaves not run when they allowed to come and go as they want." Adelbehrt struggled with his Latin. "He say it sometimes because was all slave knew, when born to slave parents. He say sometimes, like us, slaves better off than some not-slaves. I think it better to live free than in captivity, no?"

"Ha!" Paulus replied. "You're young and new to being a slave. Escaped slaves who are re-captured—and they usually are—are branded on their foreheads with the letter F, for fugitive."

"What branding?" Avelina asked. She had begun to respond to her surroundings and people in the last few days. Adelbehrt felt pleased and hoped her recovery would continue.

"They press a red hot iron in the shape of the letter to your head and it leaves a permanent mark, so you're always known as a fugitive," came the reply. He looked almost pleased at the discomfort shown by the children.

"It hurt?" the little girl asked in halting Latin.

"Yes, very much, but it does tend to put slaves off from running away."

Adelbehrt then asked, "But what if slave not caught? You say 'almost always caught.'"

The older man laughed. "They'll be fugitives for the rest of their lives. The Romans never give up. When they're caught, they might be made to wear a collar riveted round their necks that they can't take off. It'd be most uncomfortable and would rub your neck raw, I'm sure." He looked at Adelbehrt sharply. "You aren't thinking of running away, are you? You wouldn't stand a chance, being only a child, and especially with your unusual hair colour. You'd be spotted immediately."

"No," Adelbehrt lied. "Where I go? No can get home over sea."

When he said that about not getting across the sea, Avelina wailed. "But you said we'd go back to Mamma!'" She spoke in their own language and Paulus did not understand.

Adelbehrt put his arm around her and held her close to comfort her. He worried gravely about his little sister. She was still frightened, even if she did seem to be making some recovery.

Paulus ordered them sharply to speak in Latin so he could understand, then sat down on one of the benches in the garden and watched them closely, as though expecting them to make a break for freedom there and then.

No one said much for the rest of the afternoon. It felt warmer than it had the day they crossed the Oceanus Britannicus and they found it quite pleasant sitting there.

Adelbehrt whiled away the time by looking around. Marble flagstones lined the ground and the fountain was shaped like a fish. When on, it would spout water from its mouth into the pond beneath, which had a raised wall surrounding it.

Adelbehrt strolled over to it and sat on the edge, trailing his hand in the water. His eyes stung with the tears he would not allow to fall. They were now such a long way from their home that he could see no way of them ever returning. They would have to speak Latin all the time, and would probably forget their native tongue, and they would never see their family again.

Then his anger reasserted itself and his hatred of the Romans renewed. They were lucky to have found a good master, but that did not overcome his anger at losing his freedom and the brutal killing of his father. He determined to escape, no matter how long it took. He would risk the branding and being a fugitive for the rest of his life. He would also find some way to fight the Romans. There must be people in Britannia who hated the Romans as much as he did. The Romans had come to this country and taken it over. Surely, the native people would be angry about that? He would find them and join them, even if it meant his life.

The day had started to cool when Marcus came back and relieved Paulus, who had said little to them after the first conversation. They left the house through the door where they entered, and went up the passageway between the houses.

As soon as they reached the street, Marcus took hold of Avelina's hand and told Adelbehrt to be sure to stay close. People hurried past in all directions, and the boy understood why Marcus had told him not to stray. He could easily get lost in the bustling crowds.

Marcus led them towards some stalls where he saw people gathering. Here, the older slave bought food for them all. He handed them a kind of flattened bread with some cheese and herbs on it. The children ate with gusto and then drank the watered wine he handed them.

"How long will we stay in Londinium?" Adelbehrt asked as he munched his bread.

"That depends on how the Dominus' business goes. He'll want to sell as much of the wine and olive oil as he can before he goes to the country, as well as the other goods he's brought back, but I don't expect it'll be more than three or four days. The people in Londinium are anxious for such luxury goods. They can't grow olives here, and the grapes don't do very well either, so these things must be imported."

They strolled back to the domus, and when they arrived, Avelina's eyes drooped, so Marcus suggested they go to bed.

Every night, Adelbehrt spoke to Avelina in their own language, hoping she would not forget it. He told her tales of their mother and her love for her children, and reminded the little girl they had a baby brother somewhere across the Oceanus Britannicus. When Avelina fell asleep, Adelbehrt chanted his litany of hate.

❦ 4 ❧

The children spent the next few days wondering what was going to happen and when they would go to the villa. On the fifth day, the Dominus declared he had finished his trading and they should get ready to set off for the country.

The day arrived that Adelbehrt had anticipated with both dread and excitement. What were their new owners going to be like? Where was their new home going to be? Would they like it? Would it be at all like their home by the Rhenus? All these questions passed through his head as they readied themselves for the journey.

At last, with everything prepared, slaves loaded a wagon with the goods the Dominus intended to take to the villa, and hitched the oxen to it. Paulus climbed onto the driving seat. Only one wagon was to travel to the villa and so Marcus sat in the wagon with the children, with the little pony tied to a rail behind.

They passed out of the yard behind the domus, and left the city of Londinium and travelled westwards. The journey seemed long to the two children and it took a couple of days, but eventually they arrived outside a large complex of buildings.

A wall surrounded the buildings, and the Dominus paused outside the gateway. He said something to Marcus, who was now driving, and he stopped the wagon. The Dominus told Paulus to wait and watch the children while he and Marcus entered the gate and passed through a short passage into the villa.

The children heard a cry of pleasure and small feet running. Adelbehrt strained to see if he could pick up anything of what the people said, but he was too far away to hear. He heard childish laughter followed by a woman's voice.

Marcus appeared through the passageway and beckoned to them.

Once in the yard on the other side of the passageway, Adelbehrt saw two children crowding around their father, and a woman holding his arm and smiling up at him.

The Dominus gestured towards the pony Marcus led into the villa and the boy, who had his father's dark hair, and looked about a year older than Adelbehrt, ran towards it with a whoop of pleasure, making the startled pony toss its head. Adelbehrt managed to pick up that the Dominus had told his son he thought he should have a proper horse, not one of those native ponies.

He beckoned Avelina and Adelbehrt forward, and pointed Avelina out to the little girl, who had even darker hair than her brother. The girl was about the same age as Avelina and she clapped her hands with pleasure at having her own slave.

"Take her to your room, Claudia," the woman told her. "She'll sleep on a pallet at the foot of your bed since she's your own personal slave. I'll get someone to bring one into your room soon. I'll help you to train her but, for today, just take her and show her where she's to sleep and you can play for a while."

"And here is your present, Annwyl, my love." The Dominus beckoned Adelbehrt to come forward.

"What beautiful children," Annwyl responded excitedly,

"and such light hair! Where did you find them? I'll be the envy of all my friends with such a beautiful little slave."

The Dominus smiled at his wife. "I was, purely by chance, in Mogantiacum when they were having a slave auction. I was a bit worried because I hadn't been able to find you a present, but then someone told me some children were going to come up and that they were most unusual. When I saw them, I just had to have them for you."

"They're the most perfect present you could have bought for us. It's time Claudia learned how to treat a slave." She stood on her toes and kissed him. "Thank you so much, Lucius."

The Domina called Marcus over. "Take the boy and find him a room. I'll let him rest for today and I'll see him first thing in the morning."

Adelbehrt could now gaze round for the first time. He found himself in a large courtyard with grass and a fountain in the middle. On three sides, a colonnaded walkway with a roof surrounded it. Several rooms and buildings opened off the walkway. The fourth side seemed to be where they kept the wagons and carts.

Marcus led him toward a cluster of rooms to the left of the entrance, one of which proved to be an office of some kind. A woman worked in there and she stopped to regard the newcomers.

"What's this?" she asked.

"A new slave just arrived today," Marcus answered with a smile. "The Dominus bought him in Gaul for the Domina. He thought she'd like him as he's so pretty. There's also a little girl, about four. She's to be the personal slave of the little mistress."

Adelbehrt found this conversation difficult to follow, but picked up a few words here and there, so he knew they were talking about him and his sister.

"I suppose I'd better find him somewhere to sleep then. What about the little girl?"

"As she's to be the personal slave of the little Domina, she'll sleep on a pallet in her room."

The woman nodded briskly.

Marcus left Adelbehrt with the older woman, the housekeeper as he discovered. She looked at the boy. "Turn around." She twirled a finger to demonstrate.

His Latin was good enough for him to understand and he turned slowly on the spot.

The housekeeper eyed him up and down. "You'll need more clothes. I'll see to that, but first you need a bath. I don't suppose you've even had a proper wash since goodness knows when, if ever. Come with me."

Adelbehrt did not fully comprehend what she had said, but she beckoned him to follow her out of the office and back into the courtyard. They crossed to the other side where she entered a room with a pool in the centre. Steam rose from the hot water and the housekeeper indicated to Adelbehrt that he should strip and enter the pool. This he did, and she told him to wash himself all over while she went to find a clean tunic.

Adelbehrt learned there were other bathing rooms that the family visited each day but, as a slave, he only had the use of this one pool. As he discovered later, the other rooms comprised of a cold pooland a very hot, steamy room. He did not fancy either of them and so he felt grateful for only being given the use of this one, hot pool.

Shortly, the housekeeper returned with a fresh tunic and told Adelbehrt to put it on. When he had dressed, she took him across the courtyard to a small room.

There were two beds in there and she indicated one to the boy. He gathered it was to be his. At the foot of each stood a small chest for any articles he possessed. It remained empty for the moment.

The housekeeper informed him that he would share this room with another boy a bit older than Adelbehrt, himself. When he had looked around, she escorted him out of the bedroom and to a room near the back of the courtyard, but still on the same side as his bedroom. This turned out to be the kitchen and it stood next to a villa exit.

Once in the kitchen, he met the cook, a short woman of many years. She and the housekeeper passed a few words and then the cook said something to Adelbehrt that he did not understand.

She turned to the housekeeper. "Doesn't he understand Latin?"

"No. He's picked up a bit, but he's finding it difficult. He needs to learn quickly if he's to please the Domina. I've put him in with Titus. I hope the older boy will teach him some words."

"I'll ask Titus to do just that when he comes in from his duties."

The housekeeper left and the cook looked at Adelbehrt. "What's your name then?"

The boy understood this and stammered in response.

"What? Speak clearly boy! Did you say Adelbehrt? What sort of name is that? Well, I'm Anna and I'm the cook here. Go and sit down over there. I need to get on with preparing the meal."

Adelbehrt did as she told him and spent a rather boring few hours watching Anna and her helpers prepare the meal for the family and the slaves who worked in the fields and villa.

Eventually, time passed and the slaves began to return to the villa for the evening meal. Anna introduced Adelbehrt to Titus, his new roommate, a boy of eleven years who worked in the stables with the horses. Titus agreed to help Adelbehrt with Latin, and eagerly began pointing to things and saying their Latin names.

That evening, Adelbehrt went to bed and muttered his litany of hate under his breath so as not to disturb Titus.

The next morning, Adelbehrt's training began. The Domina called him into one of the triclinia, where the family took their meals and entertained guests. She instructed him to stand at one side and showed him how to pour wine and how to pass things to guests and family before they asked.

He learned how to deal with people who were not dinner guests as well. He passed bowls of fruit and nuts to imaginary visitors and kept those imaginary guests' wine goblets filled.

He managed to understand what the Domina asked him because she accompanied her instructions with demonstrations. After all, Adelbehrt could not be expected to know all the intricacies of Roman life, being a barbarian. She showed him how to behave and what to do, and Adelbehrt simply mimicked her actions.

The Domina had him sit at her feet while she told him how she expected him to behave. Adelbehrt frowned at the strange words. How could he possibly know what to do if he could barely understand the language used?

The Domina noticed his frown and sent for Marcus. "This boy can't understand the instructions. Arrange for someone to teach him more quickly. We'll be going back to Londinium in three months and he'll need to be able to understand what I want of him. I want to be able to show him to my friends there and it will be no use if he can't obey simple instructions. I'll be a laughing stock instead of the envy of them."

Marcus took Adelbehrt under his wing once more. This pleased Adelbehrt because he liked and respected the older man. In between his duties as accountant to the Dominus, Marcus taught the boy the main words he would need to know. He also recruited Titus to help whenever his duties allowed.

Titus worked in the stables and was very good with the horses. He took Adelbehrt inside one day and introduced him to the animals.

Adelbehrt patted a big grey stallion. The horse turned his head to look to see who was stroking him. Adelbehrt smiled as the stallion let out a soft whicker.

"He likes you," Titus said, smiling.

As Adelbehrt learned many new words from Titus, Marcus continued with somewhat more formal lessons; his Latin improved quickly, much to the delight of the Domina.

His lessons in how to be a house slave resumed. He found them rather boring. He sat at his mistress' feet for what seemed to be long ages.

When bored, he amused himself with thoughts of the grey horse in the stables, imagining himself leaping onto the animal's back, scooping up his sister, and galloping towards the coast where he would find a friendly captain and take a ship back home, across the extensive Oceanus Britannicus.

Some months later, when Adelbehrt had learned more Latin, Titus asked him about his mutterings before going to sleep. "Are you praying to the gods of your people? What gods do your people worship? You aren't one of those Christian people, are you? If you are, you'd better keep it very quiet. The Romans don't like them much. They refuse to worship the Roman gods and the emperor, so the Romans throw them into the arena with wild animals."

Adelbehrt thought he had better be a little careful with his reply. "No. I'm not a Christian, whatever that is. I pray to my god, Wodin." As soon as he said that, he realised he told the truth. His litany each night was a prayer to Wodin.

He asked Wodin to help him get revenge on the Romans. He knew Titus could not understand him as he always said the little speech in his own language; nevertheless, it paid to watch his step.

One morning in mid-autumn, the Dominus called for Adelbehrt. As he left his room, he noticed everyone running around, much busier than usual. He saw Avelina across the courtyard and called out to her.

The little girl answered him quickly. "I can't talk to you now, Adelbehrt. We're going to Londinium for the winter and we must get everything ready."

He noticed she had responded in Latin. It saddened him that she seemed to be forgetting their own language. He tried to speak to her in it as much as he could, but the last time he did so, she asked him to speak Latin. That had upset him, but he realised she spoke Latin all the time and her vocabulary in her native language was very limited, with her being only four years old when she left. She probably felt more comfortable with Latin now.

The next few hours were busy indeed. People sent Adelbehrt on errands to gather things, to ask people various questions, and to take messages to yet others. Soon, though, they had packed everything into the wagons, and they set off.

The group travelled the same route as the one the children used when they arrived at the villa. Adelbehrt watched the road more carefully this time. If he saw a chance of escape at any time, then he wanted to know where he was and where to go. He knew he would not be able to escape soon, though. Maybe not for many years, but he was determined he would one day get away.

Perhaps he would be able to get revenge on the Romans in Britannia … and maybe, just maybe, he could find a way to cross the Oceanus Britannicus and find his mother again. Whether Avelina would want to come, he really did not know. She seemed to like her little mistress and appeared to be forgetting her previous home. She was very young, after all. Adelbehrt thought back to when he had been four. He could remember a few things before that, but not much.

That night, in an inn, Adelbehrt managed to speak with his sister. "What do you remember of Mamma?" he asked.

"She smelled nice," the little girl answered. "She had soft skin and was kind."

"Can you remember what she looked like?"

"Did she have light hair like us?"

"No, her hair was brown. And so were her eyes."

After this conversation, Adelbehrt lay down on his bed and wondered how long he would remember what his mother looked like. Would he forget her, as Avelina appeared to be doing? He hoped not, and he squeezed his eyes shut as he tried to picture the woman who had given him life.

Eventually, they arrived in Londinium at the town house of the Dominus. The family entered through the portico, of course, but the slaves and wagons went round the back through the entrance they had used previously.

Adelbehrt had been pleased when Titus told him he would accompany them to help look after the horses. The two boys had struck up a friendship, in spite of the differences in their ages.

One day, Adelbehrt looked at the older boy, wondering what would it have been like to have an older brother? Perhaps a bit like his relationship with Titus. He seemed to have a slight memory of his father, once referring to an older child who had died, but he could not really remember very well. He thought that no one had mentioned the child again. Perhaps they had, but not while he had been listening.

Would his mother speak of him and Avelina, or would she try to forget them? He hoped she would cherish their memory as he cherished hers.

☙ 5 ❧

A few days after arriving in Londinium for the winter, the Domina invited a few of her friends round so she could show off her new pet. Adelbehrt wondered just how long these friends of hers would stay. Would they pat and stroke him as if he were a puppy? How much would he have to wait on them? This was the first time the Domina had entertained her friends. Adelbehrt's stomach churned as he wondered what would happen.

She led him through the passageway leading from the peristylium. Curious, the boy looked around. He had not been here when he had previously come to the domus and was interested to find out what lay through the passageway.

The atrium was open in the centre, surrounded by high-ceilinged porticoes. A sunken area lay in the middle, beneath the opening. It caught the rain as it fell, and Adelbehrt found out later that the water drained into a cistern beneath the house. This water would be used for washing and drinking by the family.

Some statues stood around the edges of the atrium and marble mosaics surrounded the impluvium. As he looked, he heard women's voices and the arrival of the Domina's friends caught his attention. They crossed the atrium to where she stood. The slave who had brought them bowed and withdrew, leaving three ladies with the Domina and Adelbehrt.

The Domina and her guests exchanged excited chatter about what they had been doing that summer. As the weather was still warm, the ladies elected to sit in the atrium, under a patch of sunlight filtering through the compluvium. Then the Domina told Adelbehrt to serve wine.

The boy carefully poured it into the fine goblets and handed them to the four ladies.

"Oh, Annwyl," exclaimed one of the three visitors. "Is this the boy you told us about? He's quite beautiful, and I've never seen hair that colour before. Where did you get him?"

Adelbehrt saw Annwyl smile at the praise. Why is she so pleased that I meet the approval of these ladies, he wondered. It seemed strange to him that someone so poised and in charge of herself in her own home should be concerned about three other Roman ladies and their opinions.

"He's not a Briton, is he?" asked one. "I would be surprised if you had a Briton slave, with you being a Briton yourself."

"No, he's not a Briton. But why would you think I wouldn't have a Briton as a slave? Britons take slaves just like we Romans do."

Adelbehrt sensed tension in the air. Here was something to ponder Why did the Domina emphasise her Roman citizenship? Why was she not proud of being a Briton? He was proud of his Germanic origins.

The Domina spoke to him and he roused himself from his thoughts.

"Come here, Adelbehrt. My friends want to see you properly. We've all got drinks and fruit now, and so you can come and sit by me."

The boy wandered over to where the ladies sat and knelt at his mistress' feet. One of the ladies reached over and felt his hair.

He resisted the urge to flinch, as he knew it would evoke the wrath of the Domina. Probably a slap. Not much more, as this family did not treat slaves cruelly. He tried to smile at the woman as he had been told, but he found it difficult. He did not like this petting, especially by Romans.

The Domina spoke again and so he listened. "Lucius brought them from Mogantiacum. It was pure luck. They'd been captured in a punishment raid on a village across the Rhenus. He saw them and was lucky enough to outbid another man."

"You say 'they'. How many are there?" The woman who had been stroking his hair looked at him, eyebrows raised.

"Two. The boy has a sister. Lucius gave her to Claudia as they are of an age. She'll be her personal slave and wait on her. Claudia was thrilled to have her own slave."

"I'll bet she was," the third lady replied with a haughty smile. "How old is she? Four?"

"Yes, she's four."

"Isn't that a little young to have a personal slave? Trust me, Annwyl dear, I'm not trying to tell you what to do, but only four?"

Adelbehrt felt the Domina tense.

"It's never too early to learn how to deal with slaves, Julia. At least that's what Lucius says. Personally, I might have waited a year or two, but she seems to have taken to slave-ownership quite naturally."

The conversation continued with the four women taking turns having Adelbehrt sit next to them so they could stroke his hair. Constantly, they commented upon its colour and softness.

Adelbehrt held himself still with difficulty. He felt like an exotic pet. Eventually, the Domina sent him to get more wine and he breathed more easily when he left what he considered an oppressive atmosphere in the room. On his return, the conversation had changed and he was no longer the centre of attention. He stood ready to respond to any orders, and was not petted again.

❦

The next day, the Domina decided she needed to do some shopping. She called Adelbehrt to go with her and help carry her purchases. She also took Paulus because she knew there was a limit to what the little boy could carry. She really wanted to show her little slave off in the marketplace.

Wandering around the town, friends and acquaintances frequently stopped the Domina. They all made remarks about what a pretty, little slave boy she had and remarked on the lightness of his hair.

One lady in particular seemed interested in him. He gathered she was a friend of the Domina and was also a Briton. They had been friends since before they both married Roman citizens. She made a great fuss of Adelbehrt. He shifted from foot to foot as the woman petted him and declared what a beautiful child he was, and how lucky Annwyl was to have him.

He longed to be back in the house, where at least only the Domina made a fuss over him. He wished he were back at the villa in the country. He had none of this attention from strange women there. He smiled, though, at all the people who provided remarks about him, even if it looked more like a grimace.

On one occasion, he failed to respond in the right way and received a quick slap. After that, he decided he had better be quicker to smile. His owners were not unnecessarily harsh, but they knew a slave's place and that a slave should do what pleased *them*, regardless of the slave's own wishes.

The shopping trip took forever—at least it seemed that way to the boy. They kept stopping and talking, and he had to stand behind the Domina and next to Paulus, holding his few parcels. The Domina called him forward a few times and the people she talked to stroked and prodded him. It made him feel no different from a horse or a dog. It took all his effort not to back away, or even to say something, or push a petting hand away. Eventually, and none too soon Adelbehrt thought, they made their way back to the domus.

The Dominus greeted them in the atrium. He had returned from a trip to Gaul. During the summer, he travelled away quite a lot, trading around Europe. He had even been to Rome. He had seen the Emperor too, he told them. Only from a distance, true, but the Emperor nevertheless.

The Domina sent Adelbehrt and Paulus to put the parcels away, and then she told Adelbehrt to sit with them when he returned. When the boy came back, he found the Dominus telling his wife all about the goings-on in Rome.

"The new emperor is Vespasian, Annwyl. You remember he was the man who staged a revolt? Well, he arrived in Rome while I was there."

Adelbehrt listened with interest. He had picked up that there had been a period of unrest and rebellion. There had been two emperors in quick succession after the death of the unpopular Nero, but he was unsure of the details. So, a new emperor had been crowned? He wondered if this one would last. The Dominus seemed to think he would.

"He's encouraging construction on vacant lots," the Dominus went on to say. "He's also started building a temple to Claudius, and has started restoring the Capitol. They say he's building a great arena too. One bigger and more marvellous than any ever seen before."

"I suppose it would be good for the empire to have a

period of stability," replied Annwyl, "but I really don't see how it'll affect us much, here at the edges of the empire."

"Maybe not directly, dear, but it'll affect trade, and that'll affect us."

◌◌◌

The winter passed in Londinium. The house felt warm in spite of the cold weather due to the hypocaust built into it; a furnace under the floor circulated heat around and along wall cavities. The technology fascinated Adelbehrt. He remembered being cold last winter in his home in the village. He might have hated the Romans for what they did to him and others, conquering lands far and wide and taking whatever they wanted, but he had to admire and respect them for their technology.

However, he still recited his litany of hate every evening and actively remembered his mother, father and baby brother. He determined not to forget them, nor what the Romans had done to his family.

The Briton lady they met in the town became a frequent visitor to the domus. She was a particular friend of the Domina and always made a fuss of Adelbehrt when she came. He put up with it, even though he hated being treated as a pet.

"How lucky we were, Maeve, to find Romans to marry," the Domina said to her one day. "Being part of such a vast empire is a great thing. Poor Caitlin had to marry a Briton."

"Yes, Annwyl, and we were also lucky to find such good men. I often wonder how Caitlin went on. She was in love with her Niall though. I suppose they're happy enough."

"Who knows, Maeve? Who knows?"

The women smiled at each other and drank a toast to their lost friend, Caitlin.

Eventually, Maeve said with a sour expression, "You want

to be careful of those so-called Roman friends of yours, you know. They're *not* to be trusted. They despise our Britishness, even though we're now Roman citizens and our husbands are important men."

The Domina laughed softly. "I know. They're always making catty remarks disguised as friendly ones. I can hold my own with them though. I have to entertain them for Lucius' sake."

Maeve tilted her head to one side contemplated her old friend. "Are you *sure*, Annwyl? Are you sure you're not being captivated by their Roman-ness? You must never forget we are Britons first and Romans second."

"Briton is now a Roman State," Annwyl answered with a shrug. "Thus, we are all Romans. We now have warm houses, theatres, the games in the amphitheatres, much more varied food, and slaves to serve us." She glanced at Adelbehrt. "Is it not much better to be a Roman than to shiver in smoky huts and slave in the fields?"

Eventually Maeve left and Adelbehrt sat thinking about what he had overheard. What were the Domina's real thoughts? And her friend—what about her? She seemed proud of being a Briton. More so than the Domina, in fact.

The year ended with the feast of Saturnalia. Adelbehrt was fascinated by the customs, especially the one where the roles of master and slave were reversed and, for one day, the Dominus and Domina waited on the slaves.

Marcus took the Dominus's place, but as he had not married, the housekeeper took on the role of the Domina. Adelbehrt found it all very confusing, but great fun watching as Marcus and the housekeeper ordered the family around, just as the family usually ordered them.

Then the spring came and the family closed down the domus in Londinium and left once again for the villa. Adelbehrt smiled as they left all the fussy women of Londinium.

He would have some peace at last. Besides, all the slaves helped with the harvest, and Adelbehrt looked forward to that. Last summer, he had enjoyed being out in the fields in the sunshine.

✢ 6 ✢

AD 76

The years passed. To Adelbehrt, they were years of frustration. He felt more a pet than a boy, except when Maeve came. She did not pet and stroke him like the Roman women did; even some of the men stroked his hair, like they would a dog.

He often caught the Briton woman looking at him with a slight frown on her face, and wondered about it. Did she covet him for herself? Would she offer to buy him from the Domina? If she did, he would have to leave Avelina here. He worried about this, but nothing happened regarding a sale and so, eventually, he relaxed.

One day, when the children had been slaves for six years, Marcus approached Adelbehrt.

"Have you a minute?" the older man asked.

Adelbehrt looked at him, puzzled. "What do you want?" Sitting on the edge of the impluvium, he trailed his hand in the water. The Domina did not seem to want him at the moment. In fact, the Domina had not had much for him to do for a while. He thought the novelty of his appearance might be wearing off, especially as he was now beginning to grow up.

Marcus continued to stand before the office of the Dominus. What did the accountant want? He had little reason to ask Adelbehrt for anything. Marcus was an important man, even if a slave.

Marcus finally spoke. "How long have you been here now, Adelbehrt?"

"Six years."

"That will make you about twelve then."

The boy nodded. "About that, I suppose."

"Now I don't want to worry you, but you're growing up. You're still an attractive boy—attractive enough to still be a pet—but as you get older, probably from now on," he scanned Adelbehrt's face, "the Domina will find you less like her pretty, little slave boy."

"Your unusual hair colouring is no longer a novelty. No one comments on it anymore. Soon, the Domina won't want you as her slave and will find a new pet. Or perhaps she has already." He shrugged. "Look at how she dotes on that little dog the Dominus bought her."

Adelbehrt regarded the older man. He had thought long about this himself. He noticed how the Domina played with her puppy and spent less time with him. He wasn't jealous. Not really. In fact, he often felt glad she had another toy to play with. After six years of petting and fussing, he felt heartily fed up. Still, he found it galling to be ignored.

He pricked up his ears and listened to what Marcus was saying. it did not do to ignore one's elders. "I spoke to the Dominus yesterday. It seems he's noticed how his wife seems more concerned with her puppy than you and he talked about selling you."

Adelbehrt drew in a sharp breath at that news and looked up at Marcus, biting his lower lip and frowning.

"He said he'd noticed you liked the horses and are good with them, but he doesn't need another slave in the stables. He thinks he can sell you as a stable lad though."

"But ... but." Adelbehrt did not know what to say. He

thought of Avelina. Oh, the little girl seemed happy enough as Claudia's slave, but she was still only ten summers old. She could not really remember their home by the Rhenus anymore and had completely forgotten their native language.

Claudia treated her well. In fact, they were almost like friends rather than mistress and slave, but Adelbehrt had promised his mother he would look after her. How could he do that if the Dominus sold him?

Marcus smiled at him as if he knew what he was thinking. "I made a suggestion. I'm not getting any younger you know, and the Dominus will need an accountant for years to come and after him, the young Dominus too, when he takes over the business. There'll come a time when I can no longer travel as I do now."

Marcus sat on the edge of the impluvium, next to Adelbehrt. "I pointed this out to the Dominus. He realised that, he said, and worried about what would happen then. I suggested that I teach you and you could become my successor. He agreed. Very quickly. He knows that to find a competent slave accountant would be difficult. What do you think of the idea?"

Adelbehrt's eyes lit up. "Marcus, that would be great! I won't have to leave Avelina. I can continue to look after her."

"And you won't have to worry about what sort of owner you'll get either. We're very lucky here. We're treated well. Anyway, the Dominus still has to talk to the Domina. You are, after all, her property and not his. It may be she doesn't want to release you for some reason. You'll hear in a few days."

Almost a week went by before Marcus sent for Adelbehrt. When he had heard nothing after a couple of days, the boy became anxious. He thought the Domina had decided to sell him after all. Given she had not sent for him for two days, the boy spent time in the stables with his friend, Titus, and the big grey stallion he had come to love.

As he groomed the stallion, a little slave girl came in. Her big eyes opened even wider when she saw the horses, and she wrinkled up her nose at the pungent smell.

"You're to come to Marcus at once," she told Adelbehrt and scampered out of the stables as quickly as she could.

Adelbehrt gave the grey horse one last pat and ran across the peristylium and into the atrium where Marcus waited in the office.

"Well, lad," the older slave said with a smile, "it seems the Domina has agreed to allow you to study with me. This is only when she doesn't want you, mind. You're still her slave. Since you were in the stables, I assume she has nothing for you at the moment, and so we can begin lessons immediately. The very first thing you need to learn is your letters."

Marcus began to write the letters of the alphabet and set Adelbehrt to learning their names and writing them down.

He laughed at the boy's first attempts to hold a pen. "No, not like that!" he exclaimed. "You are not eating with it, nor are you about to stab the paper to death with it. Here, let me show you."

Adelbehrt tried holding the pen the way Marcus showed him and found he could make the fine movements required to write the letters much easier. After that, he progressed in leaps and bounds.

He enjoyed the lessons. He quickly learned to read and write, and took great pleasure in it. His handwriting was not too clear at first, but with Marcus' help, he soon perfected a good hand. Adelbehrt began to learn to read and to use an abacus, essential for arithmetic in the days of Roman numerals.

"When can I start helping you with the accounts?" Adelbehrt asked one day, leaning towards Marcus and peering at the ledger in front of him..

"Well," Marcus replied with a slight smile on his face,, "you need to be more accurate with your adding. It wouldn't do to make mistakes in the Dominus' accounts. That would incur his wrath, as well as the possibility of damaging his business and reputation. Reputation is very important in trade. People *must* trust you and be sure in their minds you're honest."

⚭

Adelbehrt still had to attend the Domina from time to time, and whatever she wanted him to do had to take precedence over his lessons. He was still her slave, but the occasions she wanted him grew fewer and fewer. That pleased him. He did not really mind waiting at tables, nor serving wine to guests, but he still hated the occasions when he served as her pet; he was greatly relieved as the occasions grew fewer.

These occasions declined even more over the next two years, and by the time he was fourteen, she hardly asked for him at all. One day, however, as he attended her, the Dominus entered the room.

"You asked me to come to see you, dear," he said. "What is it? I haven't a lot of time. I'll be leaving for Gaul in a few days and I need to check the tin from Dumnonia that I'm taking to trade."

Annwyl smiled. "I believe you'll think the news I'm going to give you is worth a few minutes delay, Lucius. I'm pregnant."

The Dominus grinned, then frowned. "Annwyl, darling, don't get your hopes up too soon. You know you've lost several babies over the last few years."

"Oh, Lucius, I'm past the time I lost the others. I didn't want to tell you until I was sure that this time I'd carry the babe to term. I'm four and a half months. The baby will be born in November."

Then the Dominus did smile. He bent down, picked up his wife and swung her round. "I thought you were just putting on weight. Oh Annwyl, I'm so thrilled. Only four and a half months to wait too. How did you manage to keep such wonderful news to yourself?"

The Domina laughed. "Oh, it was so hard, Lucius, but I couldn't raise your hopes for another child until I was sure I wouldn't lose this one too."

Adelbehrt stood silent, listening to the conversation, a smile spreading involuntarily across his face. He knew the Domina wanted another child. He had been in her presence when she had discussed this with her friends, and had seen her cry when they had babies. He could not, however, understand why this was so important to her. After all, she had two children already. Still, she had not been harsh with him on the whole, even if he had hated being a little pet.

The summer passed and they returned to Londinium. Soon it came time for the birth of the baby. It was not an easy birth, but in the end, she produced a baby boy and named him Julius.

This marked the end of Adelbehrt's time as a pet. The baby became her life. She forgot all about her little slave boy, so he found he could spend all his time with his studies. He smiled with great cheer as he realised this.

7

AD 80

Time went on and Adelbehrt became more proficient at the accountancy Marcus taught him. He could now almost run the office himself. He and Avelina had been slaves for nine years; he was now fifteen and his sister thirteen.

Avelina had become a beautiful girl. Her blonde hair had not darkened as it often did on many girls. She had grown tall and slender with long legs and flawless skin. She turned male heads wherever she went.

One day, Adelbehrt found her crying in a corner of the domus. "What's wrong, Avelina? The little Domina hasn't punished you for something, has she?"

He frowned. Claudia did not usually punish her slave. In fact, Adelbehrt could not remember an occasion where that had occurred.

"No. No, she hasn't. I've not done anything wrong, Adelbehrt. Really. I've done nothing wrong." She began to sob again. "She mustn't know though."

Adelbehrt put his arms round his sister and stroked her hair. "Avelina, what is it? What are you afraid of the little Domina knowing? If you've done nothing wrong, then you've nothing to worry about. Whatever it is, tell me, please."

Avelina pulled away from her brother and wiped her hand over her eyes. "It's the Dominus. He … he tried to touch me. I was in the peristylium and there was no one around. He pushed me against the fountain and kissed me. Then he … he touched me."

"What?" Adelbehrt clenched his fists. "He tried to rape you?"

"No, not rape. A Roman citizen can't rape a slave, you know that. Even if he forces a girl, it's not rape. But no, he didn't go that far. Just touching, here.' She put her hand on her left breast. "Don't tell the little Domina, please, Adelbehrt. She would be so upset. She loves her father. She might think I'd encouraged him. I didn't, honestly I didn't." She looked up at her brother, pleading with her eyes. Sniffing, she wiped a hand over them.

Adelbehrt handed her a rag from his pocket and she used it to blow her nose.

"No, Avelina, I know you didn't. What can we do to stop him going any further?"

The girl sobbed. "Nothing. We can do nothing! We're slaves. We have no rights. He owns us and can do what he likes with us." She broke into a wail. "I liked him, Adelbehrt. I thought how lucky we are to have such a good master and mistress. I know I'll have to let him do what he wants. I'm *so* afraid."

Then they heard Claudia calling and Avelina went running to respond to her little mistress, leaving a furious Adelbehrt pondering as to what he could do.

His ideas of escape had been shelved in the last few years. He found the lessons with Marcus interesting and he was beginning to become resigned to his life. He still chanted his litany of hate every night, but it was as much from habit as anything else. Oh, he occasionally thought about escape and he still hated Romans in general, if not individual Romans, but he could see no method of escape and he had shelved the thought. In any case, Avelina seemed to have forgotten her life before slavery, and he could not leave without her. He had promised his mother to care for her, after all.

In November one day, Adelbehrt sat doing calculations for the Dominus. He was in the office with Marcus and the Dominus when the Domina strode in.

"Lucius," she shouted. "Julius told me he saw you kissing Claudia's slave!"

"Now, Annwyl, my love …" began the Dominus, but he was interrupted.

"Don't you 'my love' me! The boy wouldn't lie. He's only three years old. He would barely know what he was seeing. You were kissing that little slut. She's got a pretty face and unusual hair, and you can't keep your hands off her."

The Dominus looked shamefaced. "Annwyl, it wasn't serious. Just a *little* kiss."

"That's how it starts. Just a kiss. Soon, she'll be with child by you. She goes. Now! Before this day is ended, I want her out of the domus." She swung round and stalked out of the room with her head held high.

Adelbehrt was about to remonstrate when he felt a hand clamp over his mouth. Marcus's voice whispered in his ear. "Don't make it any worse by interfering. These are our masters."

The Dominus left the room, following his wife.

Adelbehrt pulled away from the older man and said, "That's my sister they're talking about. She's no slut! What choice did she have when the Dominus tried to kiss her? They can't get rid of her just like that … can they?"

"Yes, I'm afraid they can. They can do what they like with any of us."

Shortly after this altercation, they heard more shouting.

This time it was Claudia. "You can't take Avelina. She's my slave and my friend."

"Claudia, just mind yourself. Yes, she's your slave but, as such, cannot be your friend," her father told her. "Slaves are to attend us, not to be friends with us. It seems this is a lesson you must learn. All the more reason for this girl to go."

"Where are you taking her? I must know that, at least."

"To the brothel." This was her mother. "That's the only place for a little slut like her."

Avelina was crying. Adelbehrt rushed out of the office to his sister. Paulus happened to be crossing the atrium at the time and grabbed the boy as he passed.

"Don't make it worse," growled the slave. "There's nothing you can do."

"But they're taking her to a brothel."

Paulus shrugged. "Tough on the girl, but still nothing you can do. It could be worse. She could go to a cruel master, where she would be beaten. At least they look after the girls in the brothel. Just forget her. You'll likely never see her again."

For all his fifteen years, Adelbehrt was nearly in tears. "But I promised mother I'd look after her. How can I keep my promise if she goes?"

Marcus approached the boy. "Your mother wouldn't have expected your care to extend beyond her childhood. She's thirteen years old now and a woman. And you can't do anything about stopping the sale. The Domina has made up her mind. I think it will be a long while before she forgives the Dominus."

That night, Adelbehrt spoke his litany of hate to himself. This time he meant it. "I hate the Romans. They crucified my father; they took my family away from me;they took my home from me; they took my friends from me; they put Odila into a brothel; they took my freedom from me; they took my home-land away from me; they took our humanity and made us property; they took my sister from me and put her in a brothel."

Adelbehrt was still sharing a room with Titus. Titus had been put in charge of the horses and oxen in the villa and the domus in Londinium, and so travelled backwards and forwards with the family. It pleased Adelbehrt that the young man was with them.

Over the years, the pair had become firm friends in spite of the difference in their ages. Titus had learned about Adelbehrt's hatred of the Romans, and understood it to some extent. However, he had been born into slavery and knew no other life, but now he approached the younger man.

Whispering, Titus glanced around. "I know you want to help your sister so I'm telling you something I shouldn't know. There's a group of Britons that helps other Britons who've been captured and sold into slavery. They help them escape and get away."

"That's no use to Avelina and me," Adelbehrt responded flatly, shaking his head. "We aren't Britons."

"No, but they won't know that. You were captured when you were very young and know very little about your past. Avelina especially."

Titus lay back on his bed before continuing. "You can't speak the Briton's language, but that won't matter since you were captured so young you've forgotten it. At least Avelina has. You'd have to pretend. That shouldn't be difficult as you speak your language as a six-year-old would."

"Are you suggesting I contact these people?"

"Well, I can't really help there. I don't know who they are. I heard about them from a friend whose cousin knows someone who they helped to escape."

"That's pretty flimsy, Titus. If I did want to contact them, how could I from your story?"

Titus leaned up on one elbow, his expression solemn. "I

could mention it to my friend. He could then speak to his cousin, who may know more."

Adelbehrt shook his head. "I don't expect his cousin would know any more. After all, he just knew the escapee, not where he's gone in order to speak to him. Anyway," he continued, remembering the conversation he had with Paulus all those years ago, about what happened to runaway slaves. "The Romans always catch their slaves if they run away."

"No," said Titus, sitting up and growing animated. "They *don't* always. This man hasn't been caught—the group of Britons managed to spirit him away. He's *still* free! I'll speak to my friend when I see him next."

Adelbehrt sat up and looked at Titus. "If you wish. But what about Avelina? This is all about saving her. She has little time, being in a brothel. I want to save her before she is … well, harmed."

"Don't worry about that. She'll need to be trained first. Then she'll be kept for a special customer for her first time, as she's a virgin."

❦ 8 ❦

At first, Avelina struggled when the Dominus led her out of the house that had been her home for the last nine years. It was all she could remember. She had barely any memory of her home by the Rhenus. Even with the little she thought she could remember, she was unsure if it were a true memory or just something imagined, based on what Adelbehrt had told her.

She was crying and when they were out of sight of the house, the Dominus stopped.

"I'm sorry for this, Avelina," he said as he wiped one of her tears away with his thumb. "I'd not have you sent to a brothel, you know, but I can't do anything else. My wife is adamant. Perhaps I can visit you at the brothel sometime when I'm here on business and my wife is in the country."

Avelina stared at him in disbelief. Did he really think he could still have her?

He continued. "You're a very pretty girl, you know. Any man would want you, and I think many do when they see you walking about town. I should get a good price for you, especially as you're still a virgin, and I'll probably be able to get priority with you, seeing as I brought you here. Perhaps I'll be able to have you for a reduced price. Yes. I'll put it as part of the bargain."

Avelina was astonished. How could this man still think of her as a sexual partner after all the trouble it—*he*—had caused?

They arrived at the doors of the brothel and the Dominus knocked. A young girl a few years older than Avelina answered.

"Yes?" she asked, scanning their faces. "Come in. I'm sure we can find a girl to suit you. We have them of all kinds."

Then she saw Avelina and turned away, calling, "Mother, there's a man here!"

A sing-song voice answered from deep inside the house. "I expect there is, dear. It's *usually* men who come to a brothel. What kind of girl does he want?"

She frowned and eyed Avelina. "Seems he's brought his own."

The Dominus smiled at the girl. "No, I'm not here for a girl, nor even to have this one, although perhaps sometime in the future …? No. I'm here to sell this slave to you. She's pretty and a virgin."

An attractive, older woman emerged through a door in the back. "So you want to sell a girl, do you? Is this the one?"

She pulled Avelina away from the Dominus and towards the light from a window. She peered into the girl's eyes, forced open her mouth and looked in, and ran her fingers through the girl's hair.

"She's quite pretty and, as far as I can tell, she seems healthy. A virgin, you say? Why are you selling her? I'd have thought a rich man like you would have wanted her for himself."

The Dominus cleared his throat and looked down, shuffling his feet. The woman noticed his embarrassment and laughed. "So you did want her then. I guess your wife found out before you actually got to seducing her properly and you've got to sell her. My guess is you're hoping for a discount so you can come here and 'visit' your little slave girl after we've trained her. Well, let's begin negotiations. Julia, take our probable new girl to meet the others."

Avelina followed the girl called Julia through the door that the older woman had come through.

"What's your name?" Julia asked.

"Avelina. What if they can't come to an agreement? What will happen to me then?"

"Oh, they'll agree. My mother likes the look of you. I could tell by her eyes. It's a long time since we've had a virgin. Of course, that only lasts for the first time, then you're just the same as everyone else here. Still, you'll always be in demand because of your looks and your blonde hair, and for quite some time you'll be new and that's nearly as good as being a virgin. Now, let me introduce you to the other girls."

Shortly, the madam came through the door. "That's that, then. You're one of my girls now. You need training, of course. I take it you know what goes on in this place?"

Avelina nodded eyes downcast.

"Well, I'm not risking you escaping just yet, so you'll be with one of the girls all the time until we've finished training you. It's not just leap into bed with a man and let him do what he wishes. Oh no. You need to learn how to please him properly, and all the little tricks to increase his pleasure. That's what keeps them coming back here. Their wives don't have the training, you see, so they enjoy themselves much more here than at home."

Avelina wiped away a tear. She was stuck here. She had been thinking of running away in spite of the punishments if caught, but with someone watching her all the time, she couldn't see how she would manage it. She let out a little moan as she followed Julia up the stairs to a bedroom with two beds in it.

Julia stayed and chatted. "Mother likes you, I can tell, but

I bet she struck a hard bargain. She'll expect to make *a lot* of money from you."

Avelina wiped away another tear. "What's it like," she whispered, "being here and having to do … that … with men who come?"

Julia laughed lightly. "It's no good asking me. I'm not one of the girls. Mother is training me to take over the business eventually."

"She said I'd be trained. So I'll not be expected to do …to go with men straight away?"

"No. But I expect she'll want to start your training straight away. Probably tomorrow. Mother will want to recoup the money she spent on buying you as soon as possible," Julia told her. "She'll get it back quickly, though, I would think. You're very pretty, and your hair is so unusual." She took a strand in her fingers. "I think the men will go mad for you."

That night, Avelina cried herself to sleep. She could understand, for the first time, how her brother felt comforted by his nightly litany. She did not hate the Romans. They were a fact of life. Slaves were a fact of life, too. She was just unfortunate to be a slave and not a master.

Her mistress had been kind to her and, in fact, the two girls were more like friends rather than mistress and slave. They had grown up together, after all. As she drifted off to sleep, she wondered what her brother would do. He had always been protective of her. She only hoped he would not do anything that would get him into serious trouble.

The next morning, training began. It would take a few weeks, Julia told her. She decided to hope something would turn up to help her escape; hope was better than despair, and so she forced herself to look on the bright side and smile at the madam and the other girls.

The madam decided this meant that Avelina had become resigned to her fate and she smiled back at the girl as she told her that perhaps she could have her own room after all. She would need a private room eventually, of course, when she started working. Not many men wanted to have someone else in the room when he was with a girl. All the girls had their own rooms.

During the day, when things were a little quieter, one of the girls who was not working talked to Avelina about how she could increase the pleasure of the man who came to visit. She should always smile, of course, and look as though she enjoyed it, even if she did not. Sometimes, they had to do things with horrid men—be they smelly, fat, ugly or just plain ignorant. She must still, *always*, look as if she were enjoying it.

Then one of the girls talked about how she would sometimes be asked to do things that shocked the innocent Avelina, and she began to become very frightened.

"Don't worry," one girl told her. "You get used to it, and we often get large tips from the men, especially if they're rich and we please them a lot. Sometimes a man takes a liking to one of us and pays for her to be released into his custody. Then she only has that one man to please and he sets the girl up in an apartment of her own. That's the best that happens. It doesn't happen very often, but sometimes it does."

Avelina frowned. Would the Dominus come for her and set her up so he could have her any time he wanted? Would the Domina find out if he did? What would the Domina do if that happened?

She did not want to be the mistress of the Dominus. He was an old man. If that were going to happen, she wanted a young handsome man.

A week passed. Avelina listened to the talk of the girls in the main room, where they sat so the men could choose which girl they wanted.

One man entered with the madam. "Yes, we do have a virgin," Avelina heard her say, "but she's not ready yet. She's still in training."

"The Governor won't mind that," the man said. "He just asked me to get him a virgin. He's heard you have a very pretty one here."

"The Governor? Is that who it's for? The *new* Governor?"

"Yes, for Agricola himself. His wife isn't here yet and he feels the need of a girl. He especially likes virgins. Likes to think he's going somewhere no one has been before, great explorer that he is." The man laughed heartily.

"Well in that case, show me something that will tell me you're genuine and not some impostors trying to get a virgin for themselves for free. Is he coming here soon?"

"Well, he doesn't actually frequent brothels. He wants us to take her to him at his domus. You do allow that, don't you?"

The madam narrowed her eyes and scanned the man carefully before saying, "Yes, yes, of course, but you must take good care of her. She may try to escape if she's out of these walls. She hasn't settled down to her fate yet."

The man pulled a paper out of his pocket and showed it to the madam. She glanced at it and then eyed the seal at the bottom. It was obvious she could not read it, but she did not want the man to know and so she nodded once and passed it back.

She turned to Avelina and beckoned. "Come here, girl. You have a great honour. The Governor has asked for you. You're to go with this man and do whatever the Governor wants. Remember your training so far.

"Whatever he wants you're to enjoy, or at least make him think you are. Squeal or moan whenever he does something to you, and cry out when he finishes, as if you're enjoying the most exquisite sensation. Don't cry when he enters you though. It will hurt the first time and there will be blood. Now go and do us proud."

Avelina walked to the door where the man waited. Could she use this as a way to escape? She would have to do it before she got to the Governor's home though. Afterwards, would be too late.

The man took her by the arm, none too gently. When they had travelled some distance from the brothel, he spoke to her. "I'm not the slave of Agricola. That was just an excuse to get you out of that place. Someone's helping your brother to escape at this very moment. Come with me."

"Who are you and why are you helping us?" she asked, stunned.

"We're a group of Britons who hate seeing our people enslaved by the Romans. We help Britons escape slavery whenever we can. A friend told us of your problems and we agreed to help. We can't help everyone, unfortunately. Not if we're to remain unsuspected. Now, come with me."

Avelina followed.

9

About a week after Avelina had gone to the brothel, Adelbehrt walked through the town buying things for the Dominus when he felt someone push something into his pocket. At least he hoped it was something going in and not out. He slipped in his hand and found a piece of paper. He left it there until he got back to the domus.

As soon as he found himself alone, the young man pulled out the paper and read it: *We understand you can read so we are contacting you this way. We can help you and your sister to escape the Romans if that is what you wish. If you want to escape, reply to this letter and give it to the beggar outside the Basilica in the forum. He has a patch over one eye and a crutch. Tell no one of this.*

The note excited Adelbehrt. Here was a chance to escape the Romans' clutches! Perhaps, in the future, he would find an opportunity to fight the Romans.

He knew rebellions went on from No line break here as it's still the same sentence!time to time. He would seek one out and join. Then he would have a chance to kill Romans and exact revenge for all they had done to him and his family.

Adelbehrt stole some paper, wrote a reply, and carried it around with him. He did this partly because he did not know when he was going to be sent out to town and partly because he did not want to risk it being found if he left it in his room. He told no one of the note, not even Titus.

Several days passed before the young man again went into Londinium alone, but eventually the Dominus sent him on an errand and he found himself in the forum. He crossed to the Basilica and spotted the beggar in question. Walking up to him, he held out money to the man and, as the beggar reached up to take it, Adelbehrt slipped the note into his palm along with the money, and continued on his way without looking back.

A week later, when he was again in town, this time with the Dominus, someone jostled him. Turning, he looked around to reproach the man if he were a slave; he could not remonstrate a citizen, of course. A man was making his way through the crowds some distance away, too far away for him to say anything. He looked like a free man, not a slave, by the confident way he strolled and was, undoubtedly, a citizen.

Some time later, the young man put his hand into his pocket. He felt a piece of paper that had not been there when he left the domus. He refrained from looking at it immediately and it was with great anticipation that he waited until he could return to the domus to read it.

Meet me at the bathhouse tonight at midnight. That was all it said. He turned it over and on the back was a cryptic remark. *It's a cold night for June, yes, but not for January.*

Adelbehrt frowned. It was neither June nor January. It was, in fact, November. How odd.

How am I supposed to leave the domus to go out at that time? Adelbehrt spent a lot of time thinking. He could not just walk out of the door, so he would need to wait until everyone in the household slept before making a break. Even then, there was the danger of someone waking and hearing him.

Marcus looked up from the ledger he was working on and

saw Adelbehrt gazing into space. "What's wrong?" He put down his pen. "Are you worrying about Avelina?"

"What? Oh, er, yes," answered the boy. Adelbehrt pulled himself together and looked at his companion. "How long will her training take?"

"Well, I don't really know," Marcus replied scratching his head.. "I haven't had any experience with training prostitutes." He smiled. Then, he became more serious. "You should forget about her, you know. I know it's hard, but there's nothing you can do. She's gone and that's that."

Adelbehrt's head drooped as he returned to his work. Marcus had noticed his distraction and the young man decided he must not allow anyone to think he planned an escape. He only hoped these mysterious people into whose hands he was putting his life could manage to free Avelina too.

All too soon, night came. Adelbehrt went to bed as usual, but did not go to sleep. As soon as it became clear the household was asleep, he opened his chest and took out the money he had collected over the years, and crept out of his room, sandals in hand, towards the slave's and servant's door.

He drew the bolts. The door made a creaking noise as it opened, and Adelbehrt froze. Would anyone hear it? How come he had not heard the door creaking before now? He stepped into the shadows and waited, holding his breath. After a couple of minutes, when all remained silent, he slipped into the yard.

There were sounds: animals shifted in the stable and in the nearby distance a dog barked. Adelbehrt felt grateful that the family did not bring any dogs back to Londinium with them.

He pulled a hood over his fair hair. He reasoned it would show up in the darkness of the city, especially when passing beneath the oil lamps affixed to the walls.

Over the years, Adelbehrt had come to know the city of Londinium well. He was a trusted slave and had been out alone many times. He had money, and often went to spend it on treats or essentials and so had become familiar with the way to the bathhouse. Sometimes he accompanied the Dominus, when he went each evening, to hold his towel and do any other little tasks the Dominus wanted. The bathhouse was a social and business centre, and no Roman would miss his daily visit.

When Adelbehrt arrived at the baths, he noticed a shadow in the doorway. Was this the man he had come to meet? How would he recognise this person?

The shadow stepped forwards. "It's a cold night for June."

"Yes, but not for January," replied Adelbehrt, remembering the mysterious words on the back of the note he had been given.

"Come, follow me." The man walked away.

Adelbehrt had to walk quickly to keep up. They wound their way through the streets into the poorest quarter of the town. Here the insulae were crowded together. Fires often broke out among the wooden buildings, so the people did not cook in their insulae but bought food at the many food stalls in the vicinity.

They came to a door, on which the man knocked three times, then a gap, and then another four times. The door opened a crack.

"Ah, you're back," a female voice said. "Come on in."

The door opened and they entered. The old woman who opened the door stood back to let them pass. Adelbehrt found himself in a dark room with a bed in one corner and a table with four chairs around it in the middle. In a dark corner was another chair with a shadowy shape on it.

The woman who let them in turned to Adelbehrt. "Your sister isn't here yet. We expected her before you, but they shouldn't be much longer."

"How are they going to rescue her?" Adelbehrt asked anxiously.

"I'm not really sure. It isn't easy rescuing people from that place. Sometimes, Romans ask for girls to be brought to their homes. That is, if their wives are away!" She chuckled softly.

"I think they're going to pose as the slave of a well-known Roman and ask for her by name. Then, when they get her out, they'll bring her here."

Adelbehrt wanted to ask more questions, but another knock, in the same code, echoed through the dwelling. Two people were ushered in and a broad grin spread over his face as he recognised Avelina.

She saw him and rushed over, threw herself into his arms, and immediately began to cry. Adelbehrt stroked her hair and tried to calm her as much as he could.

"Addy, it was horrid," she sobbed into his shoulder. "I was so frightened. They were teaching me all sorts of things I didn't want to know. They said I was nearly ready for my first client. Then, this person came." She indicated the man who had brought her in. "He said his master had asked for me personally. He gave them a name and showed them something to prove he was from the person he said, and they called me over and told me I was to go with him and to do whatever his master wanted. I thought his master was going to be my first client." She sobbed again and clung to her brother.

"That's all over now, Avelina." Adelbehrt stroked her hair comfortingly. "These people are going to help us escape."

The shadowy figure in the corner spoke for the first time. "Well, young man, we'll need to do something about your hair and your sister's too. There will be notices for your recapture as soon as they find you gone. There are so few people with hair as light as yours that you'll be quickly spotted and retaken."

Adelbehrt thought he recognised the voice, but could not quite place it. He decided he must be mistaken, but then the woman spoke again. "Go and get the walnut juice so we can dye their hair."

The old woman nodded and hastened through the door,

into the street. When she was gone, the man also left; the two young people found themselves alone with the mysterious figure.

She stood and walked into the light. Adelbehrt gasped. It was the Domina's friend, Maeve.

"Yes. Adelbehrt, it's really me. You see, although I've become a Roman citizen by marrying a Roman, I've not forgotten I'm a Briton, nor have I forgotten my people. I'm a Briton first and Roman second, unlike my friend Annwyl, who seems to have forgotten she's a Briton at all. She fawns around those so-called Roman friends of hers, but I don't really think they consider her a true Roman."

Adelbehrt began to ask why she had decided to help them, but she interrupted him. "I know you aren't Britons, but I like you and your sister. More to the point, I don't like a girl as young as Avelina being forced into a brothel."

Adelbehrt thought of Odila. She was probably not much older than Avelina when the Romans took them as slaves. He was now old enough to know what had happened when the girls had been taken to the officers, and understood why they were so distressed when they returned. He clenched his fists at the thought of the mistreatment of those young and innocent girls.

Maeve continued and so he silenced his thoughts and listened. "I decided to make an exception in your case, Avelina, but knew if I rescued you, I would have to rescue your brother too. Now, the people here don't know you aren't Britons. They'd refuse to have anything to do with you if they did. They're British patriots. The fact you can't speak the language is no problem. You were taken as slaves at such a young age, you can say you've forgotten it. You've probably forgotten your native tongue anyway."

She paused to listen. "No, she's not coming back yet. There are no names here, so no one can betray anyone. You know mine, unfortunately, but I think I'm fairly safe because it's not in your interests to tell anyone."

"What if we're captured?" Avelina asked. "We could betray you then in order to save ourselves."

Maeve smiled fleetingly. "We'll just have to make sure you don't get recaptured then, won't we?" She looked at Adelbehrt and frowned. "Now, if you give your real names to our people, they'll instantly know that you aren't Britons, so I suggest you change your names. I've thought about this and suggest that you Adelbehrt take the name of Ailbert and Avelina the name of Awena. They're fairly close to your ..." She paused as the door opened and the woman who had let them in re-entered the room.

"Here's the walnut juice," she said, setting a jug on the table.

"You can begin then, and I must go or I'll be missed. Good-bye and good luck, Ailbert and Awena." Quickly, she slipped through the door.

"Right, which of you is to be first?" the old woman asked.

When Adelbehrt—now Ailbert—stepped forward, she pulled a bowl and jug from a cupboard and placed them on the table.

"Bend your head over this bowl, Ailbert is it?"

The young man did as she asked and the old woman poured the walnut juice over his hair. It was still fairly long by Roman standards, just as the Domina had always liked it.

After pouring several times, she declared him done, wrung as much of the juice as she could from his hair and turned to Avelina—now Awena—and did the same to her.

"Tomorrow morning at dawn, a man will come for you. He'll take you out of the city to a safe place. You'll need to keep putting the walnut juice on your hair though, until you're far from Londinium. Now get some sleep. You can use the bed there. I'll snooze in this chair."

A sharp knock sounded on the door. Ailbert woke with a start, looking around and, for a few seconds, wondering where he was.

The old lady roused herself from her chair and woke Awena. "There are clothes on the chair over there." She pointed to one at the table. "You'll need to wear our type of clothing if you're to escape. You'll be travelling with other Britons. You won't look right in those Roman clothes. Go through that door if you want some privacy to dress." She indicated a doorway at the back of the room.

It led to a small room that seemed to be used more as a cupboard than a room, judging by the amount of stuff in it.

Ailbert quickly dressed in the clothes left for them. He told Awena to go into the room to change, but he changed where he was. He regarded the clothes. There were undergarments in linen, which he quickly donned after checking to see the old woman was not looking in his direction. Then he pulled on a pair of woollen trousers woven in a grey-and-yellow check. A tunic, also grey and yellow, lay on the chair and this he quickly slipped on.

Awena exited the small room dressed in a red-and-blue woollen dress that came down to her ankles. She carried a blue shawl and her dress was pinned with an ornate brooch. Ailbert smiled at her and, for the first time since she entered the small dwelling, she gave a brief smile in return.

"If you're ready, we'd better go." A man broke off his conversation with the old woman. He was tall with light sand-brown hair. He sported a beard and moustache, and his brown eyes smiled at the pair. He wore clothing similar to that which Ailbert had donned.

"Put on your cloak and shawl," the woman told them. "It's cold outside. It is November, after all."

They did as she instructed, pinning them together with more brooches, then followed the man outside.

"My name's Huw. Now, we need a story to get you past the guards at the gates. They saw me come in yesterday with goods to trade and I had no one with me." He paused and looked up and down the street. People were beginning to come out now the sun was almost up.

"The story is this. You're my sister's children. You came to Londinium to see your aunt, my other sister, who lives here. I'm taking you back home."

All three climbed onto the driver's seat of the wagon and the man clucked to his oxen, who lumbered forward. The man continued talking. "They'll have discovered you're missing by now, of course, but not necessarily that you're both together. Your descriptions will have been circulated to the gate guards. The dye in your hair will, hopefully, make you unrecognisable."

He turned the oxen into the main street, heading towards the gate on the northern side of the city. "It's better to have you in full view rather than trying to hide you under sacks. Since they'll be looking for you, they'll search all the wagons leaving the city. If you're hidden, they'll find you and quickly establish who you are. The best place to hide is in full view."

The ox cart lumbered through the city streets and soon they arrived at the north gate.

A soldier held up a brawny hand to stop them. "We have to search your wagon, I'm afraid. There are two runaway slaves. A brother and sister. They should be easy enough to spot though, as they both have very blonde hair. Almost white, they say and about the same age as your two passengers. I don't suppose you've seen anyone of that description, have you?"

Awena held onto Ailbert's hand and gripped it so tightly it almost hurt him.

"Don't worry," he whispered. "You heard what the soldier

said. They're looking for people with blonde hair, not brown like ours."

The soldier continued asking Huw questions, including who the two with him were. He remembered Huw coming into the city without anyone else in the wagon. Huw gave him the explanation he had told the pair previously.

The soldier looked at them and said, "I hope your aunt is in good health."

Ailbert smiled as best he could under the circumstances and endeavoured to look relaxed. "Yes, thank you. She's quite well."

"You speak good Latin," the soldier commented. "Where did you learn it? Hardly any accent at all. You could almost pass for a Roman, you know."

Ailbert thought quickly. "We were brought up in the city," he improvised. "Our mother thought we should learn Latin, so she sent us to live with her sister, our aunt, who had married a Roman."

The soldier nodded and seemed satisfied with the answer. "No wonder you wanted to come and see her then. If you lived with her all that time, I expect she was almost like a mother to you."

Awena kept a grip on her brother's hand until the soldiers had searched the wagon thoroughly, looking under the sacks in the back, and poking all around with their swords. Only when the soldier told them they could go, and they had pulled away from the gates, did she let go.

Ailbert let out a breath as they ambled into the countryside.

"We've got away," he said, grinning.

"Well, we've got past the worst hurdle," Huw said bluntly, "but the Romans will start looking outside the city as soon as they realise you must have got out somehow. We must still be very careful."

🦎 10 🐿

Outside Londinium, the wagon rolled along through the countryside. Ailbert and Awena sat side by side, next to Huw on the driving seat. They had not been this way before, because the Dominus and Domina had their villa to the west of the city and not to the north.

After a little while, they entered a huge forest. It was comprised of mainly oak trees, and dense undergrowth crept towards the road on which they travelled. It was a paved Roman road. Few weeds grew between the paving stones, and it was clean too. No muddy patches and ridges that travellers often encountered on unpaved roads.

"How far to the village?" Awena asked after a while.

Huw looked at her and smiled. She was a very pretty girl. "Not until sunset."

They travelled along in silence until Ailbert had a thought.

"I've only a little money that I saved," His brow furrowed. "How can we pay you for all you've done for us?"

Huw laughed. "Don't worry about that."

"But that's not right. You rescued us at no little risk to yourself, and the others. You must have spent some money too."

"We have a fund. Everyone who can afford it in Treafon, that's the name of our village, gives a little towards the rescue operations. Some people from other villages give money to us too, or other types of help. We don't like our own people being enslaved by foreigners. Anyway, when you are settled in, there will be work for you to do."

"Do you fight the Romans?"

"Not directly, no. Their army's too good for us to meet them on the battlefield. Look at what happened to Boudicca. She won at first, but the Romans eventually defeated her and her daughters were raped. No, we fight them in other, little ways, like rescuing British slaves."

Ailbert looked crestfallen at that, but fell to thinking: he might not be able to join an army to kill Romans, but maybe he could find *other* ways.

The wagon trundled through the forest for a few hours. They passed charcoal-burners' huts with smouldering fires tended by people sitting on one-legged stools. The charcoal-burners had to tend the banked fires at all times, so they simply smouldered and did not burn. Awena asked about the stools.

"They're so the watcher doesn't fall asleep," Huw told her. "If he does, the stool topples and wakes him up."

Ailbert laughed at the thought. "Clever idea."

Towards evening, the forest began to thin and soon they saw a large ditch and an earthen wall topped by a wooden palisade.

"Here we are," Huw announced as they trundled across the wooden bridge and through a gap in the earthworks.

The youngsters looked around the village. They were surprised to see that all the buildings were round. They had low walls made of wattle and daub, with a doorway and a steeply thatched roof that almost touched the ground. They could see no windows, but smoke seeped through the thatch, indicating that fires burned in some of the huts.

A boy ran up and took the oxen's heads while Huw jumped off the driver's seat and helped Awena down. Ailbert leaped from the seat and continued his observations of the place while the boy led the oxen away to where he unharnessed them and then began to unload the cart.

Some pigs and a few small cattle stared at the newcomers from pens at the far side of the village, and several dogs barked at the pair as Huw led them to one of the houses.

He called through the door. "Gwen? Here are the latest rescued slaves."

A tall handsome woman with brown hair that gleamed withreddish glints stepped out of the house. She appeared about forty years old and had a broad smile on her round face. She looked enough like Huw that Ailbert could see they were brother and sister.

"This is my sister, Gwen. She can speak Latin," Huw told them. "You're going to stay with her until we decide where you're to go."

The youngsters were surprised at this.

Huw continued. "We don't usually keep runaways here. It's too dangerous for both them and us. Too close to Londinium. They would easily be found."

"How long will we stay here, then?" Awena asked, her eyes darting from side to side as she wiped her hands on her tunic..

"Until we find a safe village for you. Far away from Londinium," Gwen told her.

She took them into her house. It was dark inside, lit by firelight only, and it was comprised of a single room. Benches lined the walls, with a few low tables scattered around.

At the back of the house stood a tall frame that prompted Ailbert to frown. What could that possibly be?

Gwen saw him studying it. "That's a loom," she said. "It's for weaving cloth." She turned to Awena. "I'll teach you how to use it. You'll need to know such things if you're to live among us. We Celts always weave our own cloth. You'd have learned in your home village if you hadn't been taken. Where were you from? We can perhaps send you back there."

"We were taken when we were very small," Ailbert replied. "We can't remember where it was or much about it. Truth is, Awena can't remember anything, and my memories are very dim. I remember it was by a wide river and that's about all."

He didn't like lying to this woman and her brother, but they had been rescued in the belief that they were Britons so he had to say that. He stuck as close to the truth as he could though, but he could not tell her that he vividly remembered the village by the Rhenus and his parents … and the terrible punishment the Romans had inflicted on them.

Gwen made them sit down and busied herself in preparing food. Huw had gone to his hut where his wife and family waited for him. She asked the two about their lives as Roman slaves. What kind of slaves were they?

"We were house slaves," Ailbert said simply.

"I was a personal slave to the little Domina," put in Awena. "She treated me well. Almost like a friend."

"But she wasn't a friend, Awena," Ailbert said gently. "You must remember that. A friend would have put up more argument about you being sent to the brothel."

"I suppose so. I miss her though." Awena hung her head.

"You were sent to a brothel? A young girl like you?" Gwen gasped. "How old are you? Thirteen, fourteen?"

"I think I've seen thirteen summers," Awena told her. "Ailbert says I was three or four when we were taken and we were there for nine years."

"Why did they send you there if they liked you so much?"

"The Dominus liked her a little *too* well," Ailbert explained through gritted teeth, "and the Domina found out. It was she who insisted on Awena going. I don't really think she would have insisted on sending her to the brothel if anyone had objected. She thought they would get more money for her from there, I suspect. After all, she's very pretty, and the Dominus hadn't had his way with her yet. I understand virgins are in great demand." Ailbert's eyes narrowed as he spoke.

"This made you angry then?" Gwen asked with a sympathetic smile.

Ailbert's voice rose as he answered. "Angry? Yes! What right has anyone to put a young and innocent girl through that? What right, for that matter, has anyone to take young children from their family and make slaves of them?"

Awena put her hand on Ailbert's arm. "Calm down, please. I'm out of there and I'm fine now I'm away from that dreadful place."

The meal was ready and they sat and ate in relative silence. Afterwards, Gwen told them about herself. She was a widow and had two live children, and several others stillborn or miscarried. Her live children were now dead, as was her husband. He had been killed fighting for Boudicca. She now lived alone and had told her brother she would like to have the two young people to stay with her. They were similar in age to her own children, had they lived.

Ailbert found the atmosphere in the house oppressive. Not all the smoke escaped through the thatch and he began to cough.

Gwen frowned. "Not sick are you? I've something that will help a cough if you are."

"No," the young man replied. "I'm just not used to the smoke. I expect I'll get used to it in time. Do you mind if I go outside for a bit?"

When Gwen told him he was free to come and go as he pleased, he rose and, pushing the leather curtain aside, exited the house.

Darkness had fallen while they ate and talked to Gwen. Ailbert could hear the lowing of cattle in the pens to the north of the stockade and grunts of pigs nearby. He wandered around, trying to get his bearings. First, he made his way to the entrance where he and Awena had entered. He then started to walk round the edge of the earthwork and passed pens with sheep before coming to the enclosures of the pigs and cattle.

Ailbert made his way back to Gwen's house and entered once more. It surprised him to find more people there now. Gwen introduced them as Huw's wife, Dera and her three children, Glenda, Dewi and Gwayne. Huw, himself, had also come.

"They all wanted to meet you both," she told Ailbert, handing him a horn of ale.

The visitors threw questions galore at the young people. Where had they come from originally? What did they remember of their family? What was it like to be taken away so young? What was it like being a slave? What was Londinium like? Was it busy? How luxurious was life in the city?

Ailbert and Awena answered as best they could, but soon, Awena could not stifle a yawn that threatened. Gwen noticed and ushered the others out. When they had gone, she pointed to the benches around the walls, telling them to use them to sleep on.

As the young people lay on the beds and covered themselves with the blankets and skins, Gwen banked up the fire and lay down herself. Ailbert reclined with his eyes open for a while, thinking about the change in their circumstances before reciting his litany of hate, as he had done every night for nine years.

Then, until he fell asleep, he attempted to remember all he could of his mother, father and little brother, although he realised his little brother was now about ten years old and not so little any more.

The next morning they woke to hear Gwen bustling around the single room. Ailbert stretched and smiled. He was free. No longer a slave, a nobody, someone to be ignored unless he did something wrong or someone needed him for something. He rose and dressed quickly, took the warm bread Gwen handed him, and thanked her.

By this time, Awena started to wake and when they had both eaten, Gwen took them outside.

"I'll show you round the stockade first," she said, "then you can do what you wish for the rest of the day."

Gwen showed them the granaries, round buildings much like the houses, and the blacksmith's forge, where he was busy at work. A potter worked at his wheel, creating a large pot. There were other tradesman too, making various goods.

She pointed out the pens where the people had brought the animals in for the winter, and she told them how they had slaughtered many of them, keeping only those required for breeding. They did not have enough fodder to keep all of them through the winter and, anyway, they needed the meat for themselves. Some they salted, but salt was a rare commodity, and so they hung most in the rafters of the houses to smoke.

At the entrance to the compound, Gwen indicated the fields; they radiated outwards from the village and were small rectangular areas, separated from each other by stone walls. Here the animals grazed in the summer and the villagers grew crops.

Gwen then excused herself. "I need to do some weaving and prepare a meal for us. Explore as you wish, but don't go too far away, just in case there are Romans about. I don't expect the message about two escaped slaves has reached here yet, but you can't be too careful."

Awena wanted to talk to some of the other villagers, so they stayed in the village. Ailbert, too, thought it would be a good idea to find out more about how these people lived if they were going to settle among them. After all, their lives would be very different living in a village of Britons from the one they had led as favoured house slaves in Londinium.

He realised they would probably not be living here very long, but wherever they went, it would be similar. He could hardly believe they now had their freedom. Awena could remember nothing of life before slavery, and he could hardly remember being free. They would find it very different.

The Britons were famed for their hunting dogs, and a few trotted around the compound. They barked at the strangers. Awena moved behind Ailbert whenever they saw one. She was afraid of the cattle and pigs too. In her life as a slave to Claudia, the little Domina, she had nothing to do with animals, except for a little cat Claudia had decided to adopt.

Ailbert, on the other hand, liked them. When the Domina did not want him to attend her, and later the Dominus or Marcus, he had spent time in the stables with his friend, Titus. He loved the horses and had sometimes wished Marcus had not decided he would be a good steward one day. Then he could have gone to work in the stables ... unless, of course, the Dominus decided to sell him when his usefulness as a pet passed. At that thought, Ailbert's hands clenched into fists.

The pair stood looking at the pigs in the pen when a little boy of about six approached. He said something to them, but they did not understand him as he spoke in the native language of the Britons. Awena looked at him and shook her head to indicate she did not understand.

A boy of about fifteen came up and said something to the little boy, who shrugged and then ran off. "He not understand how you not know to speak," said the boy in bad Latin. "I learn little of Latin, but not speak so good."

Awena smiled at the lad. "You speak well enough for people to understand you. That's what matters, really, isn't it?"

"Yes," Ailbert agreed. "Speaking is about letting people know your thoughts, and you seem to be able to do that."

The boy frowned as he tried to think of the words to say. "I say to you, welcome to village."

"Thank you," Awena replied with a smile. "You're very kind. What's your name? I'm Av … er … Awena and this is my brother, Ailbert."

"I, Madoc," he told them. "Little boy, my brother. Him Bryan. Him want know who you are. I tell him you from Londinium and come visit aunt." The speech seemed to exhaust Madoc and he blinked. "I go. I do work now. Father angry if I lazy."

With that, he ran towards the cattle pens and picked up a bucket.

Awena watched him. "He seems nice," she said.

Ailbert looked at her through narrowed eyes. "We have to leave here, remember? It's no good making firm friends. When we settle somewhere, then we can think about that. Until then, we must be polite and friendly, but not get too involved."

"Addy, I can't wait to get somewhere that I know I can make friends and live permanently. I thought we would always live with the Domina and Dominus, and I'd be Claudia's slave for always. Then it all went wrong, and now we're here, where we don't even know the language and are going to be moved again."

Ailbert looked into the distance and his voice sounded far away when he replied. "It all went wrong a long time ago, Avelina." He unthinkingly used her Germanic name. "It went wrong when the Romans came and crucified our father, took us away from our mother and sold us as slaves." He turned back to the girl and his eyes blazed. "That's when it went wrong, Awena. When you were just four years old. Almost a baby still. We don't even have our names anymore."

He turned his back on his sister and strode across the compound to where the smith worked at his anvil.

Awena watched him go, but did not follow. She made her

way back to Gwen's home. As she pushed past the skin covering the door, she was grateful for the warmth of the fire.

"Ah, there you are," Gwen said. "Where's Ailbert?"

"Don't know," Awena replied with a quick shrug. "He went off. He was a bit angry, I think."

"Not at you, I hope?"

"No." She smiled. "He's never angry at me. I think it's the Romans he's angry with. Do you know he chants a litany of hate every night, saying all the things the Romans have done to us?"

"Does he? I didn't hear him last night."

"No, he does it very quietly. He didn't used to, but he's learned not to let people hear him. He'd get into trouble if they did, I suppose."

"That's the very least that would happen." Gwen sat down on one of the large logs by the fire. "Now, Awena, you should learn something of our language so you can speak to other Britons. It may come back to you when you're learning, or it may not. It's nine years since you spoke it and you were only very small then. Perhaps all memory has gone."

When Ailbert came back, he found them sitting by the fire with Gwen pointing out things, saying their name, and Awena repeating them.

"Ailbert!" Awena exclaimed. "I'm starting to learn the language of the Britons. Come and sit down, and learn with me."

Ailbert's anger had dissipated after he left her and had gone to watch the smith work. The older man seemed friendly, but as he could not speak Latin, conversation was rather limited.

Soon Ailbert had wandered off, attracted to the animal pens where he could hear the lowing of cattle.

Madoc came up to him. "You like animals?"

"Yes, I do, but I really prefer horses. I liked being with them in the Dominus's stables. They have a warm, comforting smell that I like, and when they get to know you, they're very gentle."

"Perhaps you work with animals here. See, here is hunting dog. British hunting dogs very … er … very good known." Madoc searched for the right way of putting it. "I show you to dog. She then know you not enemy." He called the dog over and 'introduced' her to Ailbert.

Ailbert held out his hand and the dog sniffed it. , He gently stroked her head. She seemed to like it and he smiled at Madoc. "She's a nice dog," he told the younger boy.

"She have pups soon. We sell pups to Romans, who take them across sea. I go now. Work to do. Must feed sheep." With that, Madoc started to leave. Then he turned and said, "Girl with you. Awena. She very pretty. She sister? She look like you."

Ailbert frowned. "Yes, she's my sister," hereplied and thought, "but you keep your hands off her. She's only thirteen."

Ailbert returned to the house and sat next to his sister.

"Awena," said Gwen, "Tell Ailbert what you've learned."

She pointed at some things in the house that Gwen had provided the Celtic name of, with Gwen occasionally correcting the pronunciation.

Ailbert tried to repeat the words his sister said, and Gwen laughed as he mispronounced Awena's mispronunciations. Soon they were all laughing and the lesson became an enjoyable game.

Awena pointed to an object they had learned the name of and Ailbert tried to remember what it was called, and then did the same for Awena to try. This way, the afternoon passed quickly and Gwen got up to stir a stew thickened with oats, ready for the evening meal. The smell of the salt beef had been permeating the house for some time and Ailbert's stomach began to rumble.

Gwen laughed. "It won't be long now," she advised the young man as she regained her seat on one of the benches.

Several days passed in a similar manner. One day, Ailbert managed to go outside the village with Madoc. They took a couple of hunting dogs, but did not manage to raise any game.

While outside the stockade, Ailbert continued his language lessons by asking Madoc the names of things they saw. He soon learned the names of a number of trees and birds, as well as the words for field and wall.

He decided nouns were all well and good, but he needed to know more words. He began to ask about movement. He could show Madoc some things, like walk and run, even sit and lie, but when it came to fly, which he wanted to know when a flock of starlings flew by, it became more difficult. He jumped up and down flapping his arms until Madoc could not contain himself and doubled up with laughter. In a short time, Ailbert was laughing too, and the pair made their way back to the village, giggling like a pair of young girls.

So this is freedom, Ailbert thought. *I've laughed more in two days than I did in two months in Londinium. I like it.*

That day, Gwen sat the pair down and said, "I've asked the chief if you can stay here with me. You're the same age my boys would have been if they'd lived, and I enjoy your company. You'll not be a replacement for my children of course, but I've been alone since the death of the three who were dearest to me. I'd like someone to share my home. He asked if you wanted this, and I said I didn't know as I hadn't asked. He told me to ask you and to go back tomorrow to see him."

Awena stood up and threw her arms round the older woman. "We'd love to stay here, wouldn't we, Ailbert?"

"Yes, if that's possible." Ailbert frowned. "But won't that be dangerous for you and the rest of the village, us being so near to Londinium? There's also the problem of our hair. We have to keep dying it with walnut juice so our light hair doesn't show. If a Roman from Londinium saw our hair, they'd know who we are and then you'd all be in trouble for harbouring runaway slaves."

"Oh, tush," Gwen replied with a wave of her hand. "Walnut juice is easy to get. Huw can get walnuts in Londinium and I can brew the juice for your hair just as simply."

The next day they got permission to stay with Gwen. The headman asked a lot of questions, but in the end decided that with their hair dyed brown they would not be recognised, so it would be fairly safe for them to stay. In fact, he said, it was sometimes better to hide in full view; the Romans would not think the escaped slaves would stay so close to Londinium, and would soon be searching further afield.

Over the next few months, Ailbert and Awena concentrated on learning the unfamiliar language. They had a few problems with pronunciation, but Gwen was pleased with their progress.

Ailbert noticed whenever he was with Madoc, Awena was coming out of the house or passing by as they prepared for a hunt or went to tend to the animals. He also noticed Madoc's eyes follow his sister as she walked by.

He scowled as he thought about this. Awena was coming up to fourteen and had started to become aware of her impact on the men of the village. Madoc was not the only one to watch her as she passed, and Ailbert felt none too pleased at the looks in the eyes of some of them, and not just the young ones either. He did not want her to be taken advantage of. She was still a relatively innocent girl who did not know much about the wiles of men. True, she had received training in the brothel, and had learned a hard lesson with the Dominus, but underneath, Ailbert could see an innocent girl still there. No question, she could easily be taken advantage of.

He had promised his mother when he was only six years old that he would take care of her. He had done so all these years and would continue to do so. Warily, he watched Madoc and the others through narrowed eyes.

The weather grew steadily colder as winter crept on. The villagers slaughtered more of the animals and Ailbert helped with that, but Awena could not bear to see them being killed and, on those days, stayed inside the house.

Awena started to learn the things a young girl would have learned as she grew up. Gwen started her off combing the wool from the sheep. She did not have much left from the fleeces the villagers had shorn the previous spring, but she found enough so that the girl could learn.

The fleece had already been washed, Gwen told her, and as she combed them to make the fibres line up, the older woman enlightened her about the dyes they used to make the colours the Britons used in their colourful clothing. Awena found this job of combing the wool soothing and, as it did not take much brainpower, she could talk to Gwen while doing it.

Gwen insisted they speak in the British language all the time.

As Awena worked, she frowned in concentration. "Would you please repeat that?" she asked in Latin.

Gwen stopped spinning and looked at the girl with hard eyes. "In Brittonic, please."

Awena looked abashed. "Sorry." She reverted to her new language. "You say again, please."

"I said, you're ready to learn how to spin the wool now."

Awena's eyes lit up. "Really? You think I can do spin wool?"

"We'll not know until we try, will we?" Gwen smiled at the

girl's eagerness. "Now, put that combed wool down and come over here."

Gwen began to teach her the techniques of spinning. She took the wool between her finger and thumb, and twisted it dextrously. At the same time, she set a spindle rotating and the spun wool twisted itself around the spindle neatly.

"Now you try," she instructed the young girl, who was watching intently.

Awena took the spindle and the thread of wool from Gwen, and tried to twist it as she had seen the older woman doing. It was not as easy as it looked when done by an expert. She found it difficult to keep the spindle spinning while twisting the wool.

After a few minutes, she held up her work and cried out to Gwen. "Look what I done! I ruin piece of wool. It all ... er ... bumpy."

Gwen laughed. "You should have seen my first attempts. They were a lot worse than yours. For a first time, that's quite good."

"No! You be kind."

"I mean it. You must keep on practising, though."

Awena frowned and continued spinning, her tongue poking out of the corner of her mouth in concentration, while Gwen picked up a tunic she was making with cloth she had woven earlier.

Ailbert, in the meantime, learned more masculine tasks. He went on hunts with the other men and learned to use a sling to bring down small game. He had killed his first pigeon only a month after beginning to learn, and felt pleased with himself. However, that had been pure luck, as he did not manage to kill anything else for a number of weeks, while the other young men all had several kills to their names.

This did not deter Ailbert because he realised the others had been learning since childhood, and while they mocked his lack of skill, it was in a friendly way.

Day by day, his skills increased. His proficiency in the Brittonic language also improved daily. He did not receive the one-to-one tuition his sister did, but he learned by doing. He quickly understood the words for various animals, both the domesticated variety and the wild ones they hunted. He absorbed the words for different trees and plants too, as well as the crops they planted in the fields.

Ploughing began and he learned to guide the oxen pulling the plough. At first, his furrows were far from straight, but the animals knew what they were supposed do and this helped him. After the ploughing had finished, they scattered seed on the ground and said prayers to the goddess of fertility, making offerings to ensure a good crop.

The months passed. Both became better at the language and could now hold conversations. They did not even speak Latin to each other now. Gwen had long since stopped giving translations when her charges did not understand, and laughed when they had problems with words. In this way, they were forced to learn as quickly as possible.

Awena became better and better at spinning, and by the time the unspun wool ran out, the wool she had spun was good enough to make blankets, if not yet good enough to make clothes.

Ailbert became quite proficient with the sling too and rarely missed his target when he shot at it; the village did not go short of fresh game when they became tired of smoked or dried mutton or beef.

11

Soon it was Imbolc, the time when young lambs were born. The villagers had much preparation to do, for they invited the goddess, Brigid, into their homes to bless them, and they prepared special food for this day.

Awena was delighted when the villagers chose her to help carry the image of Brigid around the village. She helped clean the house with enthusiasm, sweeping out all the old rushes and piling them up outside, ready to be lit into a bonfire.

Ailbert laughed at her enthusiasm, saying he had never thought of her as a domestic type.

She stuck her tongue out at him in response. "It's important that everything is ready for Brigid."

"What about the gods we worshipped in Londinium? Have you forgotten them? Jupiter, Juno, Venus and the rest?"

"They're gods for the Romans." She shook her head. "They've no use for the Britons. Only if we become Roman Citizens will they care for us, and that's not going to happen. We're now Britons and we must worship the gods that care for the Britons." She carried on sweeping while Ailbert continued walking towards the sheep pens to see if any lambs had yet been born.

He met Madoc on the way and the boy told him excitedly that one of the ewes had gone into labour and the lamb, or hopefully *lambs*, would arrive very shortly. Ailbert quickened his steps towards the pens in the hope of seeing the actual birth. Being a house slave in Londinium, he had never been present at the birth of any animals owned by the Dominus and Domina.

They arrived in time to see the ewe pushing out what turned out to be the first of two lambs. Ailbert frowned. He had not expected blood. The little lamb lay on the ground, wet, and the mother turned to look at him, for it was a male lamb. Ailbert watched as she began to lick him clean. The second lamb was born soon afterwards and she repeated the process. The lambs staggered to their feet and immediately began suckling.

Ailbert smiled. He had witnessed a wonderful thing: new life being brought into the world. He ran off to tell Awena and Gwen that the first lambs had been born, and Imbolc was due to start.

At sunset that evening, the unwed girls carried the image of Brigid around the village. The villagers had made a crude image of reeds and the girls visited each house in turn, walked three times round it, and then asked for admittance for Brigid. Each house opened the door and let the image and girls in. They gave them food and each householder added a decoration to the reed image.

For some weeks before, the women and girls had been busy making Brigid crosses out of reeds, and one hung over the door of each house.

As it was winter still, it soon grew dark. Each household put out newly made clothes, and food and drink for the goddess. They also made a bed for her in the house, just in case she decided to visit.

They ate and drank the foods made for this special day. They had a kind of porridge made from the starch left in the husks of the oats, soaked, and left to ferment. It tasted sour to Ailbert and Awena, but they ate their share as it would have been discourteous to do otherwise.

The next morning, Gwen looked carefully at the ashes that she had raked smooth the evening before, to see any disturbances that might indicate that Brigid had visited during the night, but they were as smooth as they had been when they all went to bed.

Gwen led the way outside, to be met with frost on the ground and an overcast sky. "Ah! That's good. A cold, miserable day means that the Cailleach is still asleep and not gathering wood for fires to keep her warm through the next cold spell." She turned to the young people who frowned and looked at each other.

Ailbert shrugged.

"Cailleach is winter personified. If today is bright and sunny, then she can come out and look for firewood, and so keep herself warm for longer. If it's cold and miserable, or rainy and stormy, then she's asleep and will soon run out of firewood, so Brigid can bring the spring sooner."

They, along with the rest of the village, made their way to the well. Here, they walked round it in the direction of the sun and prayed to Brigid to bring health and prosperity. They gave the goddess offerings of strips of cloth and a few coins.

Singing and dancing followed, as well as eating and drinking, and the day passed quickly, darkness coming early during this time of year, halfway between the winter solstice and spring equinox. Tired and happy with the prospect of a good season to come, the villagers finally retired to their beds.

The next morning, as Gwen went about her normal tasks, Awena spoke to her. "What do you think of Madoc?"

"Madoc? Why are you asking?"

The young girl blushed. "He keeps on looking at me when I go outside."

Gwen smiled inwardly. So that was the way it was. She wondered why Awena kept making excuses to go outside. "Do you like him?"

Awena blushed again. "Yes. He seems very nice."

"He comes from a good family. His father's the black-smith, of course. Quite a high rank here in our society. You, of course, have no actual rank, being an immigrant. We've no idea what rank your parents had. Do you think your brother might know something about that? Perhaps he remembers what your father did in your home village."

Awena looked at Gwen. What was she suggesting?

As they talked, Ailbert entered. "Ailbert," Awena said, "Do you remember what our father did in our home village?"

"As far as I can remember, he was a fisherman. I remember going fishing with him many times, but whether that was just for fun or it was his main job, I really couldn't say."

"Fisherman?" Gwen scratched her head. "We don't have fishermen here. At least not as a profession. Some of the men sometimes go out onto the river and catch a few fish, but that's all. What sort of rank would he have?"

"I've no idea. As a little boy, I didn't think of rank. Why do you want to know?"

Gwen shrugged and thought for a few minutes, then looked at Awena. "I suppose we could say he was the equivalent of a farmer. That's a bit below that of a blacksmith, but I think we could overcome that problem. How would you like it if I went to his father and asked him about handfasting between you two?"

Both the young people gasped. This was not what they had been expecting.

"H-hand-f-fasting?" Awena stuttered. "I … well … yes," she finally managed to say.

Ailbert was not so sure. "She's still very young," he told Gwen firmly. "Only thirteen, or perhaps fourteen. We can't really remember when either of us was born, so we've been calculating our ages from the day we were taken as slaves."

"She's old enough to know she's attracted to Madoc, and he to her. She's also very pretty and very innocent. More so than our own young girls. This could be a danger to her as some man or other could exploit her for his own ends. If she were to be handfasted, it would be protection for her."

Ailbert nodded, although it was with hesitation. He still thought of his sister as a little girl he needed to protect. "I suppose that makes sense. Go ahead if you wish and speak to Madoc's father. I like the young man, and if I'm to have a brother-in-law, then I would be happier if it were someone I liked."

Two days later, Gwen received an agreement from Madoc's father that they could be betrothed at Beltane. That same day, Huw came back from a trip to Londinium with disconcerting news.

"Maeve's been taken," he said as he came into the house.

"How can that be?" Gwen asked him, stunned. "She's always so careful about keeping herself the perfect Roman wife."

"I don't know the details, but it seems someone saw something. Anyway, the old woman was taken and tortured. She gave Maeve away."

"But she wasn't supposed to know who our contact in Londinium is. How did she find out?"

"I know Maeve went to her insula when Awena and Ailbert were being rescued. She has some sort of interest in them, but I don't know why. I saw her there. She had wrapped herself up so no one could see her face though, and I'd be surprised if she were recognisable. How the old woman came to know who she was, is beyond me."

"I remember Maeve," Awena put in, her expression sombre. "She often came to the house of the Domina. She was the Domina's friend. I think they both came from the same village."

Gwen looked at the girl. "Yes, they did. It was this village. Maeve is our sister and when the Roman came and asked her to marry him, she agreed in order to help rescue Britons from Roman slavery."

"She's helped many slaves to escape, but has always kept in the background until now," Huw told them. "I only hope they don't torture her to find out where she sent the slaves. That will mean danger for all of us in the village."

"Is everyone involved?" asked Ailbert, staring at Gwen.

"No. Not everyone knows some of us are helping slaves to escape. Some couldn't be trusted because they can't help gossiping, and a few others would give us away for the rewards they would get from the Romans."

"This means danger for myself, Gwen and you two especially," Huw declared. He thought for a moment. "We need to get you three away."

Gwen huffed. "I'm not going anywhere, leaving you and your family in danger. You have a wife and three little children, remember?"

Awena stared at the others. "Surely they wouldn't harm the children, *would* they?"

Ailbert looked at her. "Remember why we're here, Awena," he said. "The Romans took us because they thought we were pretty and unusual children. It wasn't for punishment. They'd already punished our village. They wouldn't hesitate to enslave Huw's children just as they did us. In fact, they might think it was justice in view of the fact that Huw has been involved in rescuing slaves."

Awena spoke after a long pause. "What about my

betrothal to Madoc? I can keep my hair dyed and no one would recognise me as the girl who was Claudia's slave."

"It's not a risk we can take," Gwen stated. "If your hair is beginning to show its true colour at the roots just when a Roman's around, then you'll be recognised as surely as if you'd not dyed it at all. They aren't stupid, these Romans, more's the pity. And they never give up searching for escaped slaves either. Unfortunately, many we rescued were re-captured. I don't want that to happen to you two. I've come to look on you as my family."

"Then we'll have to go," Ailbert said firmly. "Where will we go to though?"

"You must get a long way away from Londinium. I think north, up Ermine Street. There's a new town being developed called Eberacum. The ninth legion built a fort there about ten years ago and the town's been growing ever since."

Ailbert drew back slightly. "Are you suggesting we go and live in a town full of Roman soldiers?"

"Not at all," Huw replied. "You'll go to one of the villages nearby. It's the land of the Brigantes. They've been a bit divided about Rome over the last few years. Just before the Romans founded Eberacum, there was some trouble."

"Trouble?" Ailbert said.

"Queen Cartimandua was in favour of Rome, but her husband wasn't. There were a few skirmishes between the pair, and the Cartimandua's husband captured her. Unfortu-nately, the Romans rescued her and then they began to build Eberacum. I suppose it was to keep the Brigantes quiet. However, there are still enough Brigantes who hate the Romans to take some escaped slaves, especially if they're Britons!"

Ailbert gazed down upon hearing this reference to him being a Briton. He had not come to terms with the fact that he was there under false pretences. He sometimes wondered if he should have stayed in Londinium in order to make his revenge on the Romans easier. He had not yet done anything —not killed a single Roman soldier.

Then he looked up, excitement growing. If these Brigantes hated the Romans, perhaps they would help him get his revenge. He had begun to talk to the young men of Treavon about getting back at the Romans but, as yet, he had not managed to spur any action.

His reverie was interrupted by Awena bursting into tears and jumping up from her seat. "I've just got betrothed and now I must leave. I don't want to leave Madoc. I'm sure he doesn't want me to go either. I must go and tell him."

She took two steps to the door when Huw grabbed her. "No, girl!" He nodded to the seat. "Sit down again. If you're to go, it must be in secret. If anyone—and I mean *anyone*— knows you've gone and where, then when the Romans come here, you'll be betrayed."

"Madoc wouldn't ..."

"Oh yes he would. Under torture, he'd tell them everything," Ailbert told his sister, as he looked steadily into her eyes "Remember the old woman—she revealed Maeve's part in all this under torture."

"Ye … yes, but she was an old woman and not a brave young man, and she wasn't protecting the one she was going to be handfasted to. I'd not tell them anything if it were Madoc in danger."

Ailbert smiled gently. "Yes you would, Awena." He took her in his arms. "You'd tell them everything and more. They can inflict pain such as you cannot imagine."

Upset, Awena turned to Gwen. "Won't you come with us? And you and your family, Huw? And why can't Madoc come too?"

"If too many people leave the village and move north, then *everyone* will suffer. The Romans will suspect this village is involved in helping slaves to escape and they'll wreak vengeance on everyone. No, Gwen and I will stay here, but I'll send my family. We can say they have gone to visit relatives."

The next morning, Ailbert and Awena left with Huw and his family on the pretext of going to see if some people they had heard of further north were their family. Huw reminded the villagers that his wife's people came from further north and he gave that as a reason for them accompanying him. He advised Ailbert that they did occasionally visit his wife's mother.

Huw's wife, Dera, was a small dark-haired woman with hazel eyes that always seemed to be laughing at something, although now they looked sad. Her eldest daughter, a dark-haired girl like her mother, stood with her mouth turned down and scuffing her feet in the dirt. She was about ten years old and didn't want to go on this journey. The children had been told nothing until they got into the ox cart, just in case they let something slip.

"Come on, Glenda," her mother instructed. "Get into the cart or you'll be left behind."

"Leave me then," the girl retorted. "Aunt Gwen'll look after me until you come back, won't you, Aunt Gwen?"

Gwen gently pushed the girl towards the cart. "Get in, Glenda. Don't hold everyone up. Look, your brothers are ready."

Reluctantly, Glenda climbed into the cart and off they went.

Madoc came out of his house and called, "Where are you going, Awena?"

Huw replied for the girl, who didn't know what to say. "We're off to see if some people in a village further north could possibly be Ailbert and Awena's parents. We heard they lost a girl and boy about their age to the Romans, so we thought we'd better go and see. Then, Dera and I will visit Dera's family while we're up north."

Madoc nodded as he heard this answer and called after the disappearing cart, "See you when you get back, Awena. We can then start to plan our handfasting." He turned away wondering why his words had made Awena burst into tears.

❧ 12 ❧

Maeve sat waiting for the slave market to begin. She shivered in the cold of the early March day. She knew she was lucky not to have been tortured to give away her co-conspirators in the freeing of Britons from slavery. The old woman, sadly, had died under torture and had given Maeve away, but Maeve could not blame her for that. She thought she would have probably given away even Huw and Gwen if they had tortured her.

Agricola, the Roman governor, decided that a suitable punishment for her would be slavery for herself and he ordered no punishment that would mar her in any way. He would make a nice little sum from her sale. She still had the good looks that had attracted her Roman husband and, while not in the first flush of youth, being in her early thirties, someone would buy her for her looks as well as her usefulness.

Maeve wished again she had not given in to her heart when she had visited the old woman's insula, but had instead followed her head. She wanted to see them and make sure that Huw managed to get them away. Her mistake had been in revealing herself to them. She thought the old woman had gone, but perhaps she had caught a glimpse of Maeve on her return. She would not have known Maeve, of course, but she must have seen enough to be able to give a description— enough that someone recognised her from it and told the authorities. Then, they had come to take her prisoner.

Her husband divorced her, of course. That was to be expected. Her two children would be fine. She had to believe that. She knew he loved them, but he would be under pressure to reject them because of her criminal activities. Would people pressure him, too, because now they had become the children of a slave? Children of slaves were slaves themselves and could not inherit.

She frowned at this thought. If he remarried, as he was likely to do, and had other children, would he put them before hers? Yes, she decided. He would. At that thought, she wept for the first time since being arrested. She had condemned her own children to slavery.

Maeve heard sounds outside—people arriving at the slave market. The rumour had spread that the wife of a prominent Roman citizen had been put up for sale for criminal activities. Some knew what she had done, but the stories grew with the telling until it she had been accused of everything from theft to attempted murder.

The auctioneer came in and told the slaves to strip off their clothes. Maeve was to be the last lot of the day. She had been saved until the end because of her notoriety and because she was an attractive woman. As she had been the wife of a Roman citizen, she would know about the running of a house- hold and would make a good housekeeper for someone. As she was a mature woman, she would not be flighty either. She knew all this as she walked out onto the platform. She had been to enough slave auctions on the other side.

She shivered in the cold and goosebumps rose on her skin. She became conscious of the hardening of her nipples in response to the cold too, and blushed but stood with her head held high as she looked out over the crowd. She was a Briton and proud of it. She had rescued many of her compatriots and was proud of that too! She had *nothing* to be ashamed of. Romans would have endeavoured to free Roman citizens in her position, of this she had no doubt.

The auctioneer had done right in keeping her until the end. Most people stayed to see her sold, if not to bid themselves. *Curiosity, of course*, Maeve thought as she looked round the crowd.

The bidding began. It was hotly contested, but eventually a man she could not see won the bidding. As the auctioneer led her down from the platform, she saw Annwyl looking at her. She saw sympathy in her friend's eyes as she turned away to return to her domus with her husband. Maeve knew she would never go into that house again, nor see her friend again. As she pulled on a tunic in preparation for leaving with her new owner, a tear trickled down her cheek … the last tear she shed.

Maeve walked into the room to meet the man who now owned her. She had little interest. She now had no rights and so it did not really matter who the man was. He would treat her as he saw fit. She would do her best to come to terms with her slavery, but the fact that she would never see her sons again almost made her tears begin anew, but she held her head high as she looked towards where the man handed over a purse of money.

There was something familiar about him, and when he turned around, Maeve gasped. She had been bought by none other than her ex-husband. She began to tremble as he approached. What would he do? Why had he bought her? Did he intend to treat her badly because of the things she had done? Had he guessed that she only married him so she could rescue slaves?

He took her by the arm and told her to get dressed. When she was again fully clothed, he led her back to the domus where they had lived as man and wife.

Only when they got inside did he speak to her. He sat down on a bench in the peristylium and closed his eyes, leaning back against no line break here!he wall. When he opened them, he watched her standing in front of him for a few minutes. Then, with pleading eyes, he asked, "*Why*, Maeve?"

She held her head high as she answered his question. "You Romans had no right to enslave Britons. You Romans think you have a right to do exactly as you please with anyone. You enslaved us all, all Britons, even those whom you made citizens. You're clever enough to make us think we ruled ourselves by allowing our kings to continue in their place. But even they are under your rule."

He gazed at his feet. "Did you ever love me, Maeve? I loved you. I *still* do."

Maeve wanted to go to him, but she was now a slave and had to keep her place. "I didn't love you at first. You were a good way to find out about where the slaves are." She dropped to her knees in front of him. He would not look at her. "But then I learned what a good man you are. I never loved you as you love me, yet I learned to respect you, and like you, and yes, I love you, even if not quite the way you would wish."

Her ex-husband stood and began to walk away. Then he slowly turned. "I bought you, Maeve, because I could not bear to think of you as a slave in another man's domus. You will be my housekeeper."

As he began to walk away, Maeve called after him. "What about the boys?"

He stopped, but did not turn this time. "Sadly, your activities have made slaves of them too. I love my boys, but I can no longer treat them in the same way. They will no longer be able to go to school, nor visit their friends. They will do small tasks around the domus, but I will not make them do anything too arduous, nor will I sell them, but their position has changed."

Maeve put her hands over her eyes. Her beloved boys had become slaves. No longer the privileged sons of a wealthy Roman, but the sons of a slave, owning nothing.

❀

"I wonder what will happen to Maeve," Awena asked as they travelled northwards.

"She will probably be tortured to try to get her to say who else was involved," Huw replied. "After that, if she survives, she might be put to death or she may be sold as a slave herself. It depends on what the Governor decides. If he's had an argument with his wife, it may be death, but if he's had a good day, he may be more lenient."

"And what about Gwen?"

Huw shrugged. "Who knows? We can only pray that Maeve is strong enough to resist the torture. If she doesn't tell them, then Gwen will be safe. If she does, then she will be in grave danger, but I trust her to manage to convince the authorities of her innocence. She's a very clever woman, is Gwen. Our father always said she was the cleverest of us, even though she's the youngest."

They relapsed into silence, each with their own thoughts until young Gwayne, Hugh and Dera's youngest child called out, "Aren't they Roman soldiers?"

That brought everyone's attention to the group of people approaching them. A troop of soldiers, indeed. Gwayne had been right.

"Do you think they've seen us yet?" Dera asked, gazing toward the soldiers .

"Can't say, but we'd better not act suspiciously," Huw answered. "They aren't coming from the direction of Londinium and so may not know what's been going on."

"Should we hide?" Ailbert asked.

"No. That would make them suspicious if we suddenly disappeared into the woods. No, we'd be best carryingon and hope for the best."

The soldiers soon reached the little group. There were eight soldiers and an officer. It was the small unit called a contubernium. As they passed, the decanus, as the officer in charge was called, stopped them to ask a question.

"We're on the way back to Londinium. We heard there had been some trouble with the wife of a citizen. Something about freeing slaves, I believe. Do you know anything more about it?"

Huw shook his head. "We did hear something of the sort in our village, but we left before any more news came out."

"Well, someone said she'd not been put to death but was going to be sold into slavery herself." He laughed. "A fitting punishment it seems to me. Well, we must be on our way." He called his men together and they set off marching at a quick pace towards Londinium.

"If that's true, then she's not going to die." Huw breathed a sigh of relief, but whether from the news that Maeve hadn't been put to death or because the soldiers had gone, Ailbert could not tell.

The others smiled as they drove on northwards.

They did not stay at inns on the way, just in case anyone staying there knew what had happened in Londinium and suspected they were somehow involved. They camped by the side of the road, near a stream if possible, and ate the dried and smoked meats they brought with them, along with some cheese.

The little group travelled a long way from the village where they had all lived and it took them the best part of two weeks to get to the vicinity of Eberacum. As they drew nearer, they began to look for inhabited villages or towns showing they were Brigantii and not Roman. Eventually, they saw a hill fort ahead and changed direction to reach it.

They approached the gate, which was closed, and Huw called out. The gates opened slowly and the wagon rumbled across.

Two earthworks, one inside the other, enclosed a large open area of a thousand square metres. The town was built inside these defences. It appeared very like the village they had left, but much larger. The usual round houses were clustered in the middle and pens for the animals stood towards the northern end of the town. At the other end, the tradesmen had their workshops. There was, of course, a blacksmith and a potter, but also other tradesmen. They saw a tanner and a whitesmith. Ailbert spotted a leatherworker making the leather he got from the tanner into a variety of goods.

When he turned his attention to the animal enclosures, a grin spread over his face as he saw horses.

A group of people came across to them and interrupted his observations. They were interested in seeing why the strangers had come. A man stepped out from the group. He was a big man with dark hair and a bristling beard. He wore a gold torc around his neck, indicating that he was a man of rank.

"Welcome to Pen Coed," he said amiably. "Judging by the goods in the back of your wagon, you're traders. We're always pleased to see people with goods we seldom get here in the north. What have you got to trade?"

Huw climbed down from the wagon and began to point out various things. "I have wine and olive oil from Rome. I've also got walnuts, and glassware as well." He took out some of these things to show the people gathered there.

The crowd grew as he began to pull out his wares. The man with the torc turned out to be the headman of the town. He walked over to Dera. "Are you his wife?"

She replied in the affirmative. "And these are my three

children: Glenda, Dewi and Gwayne. The other two are Huw's niece and nephew, Ailbert and Awena."

"Why are there so many of the trader's family with him? Traders don't usually bring their wives and children, let alone nephews and nieces when travelling."

"I've been visiting my family and Huw picked me up on the way. Ailbert and Awena wanted to come with us to see their other aunt, Huw's sister, who lives in our village."

Dera knew they would need to be careful and find out exactly where this settlement stood on the subject of the Romans. If they were Romanised and in favour of the Empire, then to reveal too much would put them all in danger. It was far enough away from Londinium for them to be safe if no one knew who they were, and a day's journey from Eberacum, so there would not be much danger from that city either if the knowledge of their escapades travelled so far north.

Dera shivered. It still felt cold although spring was on the way. It did not seem to be as far advanced here as it was further south.

The headman's wife noticed her shiver and came over. "I'm so sorry. I should have invited you into our house to get warm. Come with me. I have two children about the same age as your girl and elder boy, and as you can see," she patted her belly, "another one is on the way. Since we have a boy, we're not too worried about what it will be, but another boy would be nice."

She continued chatting while leading Dera, Awena and the three children to a large round house in the centre of the settlement.

Ailbert looked towards the horses. He wandered away from the trading going on and patted a bay animal that came to the fence when he approached. A dog growled at him as he passed, but a young man about his own age kicked the animal and it slunk away.

"Don't mind the dogs," he said, approaching Ailbert. "Just aim a kick at them and they'll go away. Do you like horses then?"

"Yes, very much. I spent as much time as I could with them when I was at … er … home," he said.

"This one is a softy. His name is Blaze because of the white blaze on his face."

"He's lovely."

The other young man pulled a wizened apple from his pocket and handed it to Ailbert. "Here, give him this and he'll be your friend for life." He laughed.

Ailbert took the apple and held it out on his hand, and laughed as soft lips nuzzled his palm when the horse took the apple. Ailbert leaned his head against the animal's nose and breathed in its scent. He had not realised how much he had missed the animals.

"Told you he'd be your friend for life," he said with a smile as the horse nuzzled Ailbert to see if he had any more treats. My name is Rhodri." He held out a muscular hand.

"Ailbert. Are you in charge of the horses?"

"Not really. My father is actually in charge, but I help him a lot. Since the fighting stopped, we've not had so much work for the horses. They used to draw our chariots into battle and also carry some of our soldiers. Now they pull our wagons and ploughs." He grimaced. "Not as exciting though. I sometimes wish the wars weren't over. I was born too late to be involved. It must have been exciting to fight the Romans."

"Your people were on the side against the Romans then?"

"Hush," Rhodri looked around. "I shouldn't have said that. The Romans rule us now and we're at peace. It wouldn't do to go fermenting unrest now, would it? The Romans are bringing us so many good things."

Somehow, Ailbert felt the young man did not feel as in favour of Roman rule as he made out. He would have to find out more while he was here.

"My uncle's rather busy. I'm supposed to be helping him with the money and trade goods. He likes to have them all written down" he explained to Rhodri.

"You can write?" the other young man asked, raising his eyebrows as the pair walked back to Huw.

"Yes, and figure too. I was learning … er … I learned it at school." Ailbert found some difficulty in remembering he was supposed to be the son of a Roman citizen and not a slave. It would not do for him to say that he learned it from a slave so he could take over that job when the slave grew too old. That would put him squarely in the slave category himself.

"Ah, there you are," Huw said as the two young men came up. "I see you've made a friend. We've finished here for now. After we've eaten, we can go through the sales and you can write them down. Adair here," he indicated the headman, "has invited us to his house, so come on."

Once inside, they found Dera deep in conversation with Adair's wife, whose name was Brianne. Ailbert was glad for the warmth of the fire as it felt cold outside and he held his hands out to the blaze.

Adair offered them a drink and then food. Hospitality was very important to the Britons, and in fact to all the Celtic peoples. Not to welcome travellers with food and drink would be very remiss.

They ate the food gratefully. The cold weather had made them hungry. After the meal, they settled down to talk. Adair invited them to sleep in his house for the night.

After a while, Huw asked, "Will you tell us about Queen Cartimandua? We heard a bit where we live, but not much."

"Well," Adair replied, looking around and not meeting Huw's eyes. "When Caractacus was beaten by the Romans, he fled here from Cambria, expecting to be sheltered. Instead, the Queen had him taken prisoner and handed him over to the Romans."

At this point, Brianne, Adair's wife snorted. Dera looked at her, but she quickly regained her composure.

Adair continued. "Cartimandua decided to divorce her husband, Venutius, and to marry his armour-bearer. He, the king, was very much against the Romans and fought them when they tried to move into this area. They defeated him though, and the Romans made Cartimandua queen under Roman rule. This is a good thing as far as Cartimandua is concerned. She gets to continue her rule, albeit under the Romans."

Ailbert looked at the people gathered round the fire. Awena and Dera stared at Adair, following his story with interest, although Dera looked closely at him with narrowed eyes. His gaze then went to Brianne. She had her eyes turned down as Adair told the tale. Why, he wondered?

Adair did not make eye contact with anyone, either. This was not what he had observed in the other man previously. He had seemed open and met the gaze of everyone with whom he spoke. Ailbert wondered about this. Could it be that this tale was not one that Adair liked and, if so, what did he not like about it? Could it be that this community was, in fact, against Roman rule in the north?

❧ 13 ❧

As he still did every night, Ailbert whispered his litany of hate before he went to sleep. "They crucified my father; they took my family away from me; they took my home from me; they took my friends from me; they took my country from me; they sent Odila to a brothel; they treated me like a pet animal; they sent Avelina to a brothel;they took our names from us;they made a slave of Maeve;they tortured and killed an old woman for helping us; they made us flee from our new village;they took Awena's promised one from her."

The litany had grown over the years and it seemed to increase with almost every day.

Ailbert woke to the sound of voices. He had slept long and well, and he found everyone else already up and breaking their fast around the fire. Brianne had banked it down for the night, but it now blazed again.

Awena looked up and saw him approaching. "You've slept late. Everyone was up ages ago."

"Is the sun up?" Ailbert looked towards the open door.

"Only just," Dera answered from the other side of the fire. "You don't need to worry. You've not slept in very late."

Ailbert grabbed bread and cheese, and went out into the

daylight. Dera had been right. The sun was only just up, but the husbandmen were already tending the animals in their pens. Beltane approached when they would turn them out into the fields. With his love of horses, Ailbert made his way towards where they were penned.

He met Rhodri carrying a bucket to get water for the animals. "Get yourself a bucket, and come and fetch water for the horses," Rhodri instructed the young man as he passed.

Ailbert did not need telling a second time and he quickly stuffed the remaining bread in his pocket, found a bucket, and ran after Rhodri.

A well stood in the middle of the settlement and the two young men filled their buckets, and carried them back to the waiting horses.

The bay that Ailbert had given an apple to the previous day came over and nuzzled him, hoping for another treat.

"He likes you," Rhodri said.

"Only because I gave him an apple yesterday." Ailbert laughed. "He's trying to find another."

Rhodri laughed too as they gave the horses the water.

A reddish-brown animal came over and pushed the others away.

"Hey, Tân, wait your turn." Rhodri pushed him away.

The horse laid back his ears and attempted to bite the young man, who deftly dodged the nips.

"He's called Tân, not only because of his colour, but because he has a fiery nature as well," Rhodri told Ailbert. "He loses his temper far too quickly."

Ailbert smiled and clucked his tongue at Tân. He held out his hand and the horse sniffed it. Ailbert felt in his pocket for the bread and held it out for the horse. Tân sniffed it once, then gently took it from Ailbert's outstretched hand. Ailbert gently stroked the horse's nose and spoke quietly to him.

Rhodri, who had been watching, smiled. "What a pity you can't stay here. You'd be good with the horses. You like them and, even more importantly, they like you—even Tân, who doesn't usually like anyone."

The pair went to fetch more water for the animals and began to chat. Ailbert thought he would try to find out if the community was really anti-Roman, as he had thought while talking to Rhodri yesterday, and last night as he had watched people's reactions in the house.

"How close is the nearest Roman town?" he asked casually.

"Eberacum. That's where the garrison is. They don't bother us much unless we give them trouble. They'd like us all to be Romans though."

"And what about you? Do you want to be Roman?"

Rhodri paused and looked away. "The Romans think we're barbarians and uncivilised. We're not though. We're as civilised as they are. Just different."

"That doesn't answer my question. I asked if you want what the Romans have—baths, theatres, gladiators, paved streets and such like. You've only told me the Roman idea of civilisation is different from your civilisation, not if you would like to have theirs."

Rhodri changed the subject and started back towards the pens. "We must get this water back to the animals."

Ailbert watched his retreating figure through narrowed eyes. Rhodri's back indicated the subject was closed.

In the house, once the men had gone out, Dera asked Brianne if she could do anything for her. Dera hated sitting with nothing to do. Brianne had some wool ready for spinning and so the two women took their spindles outside and began to spin the wool. As they span the fleece into thread, they chatted.

After a while, Dera stopped spinning and looked at Brianne. "I'm going to take a risk now," she said.

Brianne raised her eyebrows.

"While we talked last night, I watched both you and Adair. When we started talking about Cartimandua, you both looked nervous and embarrassed, as though you didn't agree with her actions."

Brianne looked down as Dera spoke and stopped spinning.

"I'm going to tell you our story," continued Dera. "We are, in fact, not what we told you. Oh, Huw is a trader, that much is true, but we're here because of a different reason." She took a lengthy breath before continuing. "In our village, after Boudicca was defeated, some of us wanted to do more for those Britons whom the Romans had enslaved. It was obvious we couldn't fight the Roman army, they're just too disciplined, so we decided to set up a group to free as many of our countrymen as possible."

Here Dera looked at her companion. Brianne watched her with interest. "Fortune smiled on us and we thought the gods were approving our decision. A Roman began to show interest in Huw's sister, Maeve, a very pretty young woman. This, we thought, would be a way to find out where the slaves were. Maeve married him and went to live in Londinium. She found out where enslaved Britons lived and sent them messages with a trustworthy person from our village. We found an old woman, a Briton of course, living in an insula in the poorer part of the town, and we used her insula as the place where we took the slaves we'd rescued."

Brianne looked intently at Dera. "How did you get them out of the town?"

"That was another problem. We decided we'd use Huw's visits to Londinium to get the slaves out. He was already well known as a trader and so could come and go without much trouble." She looked around to see if anyone was nearby. When she saw no one, she continued. "Usually, we tried to get slaves out before the Romans raised the alarm. That same day, if possible. Huw hid them in his wagon or even had them sit beside him. If the guard on duty was the same one as when he came in, he would know Huw hadn't had anyone with him when he came in and, in these circumstances, he left by a different gate. We brought them to our village, but only kept them for a night, then moved them to another until they were far away.'

"Why are you telling me this? We could betray you to the Romans."

"But you won't, will you? If you were going to, you wouldn't look as you do now."

"That tells me you were subverting the Romans and doing something to aid our fellow Britons. It doesn't tell me why you're running away. You are running away, aren't you?"

Dera paused for a moment. "Yes, we're running away. Someone saw something when we took Ailbert and Awena to the insula. The Romans came and took the old lady and tortured her. Before she died, she gave Maeve away. She should never have known about Maeve, but the silly girl took a fancy to these two and went to the insula to make sure they got away safely. The old woman's description was good and Maeve was captured. We have no idea what has happened to her."

Brianne put her hand on Dera's arm. "I'm sorry about Huw's sister. So, Ailbert and Awena were slaves?"

"Yes, they were slaves and we rescued them. They have their hair dyed because it's very light and makes them easily recognisable."

"I'll speak to Adair later. I'm sure you'll be welcome to stay here."

Later that day, Adair came and spoke to Huw. He told him

Dera had told Brianne about why they had come north and invited them to stay in the settlement. They could always use more hands, and a trader would be useful to have. The boy, Ailbert, looked as though he would be good with the animals, especially the horses, and they would find a good match for Awena. New blood was always welcome.

Huw had mixed feelings about what Dera had done in telling Brianne about them. He felt partly annoyed that she had taken such a big risk, as he saw it, but then again, they could not have stayed much longer. A trader family would be expected to move on, and it pleased him they had now been accepted. This community liked the Roman occupation no more than his own did.

They would be safe here, far away from Londinium and with like-minded folk. Perhaps Ailbert and Awena could let their hair go back to its natural colour. That would certainly bring interest from the young men in terms of a handfasting for Awena.

They told the two young people that evening. Ailbert grinned at the thought they had found a new home, but Awena burst into tears and ran out of the house.

Dera followed and put her arms around her. "What is it? The people here seem nice enough and we won't have to go any further to look for somewhere to live. We'll be safe here, far away from Londinium."

"And I'll never see Madoc again." Awena sobbed into Dera's shoulder.

"You knew that when we left."

"I hoped we'd not find anywhere to live and would go back. We'd just got settled in. I'd found a young man I love and was to be handfasted to him. I learned to love Gwen, too. Everything was going so well, then we had to leave it all again. It's not fair."

Dera held her until the crying abated. "Awena, you're very young. This will be our home from now on and you will no doubt find someone to handfast here. You won't forget Madoc, but you'll forget your love for him."

Awena tore herself away from the other woman's arms. "No! There can never be anyone like Madoc. I'll not marry anyone then." She turned her back on Dera, who stood for a moment regarding the girl, then turned and walked back to the house.

Before long, they had to build their own house. They could not live with Adair and Brianne indefinitely.

First, they needed to choose a site for the house. There was space near the edge of the settlement, not far from the gate, and Huw said it would be a good place for a trader. He decided to build there. It would be handy when he went on trading expeditions.

They next needed to find wood for the walls of the house. The Britons built the walls from hazel branches woven between vertical poles, and then daubed with mud to keep out the wind. The roof they built of more poles joined together at the top, and thatched.

Most of the town turned out to help with the building of Huw and Dera's house. Ailbert and Huw went into the forest with some of the other men to look for suitable branches. Finding a sufficient number was quite a difficult job; the branches had to be tall enough to be buried in the ground and yet leave enough above the ground to serve as the walls of the building. Then, they cut another seven or so longer branches, and finally a long sapling to make the king post of the house —the central pole to hold up the roof.

In order to drag the stakes to the settlement, they took a couple of horses into the woods and harnessed them to the logs. Ailbert helped with the horses, enjoying himself immensely. This was what he had wanted to do all the time he worked with Titus in the stables in Londinium. He whistled as he led the animals from the forest to the town.

When they got the stakes back to the town, the blacksmith heated the ends to prevent rot, they buried the blackened ends of the smaller poles in a circle, adding seven taller ones in a smaller circle inside this one. The men joined all the posts together with long pieces of wood along the tops.

The sun began to set and everyone who had been helping retired to their own homes for the night. Huw, Dera and their family, along with Awena and Ailbert spent another night with Adair and Brianne.

"We won't trouble you much longer," Dera told Brianne that evening. "The house is coming along well. Just a few more days and it will be ready for us."

"Don't you worry, Dera," Brianne replied, smiling cheerfully, "but I know how you must long to get into a home of your own. Staying with someone else is not ideal."

The two women laughed. In the short time Huw and his family had been in Pen Coed, Dera and Brianne had become firm friends.

The next day it was time to begin weaving the hazel branches around the outer stakes. Several of the women turned out to do this and, with so many hands, they quickly finished the job.

Dera stood back in the light of the setting sun and smiled as she saw her home rising from the ground. Soon they would be living there and be full members of Pen Coed. Her only worry was how Gwen and Maeve were faring.

One morning, Awena went with the smaller children into the fields where the cattle grazed, carrying leather buckets. They had been given the job of bringing as much dung back to the settlement as they could find.

Awena wrinkled her nose up at this job. "Do I have to? It's disgusting."

"Awena, we want to be accepted in this village," Dera

said, with her hands on her hips.. "In order for that to happen, we must do as they do. I know this is different from what you knew before, but you aren't in Londinium anymore and we need a house, so we must build one ourselves."

Grumbling under her breath, Awena joined the others on the way to the fields. Once there, she paused by a dry stone wall as the others climbed over it and made their way between the cattle and horses, collecting dung as they did so.

Awena regarded the animals. They were so big. What if one of them decided they didn't like her and attacked? After all, they knew these people; she, however, was a stranger.

A little girl stopped and looked back. "Come on, Awena. There's lots of dung here!"

Awena swallowed and climbed the wall. A cow lifted her head as the girl passed, looked at her, then resumed grazing. Awena, eyes fixed on the cow, began to gather dung with the others.

When the dung gatherers returned, they tipped the buckets into a pit along with clay. She saw Ailbert carrying straw and water, and he too added it to the pit with clay. Then, to make the daub, some of the men entered the pit and began to tramp on it in order to mix it together.

Ailbert and Awena watched with fascination. The people in Pen Coed knew the pair had grown up in Londinium and did not know how to build a house, and they helped and explained to the young people as the house grew.

Awena watched people bring buckets of the daub to the house.

"It's time to finish the walls."

Awena jumped. She had not heard Dera coming up behind her. "Come on girl, and help."

She followed Dera to the wattle walls, wondering how they were going to apply the thick substance. Dera plunged her hands into a bucket and brought out a sizeable quantity of daub, which she plastered onto the walls, pushing it well into the wattle.

Turning to Awena, she beckoned with dirty hands. "Come and help. Don't just stand there looking."

Awena wrinkled her nose, but ambled towards where Dera and several other women worked. "Won't it smell?"

"Not when it's dry. Now, take handfuls and push them well into the wattle, between the hazel branches. We need a lot of daub. It needs to be about as thick as your thumb is long to ensure it's weatherproof."

Slowly, and with a twisted face, Awena picked up two handfuls of daub and pressed it into the wall. After a while, she found the smell didn't bother heranymore; in fact, she found it quite satisfying work.

Ailbert watched as men climbed up and attached wooden crosspieces to the long poles of what would be the roof. After a few minutes, several more men appeared, carrying a long snake of reeds tied together. This snake they placed around the bottom of the roof, on the top of the now finished walls.

As he watched the procedure, it became clear why they needed this 'snake'. The men pinned bundles of straw to the snake before fastening them to the crosspieces on the roof structure. Gradually, as the men climbed up to affix more bundles, the roof took shape.

One young man named Gareth, a friend of Rhodri, asked Ailbert if he would like to help. Ailbert looked at the roof with the men crawling over it. In Rome, people did not build their own homes but had specialists to build them. He decided, though, that since he was to be a Briton from now on, he had better learn these tasks.

He climbed slowly onto the roof. The others were used to doing this, but his palms sweated, threatening to make him slip. What if he fell? What if his weight caused the roof to collapse?

Rhodri laughed at him as he crawled to where the next bundle of reeds lay, but the roof held, and Ailbert managed to fix the bundle to the one underneath with no ill effects.

"Make them tight," Rhodri instructed. "You don't want it to rain inside the hut. It's bad enough when it rains outside. And if they're not tight, then the wind'll get in … and perhaps snow, too."

Ailbert did not look at his friend, but kept a tight hold as he fastened another bundle.

Slowly, the roof neared completion. Gareth turned to Ailbert. "Here we don't pin the bundles so tightly together. We need to leave them a bit looser so the smoke from the fire can escape."

Ailbert sat back on his heels. This was hard work. He had been a house slave and not used to doing manual labour. He puffed loudly.

"Not tired, are you?" Gareth laughed.

Ailbert stretched. "Not at all." He picked up another bundle of reeds and pinned them to the one below, taking care to leave it a little looser.

Once they had finished building the outer part of the house, they dug a fire-pit in the centre and lined it with stones. When lit, the smoke would seep through the looser bundles of reeds near the top of the roof.

Everyone in the settlement had lent a hand with the building and furnishing of the house, everyone having wanted to do their part to welcome the new family into the town.

When the house had been completed, and the daub had dried, Dera brought her cauldron from the wagon where it had been all this time, and Huw carried in the firedogs. Dera told Awena to get water and when the girl returned, she poured it into the cauldron. Huw lit a fire while Dera and Awena sliced vegetables and smoked beef that Brianne had given them. Then Dera hung the full cauldron over the fire and turned to the rest of her little family with a big grin.

'We've now got our home, thanks to these kind people. I'm sure we'll be very happy here.'

The children clapped and Huw went over to her and gave her a big hug. All they had left to do was throw blankets over the wooden trestles around the walls and sit on the logs around the fire.

Not long after the townsfolk had finished helping with the building of Huw and Dera's house, Ailbert decided it would be a good idea for him and Awena to have their own, and so the procedure started all over again.

This time, Ailbert could help much more, and he and Awena moved into their own house in what seemed like record time.

"Our own home, Ailbert," Awena said as they crossed the threshold for the first time. "Who would have thought it only a year ago? I can cook a bit now, too. Dera taught me, but I still need help with some things."

Ailbert hooked an arm round his little sister. "I'm sure whatever you cook will be excellent," he told her with a smile.

"And I'll need a loom, eventually," Awena advised. "At the moment, I'm not good enough to do much weaving, but I'll need one so I can weave cloth to make into clothes for you."

Ailbert laughed and told her he would find out how to make one, but that it might not be very good.

They laughed again at each other's inadequacies in this new life and promised each other they would learn as fast as they could.

Then Awena banked up the fire and they slept for the first time in their very own home.

🦋 14 🦋

One morning, Huw got up and said that he should go to Londinium.

"Why?" asked Dera, frowning.

"I'm a trader, dear. I need to trade. I can buy stuff from the people here to take to trade, and I'm sure the folk in Eberacum will be grateful for some of the things I can get in Londinium. Look how anxious the people there were for things like wine and olive oil. If I can get some at a good price, then I'm sure I can sell it in Eberacum for a profit."

"But what if you're recognised as Maeve's brother?"

"No one knew Maeve had a brother. Her work was secret."

"Who knows what she told them under torture!"

Huw put an arm round his wife. "Look, Dera, I know you're worried about it, but I'll be very careful. If you like, I'll go to Treavon and find out exactly what's going on as regards our old enterprise. If there seems to be any danger whatsoever, then I'll come straight back and do no trading at all … well, perhaps a little on the way."

Dera gave up. She knew it was no use arguing with her husband if he had made up his mind. She turned to the cauldron hanging over the fire and stirred, saying, "Go then, but if you don't come back all in one piece, then you'll be in even smaller pieces when I've finished with you."

Huw chuckled and ducked through the door to bargain for goods he thought people in Londinium might want.

Two days later, Huw was ready to leave and he harnessed the oxen to the loaded cart. He felt a little dubious about one of the boxes. It contained three hunting dog pups. He knew hunting dogs from Britannia were in demand by the Romans, but taking three pups in a box down the long road to Londinium was quite an undertaking. He would have to take food for them and ensure they could relieve themselves. Still, he could make a good profit from them, so he decided it was worth any problems it may entail.

Dera watched as the wagon trundled through the gate and onto the road south; then, with one last wave, she shook her head and returned to the house.

"How long will daddy be away?" asked Gwayne.

"I don't know, really," replied his mother, smiling at the little boy. "It could be three weeks, or even more. It's a long way to Londinium."

"I know that! We came a long way, and it's farther than that."

His mother smiled again and said, "Of course you do. Come on, let's go back to the house now."

Two weeks passed, then one more. Ailbert became quite competent with the general work in the settlement. He helped with everything he could, but as a house slave in Londinium he had had next to no experience in farming.

He decided he must do his best though, and he learned quickly.

He helped plough the land for the sowing of spring crops. He enjoyed this task as it meant he could work with the horses. The villagers decided the horses had better be used for something, as they were not going to be used to pull war chariots.

One day, Rhodri, with whom Ailbert had struck up a firm friendship, called to him. "Ailbert, are you very busy?"

Ailbert shook his head.

"Then come here. This cow is about to have her calf. She might want help."

Ailbert crossed towards where Rhodri stood by one of the animal pens. He felt a fluttering in his stomach. Would he be able to help if the cow needed him?

The cow managed perfectly well. She had calved before and knew what she was doing. Soon, a little creature, still wet from the birth, struggled to its feet and began to suck at its mother's teats.

He remembered the first time he had seen the birth of an animal—the lamb that had been born when they had stayed in Treafon. He stood watching alongside Rhodri, his eyes aglow at the miracle of new life.

He was brought back to reality, however, as Awena rushed over calling, "Huw's back! He's got lots of things to trade in Eberacum!"

Ailbert dragged himself away from the calf and its mother, and ran to his sister.

"Look what he's brought me." She held out a brooch made from an orange, translucent material. "He brought Dera a necklace made from it too. It's called amber and comes from a long way away. They find it in a land near the Mare Balticum. There's lots of it there, Huw claims. Isn't it pretty?"

She ran back towards their home. Ailbert apologised to

Rhodri and followed his sister to see what Huw had managed to get to trade in Eberacum.

As he left, Rhodri called after him. "Some of us are meeting this evening. Come to the well at sunset."

Ailbert waved his assent and wondered what it was about. Still, he would go, if only out of curiosity. They were probably planning a big hunt or something.

Once back at the house, he saw Huw's wagon loaded with goods. The trader had brought back amphorae of olive oil and wine, of course. That he had expected, but he noticed a number of boxes too. Huw opened one of them. It contained more amber jewellery like the brooch that Awena showed him.

"A shipment of this stuff had just arrived when I got to Londinium," Huw told him. "It wasn't cheap, but I think I got a reasonable price. Enough to make a profit, anyway. Here's a box of the raw stuff. I can sell this to a silver or goldsmith, who can make items himself."

He opened another box containing glassware, then another of fine pottery. His family gasped at all the wonderful goods he had managed to acquire.

"These things are much better than you got when we lived near Londinium," Dera rubbed her hands together as she looked at his purchases.

"I was concentrating more on the release of our people then, dear. Now I can give all my attention to trading."

"I worry about you travelling the roads. If you've to keep going to Londinium or beyond, I'll be anxious about you being attacked."

"The roads are a lot safer now the Romans are here. They patrol them with their soldiers. Bandits don't try to attack nearly as much as they did."

Everyone was impressed by the goods Huw brought back. He decided he would go to Eberacum in a couple of days, giving him time to rest and to sort through the goods he had brought back. He told Ailbert he wanted him to go with him to help. The fact that the young man could read and write, as well as having a little experience, would be a great asset in the world of trading.

Ailbert agreed, looking forward to going to the city. He had not ventured far from the settlement except to do a bit of hunting in the surrounding forest, and he wanted to see if Eberacum looked anything like Londinium, which was the only city he could say he had seen. The places they had passed through, and stayed at on the way to Britannia, were vague memories he felt he could not trust.

As the sun began to set, Ailbert made his way to where Rhodri told him the young men were meeting. As he approached, one young man of about eighteen looked at Rhodri and asked gruffly, "What's *he* doing here? He's a stranger. We don't know if we can trust him."

"Come on, Rees," Rhodri stated. "He can be trusted. I know he hates the Romans as much as the rest of us."

Rees turned to Ailbert. "Rhodri says you hate the Romans. Tell us why."

Ailbert looked at the other young man and chanted his litany of hate. "They crucified my father; they took my family away from me;they took my home from me; they took my friends from me;they took my country from me;they sent Odila to a brothel;they treated me like a pet animal; they sent Avelina to a brothel;they took our names from us; they made a slave of Maeve;they tortured and killed an old woman for helping us;they made us flee from our new village;they took Awena's chosen man from her."

Upon hearing this, all nine of the young men gathered round the well stared at Ailbert. This litany could not have been made up on the spur of the moment, so they knew some of it at least must be true.

Gareth, who appeared to be their leader, said, "It seems you have a great deal to hate the Romans for. You can join us if you wish. We're planning an attack of some kind. It would be great if we could stir a full rebellion, but I don't think the older men would join us. We need to decide what kind of things we can do to disrupt the Romans as much as possible, and even kill a few. If we cause enough trouble, then maybe they'll decide it's not worth staying here and go away."

"Boudicca nearly succeeded in the south," put in Ailbert. "Unfortunately, the Romans came back from Mona before everything had settled down."

"And perhaps Venutius would have had some success if Cartimandua hadn't been so difficult. If she'd fought the Romans with him and Caractacus, perhaps we wouldn't be under Roman rule now," someone said solemnly.

Gareth looked around. "Now, how are we going to fight the Romans? Perhaps we could send a message around the other settlements, asking people to join us. Then, when we've gathered enough men, we could fight a battle that we could win."

"We'd need *thousands*, Gareth," Rees stated from the back of the group. "How are we going to get so many?"

"When people hear about our proposed rebellion, then they'll come, I'm sure."

"No, not enough, Gareth. We can't fight the Romans. Have you seen their organisation? That's the reason we've never won against them. This meeting is a waste of time. The Romans are here to stay and we'll have to get used to it."

"Don't be so defeatist, Rees," piped up someone else. "There must be *some* way we can fight them."

As Ailbert had been listening to this, he had been thinking all the time. He then spoke with an idea that had been going round his head. "You're all good hunters and are successful in killing your prey. Why is that?"

Silence fell as the young men looked at him and wondered what this had to do with attacking the Romans.

"We all know how to be stealthy and to hide. We only shoot when the animals are confident and not easily spooked."

Rees said, "This is all nonsense. Hunting has nothing to do with raising a rebellion against the Romans. I'm out of here."

"Wait, Rees!" Ailbert's voice was firm and confident. "Hear what I have to say before you go."

Rees settled down with a humph and grumbling no one else could understand.

"You're all successful hunters because you know your prey. You know where they'll be and when. Then you hide so you can't be seen, and shoot from cover. The animals don't know what's happened. This can be used against the Romans." Ailbert looked to the back of the group and his eyes found those of Rees. "I agree, Rees. We can't fight them out in the open and so I propose we hunt them instead."

Ailbert was surprised when a round of cheering erupted.

Gareth spoke. "Ailbert has some excellent ideas. I suggest we make him our leader in this. I couldn't have come up with a plan like that."

They greeted this suggestion with another round of cheers; in this way, Ailbert found himself the battle leader of a group of young hotheads who wanted to fight Roman soldiers.

❧ 15 ❦

Ailbert dismissed the young men at that point, telling them he would need to consider a more detailed strategy. As well as that, he would need to think how he could discover the movements of the Romans so that their 'army' could lie in wait for them. This would not be an easy task and he wandered back to his home deep in thought.

He liked the idea of attacking the Romans. He had no real thoughts that they could win, or even make them think that staying here was not worthwhile, but he liked the idea of disrupting them and killing some of them. His hatred truly ran deep.

Ailbert entered his home as darkness started to fall. The siblings ate the meal Awena had prepared and then Ailbert said he felt tired and retired to bed. In reality, he wanted to continue thinking about plans to attack the Romans.

He rose the next morning and went out to feed the livestock. He still enjoyed working with them. One of the dogs ran up to him and he bent to pat it, then proceeded to where the horses and cattle lived for the winter.

On reaching the enclosure, Ailbert picked up a bucket and

went to get water for them. On the way, he met Rhodri, who picked up another bucket and accompanied him.

"Your sister ... well, what I mean is ... she's beautiful. I like her a lot."

Ailbert stopped and looked at his friend. "What is it? What are you trying to say?"

"This is difficult," Rhodri began with a faltering smile. Then he released the words all at once. "I'd like to handfast her. Do you think she'd have me? Should I ask your uncle? Will he approve?"

Ailbert laughed. "Well now, there are a lot of questions there. First, I'd make sure she wants to handfast you before asking anyone else. Second, I can't say what she thinks of you. She's said nothing, but you know she was promised before we came here, don't you?"

"I'll have to talk to her then." Rhodri walked towards the animals with his bucket of water.

"You do that, then go and see Huw, and see what he says," Ailbert said to the retreating figure. "I don't suppose he'll object."

Rhodri stopped as he poured water into the trough. The cattle jostled for position, nearly knocking the young man over. "Do you think she's got over the other one? The one she was promised to before you came here?"

"I really couldn't say." Ailbert added his bucket of water to the trough. "She isn't moping like she was at first, so that's a good sign. She doesn't talk about him either, but whether that's because she's over him, or because she finds it too painful, who knows?"

The pair went about their daily tasks and spoke no more about it.

That evening, Awena greeted Ailbert as he came into the house. "Rhodri has asked me if I'd like to handfast him. I'll need your permission, of course, as my nearest older male relative. What do you think of him?"

"Awena, I like him very much. He's become a good friend to me since we arrived here." He paused and looked at her. "But do you want to handfast him? It's not enough to say you like him. You'll be spending the rest of your life in his company."

He looked into his sister's eyes as though seeking the answer to a question. Awena stared back. "You're wondering if I've got over Madoc, aren't you?"

Ailbert said nothing, but turned his eyes away from hers.

"You are. Well, for your information, I've not thought about him for months. He was just a child in comparison to Rhodri."

Ailbert smiled at that thought. Awena was still a child herself, in his eyes, although of an age to be handfasted. She always would be he suspected. He had looked after her for as long as he could remember. Even before they were taken as slaves his mother used to ask him to mind her while she tended to the baby.

His face fell as he thought about his real family. What was his little brother called? He could not remember. He then wondered if his mother had remarried and had more children. She had not been old when the Romans took him and Awena as slaves, although at the time he had thought of her as such. He sank down onto a log by the fire-pit.

Awena strolled over to him and sat down on the log as well. She put a hand over his. "What's wrong? Don't you want me to handfast Rhodri?'

Ailbert shook his head. "It's not that, Awena. I was thinking about our parents and wondering how our mother has managed all these years."

"I expect she got married again. She'll have more children now to replace us. She's probably stopped thinking all about us." She stood up and smiled, forgetting about the mother she could not remember. "Anyway, what about me and Rhodri? Will you give your permission?"

Ailbert smiled, realising she could not remember anything of their life before slavery. She had been such a little girl. Her attitude now was not because she did not care, but because she could not care. How could she care about something she could not remember?

Ailbert stood and hugged his little sister. "You have my permission, Avvy." He used the nickname he had given her when they were both small and she was called Avelina. Then he released her and said, "You realise though, that everyone here thinks Huw is your uncle. As such, it'll be him that Rhodri goes to for permission."

Awena's hand went to her mouth and her eyes widened. "Oh, do you think he'll refuse?"

"I think he'll not know what to do. He's not actually your uncle. I'm your only blood relative here, but no one knows that." He paused for a few minutes and then slapped his fist into his hand. "Got it! I'll tell Huw I approve of the match and he can tell Rhodri. That way, I'll be giving permission, but everyone will think it was Huw."

Awena flung her arms round her brother, extolling his cleverness in thinking of a way round the problem.

The conspirators met to discuss plans. Some of the more hot-headed of the lot wanted to rush out and ambush Roman soldiers immediately, but Ailbert forbade them.

"We need to make sure we can succeed before we attack any Romans," he stated. "They're well-disciplined and unless we work together and disappear quickly, they'll catch us. Then it'll all be over. Not only for us, but probably for the rest of the town too. The Romans don't take kindly to people who attack them." Ailbert's eyes peered into the distance as he remembered long ago and how the Romans took revenge on his village.

The conspirators met in a clearing in the forest because Ailbert decided that meeting in the centre of the village would not be a good idea. He walked around the little group, talking all the time.

"As you all know, I've been travelling to Eberacum with Huw on a regular basis. While I was there, I often saw the patrols leaving the city. What I need to know is how often they go out, where they go, and if the patrol routes are regular or random."

He reached the back of his men, as he had now come to think of them. They all turned to face him. He smiled. Every one of them accepted him as leader. Even Rees. Ailbert had felt reluctant to accept the position at first, but now he found he enjoyed having a group of young men hanging on his every word and expecting him to set plans in motion.

"If they're regular, that'll be easy, but it'll be difficult if they aren't. That I'll try to discover when I go to Eberacum. The rest of you need to practice your shooting skills, as well as stealth."

"We'll need to go out to the forest to do this," Gareth pointed out. "We don't want people wondering what we're doing."

"You're right. It's best kept secret. The fewer people who know, the better. In fact, we should keep it entirely to ourselves."

Rhodri fixed his gaze on Ailbert. "Even our wives and promised ones?"

"Especially them. They'll worry, and worried women can be unpredictable."

Rees spoke. "How are we to practice then? We'll need to get away from the women, and the older men too. Tell me that?" Rees folded his arms and stared Ailbert in the eye.

Ailbert breathed deeply. He had thought Rees had come to accept his leadership, yet he still argued and tried to find problems with everything Ailbert suggested. "We'll organise a hunt. Just for us, of course. We can then put the skills we'll need to practice."

Rees huffed loudly, but settled down. Ailbert looked at him closely. This young man could make trouble, he thought. Gaining his trust and confidence would not be an easy task.

The rest of them decided they would go on a hunt in two days.

۞

The young men met at sunset in the usual clearing at a time when the deer, in particular, came down to the pools and streams to drink. All arrived early, bows at the ready, with knives for skinning and preparing the carcass of any kills they might make.

Ailbert looked round his little group. There were ten of them, including himself. He decided to split them into two smaller groups for the hunt, as too many people might alert the game.

"Now, there are two places where the deer drink," he reminded them. "I, and my group, will go to the stream. The rest of you go to the pool near the big rocks, where our stream meets another."

He stooped to pick up his bow. "Don't forget we're practising being silent and disappearing quietly afterwards. Stay downwind or the animals will scent you. Hide up trees or behind rocks, or anywhere else you won't be seen. Good hunting!"

The two groups left the clearing to go to their separate destinations. Ailbert and his group arrived at the drinking area in half an hour. He set his men where he thought the deer would not see or scent them; then they settled down to wait.

It seemed an interminable time as he waited up the tree where he was perched. He felt his foot going numb, but dare not move. He told everyone they had to remain completely still and silent and, therefore, he could not move himself.

The deer arrived. The little herd of does and last year's fawns approached the stream. They scented the air and flicked their ears, listening, on the alert for predators. Wolves abounded in the forest and they knew this would be a good time for them to find young deer.

After looking around and scenting the air once more, nostrils quivering, the does approached the water. Ailbert decided to shoot. Earlier, he had thought this was the best way to initiate the attack, as calling out would warn the animals of their presence, and in the event of pursuing the ultimate goal of attacking Romans soldiers, it would warn them to be prepared.

His arrow flew true, shortly followed by four others. Three of the others missed, but as luck would have it, Ailbert's and one other hit the same doe. She threw her head up and leaped for the other side of the stream, followed by the rest of the animals. She did not get far before she stumbled and fell to the ground.

The men remained where they were until Ailbert climbed down from the tree and noiselessly made his way over to the dead animal. They then followed, maintaining their silence.

Ailbert smiled at his men. "Well done. That was an excellent trial. We'll need to practise more though. What we'll need to do after our attack on the Romans is to escape, not to go down towards them as we do in a hunt. They won't be running like those deer, but actively hunting us."

He patted each of the four on the back, then began to skin the deer.

"I wonder how the others went on," Rees said. "We were lucky here. Were *they* so lucky?"

Ailbert stopped skinning and looked at the other young man. "This was not luck, Rees. This was well planned and executed. Everyone did his part well and followed orders to the letter. The deer had no idea we were there, so we could shoot them easily." He continued skinning, helped by the others.

On returning to the town, the townsfolk greeted them with enthusiasm. The venison would help them through the winter months.

The two groups met on the way back. The second group had failed to catch anything. Later, Rhodri told Ailbert someone had sneezed and spooked the deer.

Ailbert was not impressed by this and told the culprit so.

"I'm sorry, Ailbert," replied the young man ruefully, "but I couldn't help it."

"If you do that during an attack on the Romans, then that'll be the end of you and everyone with you. Even sneezes need to be controlled."

The young man walked away looking guilty, wondering how anyone could control a sneeze.

"People are asking me why you're going hunting so much, Ailbert," Awena mentioned one day. "I can't answer them. We've got enough meat to last all the winter and into the spring. There's no need for any more."

Ailbert looked down at his feet. "We enjoy hunting, that's all."

"But you don't take the hunting dogs. That seems odd. Surely you can hunt better with the dogs?"

"We want to do it ourselves. Yes, it's easier with the dogs, but we get more satisfaction without their help. We can find the animals with our tracking skills instead of the dog's noses, and we kill them with our own weapons, not the dogs' teeth."

"I don't know what you're up to, Ailbert, but I don't believe a word. Oh, you're going hunting all right. You bring meat back. But there's more to it than that. Are you going to tell me?"

Ailbert walked out of their house without another word. He did not know what to say to his sister. He would have liked to take her into his confidence, but having forbidden the others from telling anyone, he could not tell her. He shook his head and walked over to the horses, where Tân trotted over hoping for a titbit.

Ailbert stroked the horse's nose. "Sorry, boy, I've not brought you anything."

Tân eyed him, appearing as if he might berate him for not bringing anything. Ailbert leaned his head against the animal's neck and told him all about what they were doing and how he wished he could tell Awena. The horse nuzzled him.

A voice sounded from behind Ailbert. "So that's why you've been doing all this hunting. You're practising to hunt Romans."

Ailbert whirled to see Huw, who had been leading his oxen back to the pens after going on a trading mission.

"Huw, you startled me. I didn't see you coming."

The older man frowned at Ailbert. "Obviously. How many of you are there? Do you want to get yourselves killed?"

"I'm not saying any more, Huw."

"Look, lad, I know you hate the Romans, but this isn't the way. Come back to the house and we'll talk about it."

Ailbert followed Huw back. Dera was not in, having gone to visit Brianne. The two had become great friends since Dera helped in the birth of Brianne's baby. Huw's wife had learned something of medicine before she married Hugh and found her expertise useful. She had become pregnant herself since arriving in Pen Coed, and Brianne had promised to help her when her time came.

Huw and Ailbert had the house to themselves.

"Now, tell me about this wild plan of yours. If you want to

kill Romans, it's not fair to drag others in too. You'll get them killed as well as yourself."

Huw sat down and Ailbert sat next to him. "It wasn't my idea in the first place. I've just refined it. The others wanted to build an army and attack the Romans on the open field, in battle."

Huw ran his fingers through his hair but remained silent, and Ailbert continued. "I pointed out it was a stupid idea, and they couldn't possibly fight the Roman army. They just saw glory and the hope of driving them out."

"So what did you tell them?"

"I said we'd need to attack by stealth. Kill a few Romans when they were out on patrol and then melt away."

"Hmm. Seems a better idea than open battle. What's your aim though? A few dead soldiers won't defeat the Romans."

Ailbert raised his head and looked into Huw's eyes, his own blazing. "Vengeance."

"For you, perhaps, but for the others?"

Ailbert looked away. "I'm not sure. Excitement? I think some of them hope if we can harry them enough … they'll think it's not worth staying here and leave."

Dera waddled in. Her time was getting close and she found it more and more difficult to get around. "Hello, Ailbert." She pecked Huw on the cheek. "Good to see you. What were you two talking about?"

The men looked at each other and an understanding passed between them.

"Nothing much," Huw told his wife. "Just this and that. We've not had a chat for a while."

"You see each other often, Huw. Have you forgotten that Ailbert does your finances?"

"No, of course not, but that's business, no time for chitchat then." He turned to Ailbert. "That reminds me. Will you look at the books tomorrow?"

The look that Huw gave him told him that he would not

tell Dera about their conversation, but that he would continue it the next day.

Ailbert poured over the accounts. He had an abacus in front of him and moved the beads quickly, adding up the money Huw had made. The beads clicked as Ailbert slid them along the wires. He concentrated, with his tongue sticking out of the corner of his mouth. When he had finished, he handed the paper on which he had written the accounts to Huw.

Huw glanced at the paper and pushed it aside, and turned to the young man. "I think you should consider coming with me on a regular basis and learning more about the merchant trade."

Ailbert merely looked at him.

Huw continued. "I'm going to train my sons eventually, but a second person will be useful. You could perhaps find out more about the timings and routes of the Roman patrols while we're in Eberacum."

Ailbert raised his eyebrows. This came as a surprise. He had not expected it. He had thought Huw intended to berate him about his plans, but he seemed to like the idea. "You've decided to help us then?"

"No, not exactly. I still think it's foolish, but I also realise I can't stop you." He grinned then. "And I'd be pleased to see the Romans a bit put out."

A week later, the pair set out for the market in Eberacum. The oxen plodded along. Ailbert sat on the seat next to Huw, willing the miles to pass and the oxen to speed up, but the beasts had their own pace: slow. He wanted to get to the city as soon as possible to start his observations.

A patrol met them as they neared the gates. The patrol headed along the road in the direction of Pen Coed. Ailbert watched and saw them turn off to the left towards the village of Blaenafon. He did not know that road, but he resolved to go along it as soon as possible to look for suitable places for an ambush.

When the traders arrived at the marketplace in Eberacum, Huw set out their stall. People soon came to inspect their goods. A new trader in town would always bring people to see what he sold. Huw specialised in luxury goods, so it was mainly the richer folk who approached.

A man in ragged clothes drew near.

"On your way," Huw shouted at the man. "Nothing here you can afford."

The man slunk into the crowds.

"You have to be careful of thieves," Huw told Ailbert. "Sometimes the beggars and poor folk try to steal things to sell."

After a very short time, Ailbert became too busy to think about anything other than attending to customers. People bought much of the wine. Of course, he remembered, it would be Saturnalia soon, and the wine would be for the feast. At this time, the Romans also had the practice of giving gifts, so other things, like the jewellery made by the silversmith in the village and the game of knucklebones, also made in the village, were in great demand.

Huw had the carpenters create wooden toys for people to buy for their children as well. These sold quickly too.

"If you want to, go and have a look round the market," Huw said when there was a lull in the many buyers. "It's probably best if you go now while there aren't so many people."

Ailbert thanked him and wandered off. Many stalls filled the marketplace, several selling food. There were not many people like Huw, who went far to gather their goods. Most of the stallholders were local farmers selling their own produce and a few craftsmen selling their wares. No wonder Huw's stall seemed so popular. Few, if any, had wine and olive oil, nor the lovely amber jewellery that Huw sold.

The day ended and the merchants packed their things, and set off to their various homes. Huw and Ailbert hitched the oxen up to the cart and began the long journey home. They did not arrive until well after dark.

Dera welcomed them and gave Huw a hug. "Did you do well today?"

"Yes. With the Roman feast of Saturnalia coming up people were in the mood to buy. It was very successful."

Ailbert left to go to the home he shared with Awena, his head not filled with merchandise and profits but with possible ambush places on the road to Blaenafon.

The next morning, Ailbert and Rhodri left the village to look at the road the patrol had passed along. They reached the turning just before mid-day. After stopping for a brief rest and something to eat, they strolled leisurely along the road.

It passed through fields for a while, then the sides of the road rose up to create a steep valley. Rocks lay by the side of the road and up the steep slopes. However, there were no trees of ample size to hide in or behind.

"Look away, Rhodri, and I'll go and hide. Tell me if you can see me at all."

Rhodri turned and Ailbert climbed up the roadside and crouched behind a large rock. Rhodri turned and looked all around. He could see nothing of his friend at all and called to that effect.

Ailbert stood and waved, and then he called, "Go a little way down the road and see if you can see me from there."

Rhodri duly did as his friend instructed. When he looked to where he had seen Ailbert stand up, he could see the other man crouching there. "No good, Ailbert. I can see you from here. This is where the Romans will come from."

The pair decided that would not be a good place if they

could be seen by anyone coming along the road and so they pressed onwards. A little further along the road, the steep slopes dropped and a small stream crossed the path. The road narrowed here and thick woodland grew along the banks of the stream.

"A-ha," Ailbert exclaimed, gesturing. "Perhaps this would be a good place."

They repeated the procedure and this time Rhodri could see nothing of Ailbert. Then Rhodri hid in a different place. The pair tried hiding in eight or ten different places; as most were hidden from the road, they decided this would be the best place for an ambush.

It took them a long time to get back to Pen Coed, but both felt pleased and elated by their day's work.

❧ 16 ❧

Ailbert continued to travel to the Eberacum market with Huw, until two weeks later, just before Saturnalia.

He had managed to establish the routine of the patrol. The young men prepared to leave so they would be in position well before the patrol arrived. On arriving at the chosen spot, Ailbert sent each man off to his hiding place with strict instructions to remain still, especially when they heard the Roman soldiers coming along the road.

"I want you to be so still the birds will think you're rocks and land on you," he told them firmly.

Rees snorted at this, but at a look from Gareth, he quietly went to his allocated place.

They waited an age before the sounds of marching feet could be heard further along the road. Ailbert silently sympathised with his men; he found it difficult to stay still as well. He thought he could sense excitement in the wood and felt sure the Romans would feel it too.

Then they appeared. A patrol of two contuburnia, each led by a decius. Eighteen men. Ailbert's little band was only ten. Would they succeed? *Could* they succeed?

Be that as it may, they did not intend to defeat this patrol, perhaps just injure one or two … give the Romans something to think about … then melt away, as though into the mists.

Ailbert raised his bow and remained crouching as he fired his arrow straight at the nearest soldier. The arrow struck true and the soldier went down, clutching his side. Nine more arrows flew. Three struck soldiers. One soldier went down and lay still. The others were hit only glancing blows.

Now came the time to make a silent getaway. Ailbert hoped the practice they had put in to move silently and stealthily had paid off; they had decided not to leave as a group, but that each young man would make his own way back to Pen Coed. That way, if the Romans caught any of them, the rest would live to fight another day. Slowly, Ailbert crept backwards along the bank of the stream, hidden by the dense bushes growing there.

The Roman patrol milled around the banks of the stream. They had not anticipated this attack and it took them a few moments to organise themselves. Once their commanders had re-established order, they immediately slipped into the formation they called the testudo. They formed closely and held their shields over their heads and round the sides, making an impenetrable cover. It was too late, though. Four of them were hurt and possibly of those was dead.

Soundlessly, the attackers crept out of the ambush and headed back overland to Pen Coed. The testudo could not follow, even if they knew where their enemy went.

Back at the village, the young men clapped each other on the back at the success of this initial ambush, and the resultant injuring of the Roman soldiers.

Ailbert joined in the excitement. He had done it! He had given the Romans something to think about and injured some of them in the process. He could not stop the grin that spread across his face. However, he knew next time would not be so easy. The Romans did not expect any resistance, at least not since they had put down the rebellion of the Brigantes, but they would be more on their guard in future.

As Ailbert continued to accompany Huw to Eberacum, he gradually found out more about the movements of the patrols.

"They say they're for our protection," Huw told him one day, "but they're really to keep us down. Who's going to rebel if they think soldiers will attack them if they do?"

He had winked at Ailbert as he said this, and Ailbert smiled inwardly.

The ten young men had begun to refer to themselves as Ailbert's Army. Rees had objected at first, but the others shouted him down.

"Who's planning all this and finding out about the patrols and where they go?" Gareth asked. "Ailbert. Who searches out the best ambush places? Ailbert. Who taught us the best way to attack and harry the Romans? Ailbert!"

Rhodri offered his opinion. "We'd have gathered a load of hotheads from here and other villages and called ourselves an army. Then, we'd have gone and challenged the Roman army on the battlefield and lost. We'd all be dead and probably many of our families too, not to mention being taken into slavery."

"If they find out who's attacking them, they'll still do that," Rees responded.

Ailbert raised his hand. "No more. We must remain as a unit. If we fall out among ourselves, we'll get nowhere."

The others fell silent and listened to the next plan.

Ailbert's army attacked three more patrols that winter. Then the Romans became more alert, watching for new attacks.

One young man took an arrow in the leg in the last ambush. It was nothing serious though, as it had only been his thigh and would only leave a long scar. Nevertheless, Ailbert's Army decided to abandon the harrying for a few months.

"Let the Romans think we've given up," Ailbert told them. "Then, when they relax their guard a bit, we can start again."

❧ 17 ❧

Beltane approached rapidly. This was a time for handfastings and Huw agreed that Awena and Rhodri could become handfasted at the ceremony.

The morning of Beltane arrived. Awena was dressed in the new clothes Dera helped her fashion.

Dera's baby had been born earlier in the winter. The little boy only lived for but one month and the woman needed something to take her mind off her grief. Helping make Awena's clothes came at a good time for her.

Awena stood in the centre of Dera and Huw's home. Her stomach churned as she thought of the ceremony to come, and how her life would change.

She looked at Dera anxiously. "I feel a bit sick."

Dera regarded her and reached for an infusion of camomile. "Here, drink this. It'll help settle your stomach. I expect you're feeling quite nervous."

Awena nodded. "But excited, too." She walked to the door, sipping the camomile tea, and peered outside. The day had dawned, fine and sunny, though not very warm. Every household put out the fires that had burned throughout the winter so no smoke rose from the thatch of the houses. Every home had brought in flowers and the inhabitants laid new fires, ready to be relit from sacred bonfires.

Awena and Dera, along with the rest of the village, left to go to the sacred place, where the druid would light the bonfires.

Once there, the ceremonies began. The druid prayed to the god and goddess to bless the village with fertility, and then the farmers drove the livestock between the two fires.

When they had completed this, the time arrived for the handfasting of three couples. The druid heard their vows and then tied their hands together with a red cord as a symbol of their commitment to each other. After that, they jumped the fires, laughing and hoping they would make it across. All did, of course, but Awena and Rhodri both breathed a sigh of relief, looked at each other, and burst out laughing.

The feasting started, causing much merriment as the couples tried to eat with tied hands—for the cords would not be untied by the druid until the feast had officially ended.

Awena thought she and Rhodri would never stop laughing. She reached out for something—as he was raising his hand to put something in his mouth, Then he dropped it, of course. Eventually, they managed to coordinate their eating so they both managed to eat enough to satisfy them.

After the meal, the druid came over to the newly handfasted couples and ceremonially untied the cords, which demonstrated that the untying showed that the couples would stay together of their own free will.

Thus began Awena's life with Rhodri. They would live together in the home she had shared with Ailbert. This arrangement would last for one year and a day; then, if they did not wish to stay together, they could part ways.

Ailbert moved back into the home of Huw and Dera to allow the young couple their privacy. It made the house crowded and Ailbert privately thought it was perhaps a good thing Dera's baby had not lived. That would have made it very uncomfortable indeed.

The summer passed quickly and, with it, the festival of Lughnasa, the beginning of the harvest season. The bonfires had been lit on the hills and Lugh appeased for another year so he would not send storms to ravage the crops.

Awena had become pregnant with her first child, due just before Beltane the following year. This delighted her, but also made her afraid. After all, many women died in childbirth, and many children did not survive. Dera comforted her fears, however, telling her that she was a healthy young woman and there was no reason why she should not have a strong child.

Not long after this, Rees began talking to the others, declaring they should resume the attacks on the Romans. "We've not made any attacks for months, and the Romans must think by now we've given up. A new series of attacks will surprise them."

Ailbert cautioned against starting again too soon.

One day, one of the men came up to Ailbert and advised him that Rees had threatened to take the men himself and resume the attacks.

Ailbert felt he had enough on his plate at the moment; he had been travelling to Eberacum on a regular basis with Huw, and was beginning to enjoy the life of a merchant. Huw had taught him how to value a variety of goods and promised to take him to Londinium next time he went.

"What if I'm recognised though, Huw?" Ailbert asked, knitting his brows.

"It's been over a year now since you escaped and, anyway, you can dye your hair again. I don't think anyone will recognise you with brown hair. In the last year, you've grown from a boy to a man."

Ailbert called a meeting of Ailbert's Army after Rees' threat to take the men himself. Gareth told him not to worry, that the men would never follow Rees, but Ailbert wanted to ensure all was clearly understood. There could be *no* divisions in the troop if they were to succeed.

They met as usual in the clearing in the wood.

"Now, Rees," Ailbert began when they were all assembled, "what's this about you starting the attacks again?"

"Who told you?" Rees snapped, looking round the clearing at those gathered there.

"It doesn't matter. What matters is that we stand united. If we split, then we've lost. We can't do what we've been doing with fewer men."

"You think not? I disagree." Rees scowled at Ailbert. "This shooting and retreating could be done with fewer men quite easily." He gazed round to see how many of the assembled group were nodding in agreement. A few were, but the majority watched at him with hard eyes.

"The important thing is not splitting the group," Gareth affirmed. "We can't afford to have two rival groups fighting the same battle."

"Why not? My group could attack one lot of Romans while Ailbert's group attacks another. Wouldn't that confuse and disrupt the Romans even further?"

"First, you need to *have* a group," put in Rhodri. "How many of these men would go with *you*?"

Ailbert looked around before speaking again. "Rees, how about first seeing how much support you have here? You want to start the attacks again, but I say we should wait longer, so the Romans think we've stopped because one of us was injured in the last attack." He walked to one side of the clearing. "Those of you who agree that we should hold off attacks for a little while longer, come over here and stand with me, while those of you who think, like Rees, that we should start again immediately, go over there with Rees."

There came the sound of shuffling feet among the men. Gareth and Rhodri did not hesitate, and came immediately to stand by Ailbert. The others looked at each other, no one wanting to be the first to decide. Then three went over to Rees and that seemed to make the others decide. There was a rush to Ailbert, leaving one young man standing alone in the middle of the clearing.

He looked undecidedly from one to the other. Rees had three and Ailbert four. Which way would the last man decide? Eventually, he seemed to shake himself and walked slowly over to Ailbert, to the catcalls of those supporting Rees.

Ailbert looked at those who had come to his side of the clearing. He had felt certain he would have been able to carry the majority of the group. Yes, he had five to Rees' three, but it was a serious split in his army. He would have to do something about reuniting them.

"Rees," he stated, "we should have a meeting. Just we two. Four of you can't do much against the Romans, even if it's an ambush."

Rees regarded him intensely. "That's what you think. "I bet we'll take out as many Roman soldiers as you." He turned to his supporters. "Lads, we'll go on a raid in three days time. We know the routine of the patrols now. We don't need Ailbert to tell us." Then he left the clearing, followed by his small group of men.

Gareth turned to Ailbert, appearing discouraged. "What now? Our army's nearly halved."

"I need to think about this," Ailbert replied calmly. "We may not be able to reunite, but perhaps we can cooperate. Perhaps what Rees suggested, two raids at the same time, would be an idea we could pursue."

Three days later, as Ailbert and Gareth crossed towards the

animal pens, Rees came in through the gate followed by two of his three men. The two carried something between them. When they put it down, Ailbert realised it was the third man. He walked across to where Rees stood staring down at the fellow at his feet.

"What happened, Rees?" Ailbert asked softly.

"He wasn't quick enough. A Roman saw him and chased him. When the Roman caught him, he tried to fight back. The Roman stabbed him with his gladius."

Ailbert knelt down before the young man and felt his neck for a pulse. "He's dead, Rees."

"He was alive when we picked him up," said one of the men who had carried him back. "We thought your aunt, Dera, could help him. We came as quickly as we could." He blinked rapidly and brushed a hand over his eyes.

Ailbert gazed at him from where he still knelt. "Four of you on a raid isn't enough—not enough to throw the Romans into confusion as to where the shots are coming from, and not enough to split their forces when they come after you." His gaze returned to the young man, and then he stood and turned to Rees. "You must go and tell his mother. You're responsible for this, so *you* must do the decent thing." Ailbert turned on his heels and strode back to Gareth and the feeding of the animals.

Ailbert and Rees met the following day. Rees reluctantly agreed to join forces once again. Since the death of one of his men, thus leaving only three of them, he realized he could not continue with his rival army. Even he could see that three were not enough.

Ailbert planned a bigger attack than ever: a night-time raid on a camp where the Romans usually slept when on a longer patrol.

Once they arrived where the Romans usually camped, Ailbert sent four of his men off to hide themselves ... if possible, in the trees within the camp area. He set Gareth in charge of these men. The other three men and Ailbert hid in the dense bushes that surrounded the camp.

Soon, they heard the sounds of marching feet and the Roman patrol appeared. Now came the worst time of all. They had to wait in utter stillness until the patrol slept.

The patrol erected tents and settled down to cook and eat a meal. Then the guards went to the perimeter of the camp, where they set six guards. The rest of the patrol crept into the tents to sleep.

Ailbert decided to wait until after the first change of guards. That way the guards would all be a bit sleepy; those who had just woken would be rubbing their eyes and trying to wake up while the ones going off would be tired and anxious to get to their beds.

After what seemed an age, the change came about.

"Nothing to report," the guards told those replacing them. "It's a quiet night. I don't suppose there'll be an ambush. I think, after we got one of them last time, they've given up. Cowards all."

"Can't be sure of anything with those barbarians," a new guard stated, and the changeover took place.

Ailbert decided to wait for a half hour before beginning his attack. After that time, he shot at one of the guards. He deliberately missed and jumped from his hiding place. The others followed his lead.

"Look, there are only four of them," called the guard Ailbert had shot at. "We can easily take them."

As he had hoped, the six guards all left their places and ran after the now fleeing men, who periodically turned and shot at them to make sure they were followed.

While this went on, Gareth led the other four down from the trees where they had been hiding within the camp.

There they each entered a tent and silently killed a sleeping soldier.

That done, they took themselves in the opposite direction from that which Ailbert and his men had taken. They looped round and quickly moved behind the guards chasing Ailbert and his men, where they easily killed them with accurate shots.

When the nine got together again, they whooped with joy. This was the best ambush of all.

"We must have killed at least eleven Romans," said Rees gleefully.

Rhodri turned to him. "Do you still think you can plan things better than Ailbert?"

Rees appeared guilty. "No. I'll hand it to him. He planned a superb attack this time. But what about next time? We can't do the same thing again. The Romans will be ready for us."

"Ailbert will think of something," Gareth affirmed.

As Ailbert listened to the discussion, he realised Rees was right. The same tactics would not work again. At least not for quite some time. He would need to think hard to come up with something new.

The next time Ailbert and Huw went to the market in Eber-acum, all they heard about was the night attack on the patrol.

"It can't have been humans," one elderly woman said to them. "They melted away into the night, just as they have done every time they attacked. This time though, they later reappeared out of nowhere. It must have been a ghost attack."

"Perhaps the ghosts of some of the barbarians we killed when they rebelled," her friend suggested.

The two wandered into the market and Ailbert could hear no more.

In Eberacum, at least, Ailbert's Army began to be dubbed the Phantom Army.

It began to get colder now and ice formed on the ground and ponds. Waterfalls turned to ice after a long cold spell, creating beautiful glassy structures. Ice even formed at the edges of fast-flowing streams.

Ailbert decided to return to the original plan for raids on patrols, at least for a while. He needed to keep the bloodlust of his Phantom Army satisfied. He could not afford to have another disastrous split like the one with Rees that led to the death of a young man.

They did a couple of raids, one of which resulted in a slight injury to Rhodri. Awena was not pleased. She pressed him until he admitted to the raids and she forbade her husband to go on any more. Rhodri made her promise not to tell anyone, though. He knew Ailbert would be annoyed at his breaking of the rule.

"I don't want our baby to lose his father before he's even born," she stated angrily.

Rhodri raised his eyebrows. "How do you know it's a he?"

Awena smiled. "Just a feeling."

The Phantom Army was thus reduced to eight.

"Do you think we can manage with only eight?" Gareth asked Ailbertwith puckered brows.

"Perhaps we ought to try to recruit some more," replied Ailbert.

The current eight army members discussed who to include. There a few younger men in Pen Coed, but most were too young. The youngest of the Phantom Army was sixteen and he was a little hot-headed at times. Anyone else from Pen Coed would be even younger than that.

They decided to leave it for a while until Ailbert had planned another attack. If that did not go well, then they might try to raise help in another village. It would have to be one they knew they could trust, though. Some people had accepted the Roman occupation and even become Roman citizens themselves.

❧❦❧

Two weeks later, Huw and Ailbert went to Eberacum as usual. As he had done before, Huw told Ailbert to have a look round. Ailbert decided this time he would listen for any young men objecting to Roman rule.

It started to snow as Ailbert climbed the steps to an inn. As he neared the top, his feet slipped from under him and he fell down five steps. He landed very awkwardly and felt something crack.

A passing man hurried over. "You had a nasty fall there. Can you get up?"

Ailbert tried, but found he could not.

"You've done something very nasty to your leg. I suspect you've broken it. Here, let me help you."

The man assisted Ailbert to his feet and then hailed a man with a cart. "This man has broken his leg, I think. Help me get him into your cart and take him to my house. I'll pay you well."

Ailbert objected, but the man insisted and Ailbert soon found himself being carried into a domus, much like the one where he had been a slave.

He shivered as they crossed the threshold. All his conditioning as a slave—that he could not use the main entrance to the domus—came to the fore. He could not tell this man why he shivered though, as that might result in both him and Awena being taken back to Londinium to suffer punishment as escaped slaves.

The Roman called for a slave to help Ailbert into a bedroom. Here he laid him on a bed before sitting down on a chair next to him.

Ailbert tried to get up. "I must go. Thank you for your

help, but I must go back to my uncle. He'll wonder where I am."

"Wait," the Roman said. "You've got yourself in a bit of a mess. I think we need to have a doctor see to you. If I'm right, and you have broken a bone, then it needs to be set properly or you'll have a permanent limp, and might end up a cripple."

Ailbert looked quickly at the other man. He could not afford to be either crippled or walk with a limp. How would he fight the Romans in that case? He decided he had better do as this man said.

"My name is Flavius. Yours is …?"

He lay back. "Ailbert." He sat up again, wincing as pain shot through his leg. "My uncle. He'll wonder where I am."

"I'll send someone to tell him," Flavius replied. "What's his name?"

"Huw. He's a merchant in the market. He sells luxury goods like wine and olive oil."

Flavius smiled. "I know him. I've bought some things from him. I got a lovely brooch for my wife for Saturnalia. A strange yellow stone. I think he said it's called amber."

"Yes, that's right. He got the amber from a merchant in Londinium. It comes from the Mare Balticum, over in the east. Our silversmith sets the amber in silver."

"Beautiful it is too. All that intricate work, weaving in and out."

Ailbert moved again and that prompted another wince.

Flavius stood. "We need to get a doctor here as soon as we can." He walked to the door and called for a slave, and gave instructions for him to tell Huw where his nephew was.

"Tell him he's hurt his leg and I've brought him here so a doctor can see to him," he instructed the slave, who departed immediately.

Soon Huw arrived, followed almost immediately by the doctor. The doctor ushered everyone out of the room, much to the annoyance of Huw, who had not had time to speak to Ailbert.

Flavius took the man by the arm, talking to him and telling him that the doctor could do his work better without an audience.

The doctor ran his hands down Ailbert's injured leg. It made him wince as the doctor's hands passed the injury.

"Ah! Flavius was right. You have broken it. I'll need to set it, and then you must keep off it while it heals."

He reached into a bag he had with him. First, he manipulated the leg to ensure the bones were in place, eliciting a cry from Ailbert. Next, he took two sticks and placed one on each side of the leg, and tied them in place. He called for Flavius and spoke to him quietly.

Before Flavius and the doctor left, the doctor gave Ailbert strict instructions not to move his leg until he returned.

Shortly thereafter, the doctor returned and wrapped bandages soaked in some sort of mixture around the splints.

"What's that?" Ailbert asked.

"Cloths soaked in starch. The starch stiffens the cloth and it's better for holding everything still." He stood up and looked at his handiwork. "Yes, that'll do. Now, don't move around. Stay here in bed, and I'll come back in a few days and change the bandages."

"I can't do that," Ailbert began, but the doctor hastened into the corridor.

Flavius entered several seconds later, as Ailbert struggled to sit up. "The doctor says I'm to stay here, and he'll come back to change the bandages in a few days. I can't do that."

"Why not?" Flavius asked, perplexed.

"You've done enough for me already. Brought me here, got a doctor to see to my leg, and kindly lent me a bedroom. You must tell me what I owe you. The doctor doesn't come free."

Huw entered and agreed with Ailbert, but Flavius was having none of it. "Look, I know the doctor well. I'm the

Primus Pilus of the legion here in Eberacum. That doctor sees to the men under my command. He'll give me special rates."

Huw became insistent. "You *must* let me pay something."

"Nonsense. I can afford it. As to leaving, I won't allow it. Ailbert will stay here until he can walk out on his own. This I insist."

After further arguing, Huw and Ailbert gave in, and Huw left to return to Pen Coed with the news.

Ailbert felt uncomfortable. He found himself staying in the home of one of the hated Romans. And a soldier at that. In his head, he heard the sound of his mother's screams as the Roman soldier dragged him and his sister away from her. He heard the hammering of the nails entering the flesh of the men being crucified and their screams, and heard Avelina's sobs as she missed her mother. Once more, he saw the tears of Odila and the other girls who had been taken to the soldiers every evening. He felt the petting of the Domina and her friends, and the rejection when no longer the pretty little pet.

Anger crept within as he remembered how the Dominus had tried to compromise Avelina and the Domina's revenge, sending the girl to a brothel. His anger mounted as he recalled why he and his sister had needed to change their names.

He wept for the old woman, killed for helping them, and for Huw's sister, losing her life of luxury to become the slave of the man she had married. He wept for her two little boys, not knowing why they were no longer pampered children but slaves too.

Then there was the uprooting from their new home to come here, and Avelina's distress at leaving her betrothed, although the anger cooled a little as he thought of her new life with Rhodri. She seemed happy enough now.

But he still lay here, in the home of a Roman soldier. He did not want to be here. He was tempted to walk out, but as he raised himself, the room span and his leg pained greatly. With a sigh, he lay back.

❧ 18 ❧

Ailbert fell asleep in spite of the pain in his leg. He woke to hear a slave girl in his room. He opened his eyes and, as he focussed, a voice came to him.

"Ah, I see you're awake. I've brought you something to help with the pain."

He struggled to sit up, which provoked a yelp, and he took the proffered drink, sipping slowly.

The girl smiled.

A lovely smile, Ailbert thought.

"I hope it helps," she said. "Pater told me to bring it every few hours. He doesn't trust the slaves to remember, you see."

"Your father? Then you must be Flavius's daughter."

"Yes. Pater went to see about something in the legion. Something about the patrols. They're being attacked, you know. The last one, we lost about ten men. It was quite a disaster. They're sending two contuburnia together now, because of the attacks."

Ailbert smiled inwardly. Perhaps he could find out more to make his attacks even more effective. If they could kill one complete patrol, that would be excellent. The girl may know more than she realised.

"What's your name?" he asked her.

"Sylvia. Pater said your name is Ailbert."

He nodded as he studied the girl. So this was Flavius's daughter? She was pretty, although not what people would call beautiful. She had brown hair that glinted with golden highlights as she moved her head. He looked at her appraisingly when she took the goblet that had held the painkilling drink. He noticed light brown eyes that sparkled with fun, and that lovely smile. She was small. He estimated she would come just past his shoulder.

She put the goblet down and turned to him. "I must go. Mater is going to see you in a few minutes." She slipped through the door.

Almost as soon as she had gone, an older version of Sylvia entered with a couple of boys.

"So you're Ailbert," she said, head tilted to one side. "My husband told me you've broken your leg and must stay here until it's mended." She frowned as she regarded him.

Not much like her daughter in attitude, Ailbert thought. *I don't think she wants me here.*

The woman began talking again, all the while looking him up and down. "My name is Octavia. You've already met my daughter, Sylvia. These are my sons, Laurentius and Quintus."

Ailbert looked at the two boys. Quintus looked about twelve or thirteen and had brown hair and light eyes like his mother. Laurentius, on the other hand, was dark like his father and his eyes seemed almost black. He looked at Ailbert and scowled. Ailbert estimated him to be about fifteen, just a little younger than his sister. He smiled at the two boys. Quintus smiled back, but Laurentius' scowl deepened.

Ailbert smiled at Octavia.

She did not smile back either, but said, "My husband has told me to tell you that you are welcome here. He said you wanted to leave, but the doctor advised it would not be a good idea if your leg is to heal properly."

She turned to leave, then turned back. "I hope you're not in too much pain. If you are, just ring the bell I'll send to you, and a slave will come and bring you something for it." With that, she swept from the room, taking her sons with her.

At the door, Quintus turned and gave a beaming smile.

"Well, at least one of the household thinks I'm welcome," he muttered. "This is not going to be pleasant if the rest of them think differently."

It seemed only Octavia and Laurentius felt Ailbert was an intruder. The slaves were attentive, but not talkative, even when he tried to engage them in conversation. He understood that. He had been a slave himself, after all, and knew what was expected of them.

Sylvia and Quintus, though, came to visit whenever they could. He liked the young boy. He had a little brother of his own, somewhere, who would be a similar age to this young man. Ailbert welcomed his company and questions.

Sylvia he welcomed as someone nearer his own age to whom he could talk. She was an intelligent girl who understood much about the politics of the Empire. She questioned him about life in a Celtic town.

"I'm surprised you can read and write," she told him one day. "I always thought the bar ... er ... Britons were uncivilised. That's what we've always been taught."

"I grew up in Londinium. That's where I learned to speak Latin."

"I've never been to Londinium," she said, a wistful look in her eyes. "Is it as grand as they say?"

Before he could answer, a voice called, "Sylvia. Sylvia, where are you?"

"I must go,' she jumped to her feet. "Mater is calling. She doesn't really like me spending too long with you."

No, thought Ailbert, she doesn't like anyone spending too much time with me.

The doctor arrived a couple of days later and removed the stiffened bandages. He called to Octavia to soak the ones he had brought with him in the starch he had given her.

Octavia smiled warmly at the doctor. "Of course. How is his leg mending, Doctor?"

She means how long will I be here.

"Oh, it seems to be quite straight," the doctor replied. "I'm pleased with the way it's going so far. As long as he does as he's told, I have every confidence he'll make an excellent recovery."

Octavia simpered. "Oh, don't worry. We'll all make sure he's a good boy and then he can make the best recovery ever."

She means 'quickest recovery', I think.

Sylvia came to see Ailbert whenever she could, as did Quintus. Laurentius he never saw again while he was in the house.

If she thought the pair were visiting Ailbert, Octavia always found them something to do elsewhere. Ailbert found this very uncomfortable. The only times Octavia acted in any way more than civil was when either Flavius or the doctor were around.

Eventually the doctor said Ailbert could go and sit in the peristylium, if he wished. Even though it was winter, and snow lay thickly on the ground, Ailbert could not help but smile at the thought he could leave his rooms. The doctor gave him a crutch to use and he hobbled from the bedroom and into the peristylium.

Once in the peristylium, Ailbert shivered, but he relished being outside where he could look at the garden. He hobbled to a seat and sat down to watch the comings and goings of the house.

Slaves ran from one place to another, ignoring him for the

most part. Sylvia came out of one of the rooms and smiled when she saw him. "Aren't you cold out here?" she asked.

"A bit, but after being cooped up inside for days, I'm enjoying the fresh air."

She sat next to him. "As I said before, I've been taught that you people have no culture. You seem not to be like what I've been taught."

"It all depends on what you call culture," Ailbert said. "We have our own, but remember: I grew up in Londinium, so I'm not really like Britons who've always lived in villages."

"Are you saying you have no culture then?"

"Not at all." Ailbert frowned. "We have our own. We have gods and goddesses who protect us and whom we worship, but we don't use temples built of stone. We have people who make the jewellery you Romans like to wear."

Fascinated, she regarded him as he went on to tell her all about life in a Briton village. Eventually, she began to shiver.

"You should go inside," Ailbert told her.

"You come in too. Quintus is there. I'm sure he will want to talk to you as well."

Ailbert looked around. There was no sign of Octavia and he asked Sylvia about her. "I get the impression she doesn't like me being here."

"Perhaps not, but Pater says you must stay. He's a kind man, is Pater. Mater thinks you're a smelly barbarian."

They laughed at that and went through the passage leading to the atrium where they sat next to the pool in the centre, As in all Roman houses, a hole in the roof allowed rainwater or, at this time of year, snow to fall into the pool. In spite of the hole in the roof, it felt warmer here than in the peristylium due to the hypocaust beneath the floor.

Quintus jumped to his feet when Ailbert and Sylvia entered. The twelve-year-old appeared as anxious to talk to Ailbert as his sister had. He questioned him on all sorts of things, but was especially interested in hunting.

The afternoon passed quickly and soon it was time for the family's evening meal. Flavius returned and invited Ailbert to dine with them. Ailbert declined. though, saying his leg was hurting and he would rather take his meal in his bedroom. Flavius looked a little disappointed at this, but agreed, saying he hoped Ailbert would be able to join the family in a few days.

In spite of the unwelcoming attitude of Octavia and Laurentius, Ailbert found the time passing relatively quickly. He thought Octavia and her elder son to be typical of Romans—full of superiority to others, but he liked Flavius, Sylvia and Quintus. These three, he thought, were not like Romans at all.

He, Sylvia and Quintus spent a lot of time together and Ailbert knew he would miss them when the time came for him to leave.

That day finally arrived. Ailbert now walked with a stick in place of crutches, and he walked from the domus into the street, followed by Sylvia and Quintus. Sylvia held out her hand for him to shake, which he duly did. Then he thanked Octavia, who had come out to see him off.

To make sure I've really gone, thought Ailbert.

Huw drew up with the wagon. He had made enough money that he could buy a horse and so it was this creature that pulled it. Ailbert went and patted it on its nose, then climbed into the back where he could stretch out his leg. Huw clucked to the horse and it moved off towards the gates of Eberacum.

❧ 19 ❧

A ilbert settled back into his work with Huw. At first, Huw would not allow him to go to Eberacum with him, but Ailbert became ever more frustrated. He spent a lot of time with the horses as they and the other animals were settled into their winter pens in the village.

Tân was pleased to see him and trotted over as soon as he appeared.

"I swear that horse missed you," Rhodri said one day.

Ailbert turned to his friend and grinned. "Of course he did. He's a very intelligent animal. How's Awena, by the way?"

Beltane approached once more, and Awena's baby was due any day.

"She's large and gets tired easily. No sign of the baby coming though."

Just as he finished speaking, Glenda, Huw and Dera's daughter, came running up. "Rhodri," she called anxiously, "The baby's coming!" She stopped to catch her breath. "Mother's with her, but she thought you should know."

Rhodri stood as if turned to stone. He paled and then grabbed Glenda.

The girl winced as his grip tightened on her arm. "Ow, Rhodri, that hurts."

"Sorry, but how is she? How long will it be? Is she in much pain?"

Ailbert was not much calmer than Rhodri. After all, he had been brother, father and mother to her since she was four years old. He felt a responsibility to her that most brothers did not. He took Rhodri by the arm and led him away from the animals. Tân whinnied in disappointment as he had not had his treat from Ailbert, and then trotted off to join the other horses, kicking in frustration at a mare who got in his way.

Ailbert led Rhodri to Huw and Dera's home. Rhodri paced backwards and forwards. It was noon and Dera had been preparing the meal when she went to help Awena.

The meal was ready and Glenda served them all a portion, but neither Rhodri nor Ailbert could eat anything. Huw, however, polished off his plate and half of Ailbert's. Then, they all sat waiting for the news.

Hours passed. Rhodri stood and paced, then sat down again. Ailbert stood and paced, then sat down again. They both stood and paced, until Huw snorted with impatience.

"Sit down, you two! Pacing around won't make it happen any quicker. Babies come when they want and not before."

"But is she alright?" Rhodri sat once again and closed his eyes. "What if she should die? Women do, you know? What would I do then? It's taking so long." He hopped to his feet and started pacing again, then stopped and looked at Huw. "Should it take so long? It seems like it's been far too long."

Huw smiled. This was Rhodri's first baby. He would learn about the time it takes for a child to be born. "Rhodri, birthing a baby is not like birthing a lamb, calf or foal. It always takes a long time. I don't know why, but women seem to have more difficulty than animals. We'll hear soon, don't you fear."

Darkness fell and still no news came. No one could sleep

except Huw's two boys. Then, in the early hours of the morning, a weary-looking Dera entered the house. She gazed at the three men and Glenda. "You should be in bed," she told her daughter and turned to Rhodri. "You've got a lovely little boy."

Rhodri was out of the house before Dera could say any more. She slumped onto a bench.

"Was it difficult?" Ailbert asked.

"No more than any. She's young and strong. The baby is healthy too. Now, I must go to bed, if you don't mind." She moved away from the fire and lay on one of the benches around the side of the house, and pulled up a large section of fur. Within minutes, she was asleep.

❃

Beltane came and went, and Ailbert helped drive the livestock to their summer grazing. Awena and Rhodri completed their year and a day, and made their handfasting permanent. They both delighted in their son, and Rhodri could talk of little else. This meant he would not even consider going on the raids with the others, and so the reduction to eight members became permanent.

Ailbert had decided to make another attack when Huw said he was going to Londinium and would like Ailbert to accompany him this time.

Huw knew about the raids the Phantom Army had made. Since his hatred of the Romans was only slightly less than that of Ailbert, he had said nothing, not even to Dera.

When he told Ailbert he wanted him to accompany him to Londinium, Ailbert objected. "I'm planning another raid, Huw. How about leaving it until your next visit?"

"That won't be for months. I want you to come on this one. You can do all your raiding when we get back."

Ailbert shrugged and went to tell the rest of the Phantom Army the raid would be postponed.

"Can't we go without you?" Rees begged. "We know the plan. You've told us all the details."

'There'll be only seven of you. Not enough. Don't go doing anything silly in my absence."

Gareth said, "Don't worry. I'll see no one becomes stupid, and I'll ask Rhodri to help too."

Ailbert laughed. "Rhodri's too engrossed with young Bran to do much helping; still, you can ask."

Huw and Rhodri set off for Londinium the next day. Ailbert had not been back to the south since their escape and he felt a bit apprehensive. Dera suggested he dye his hair again because, although it had been a couple of years since he left, his ash blonde hair was extremely unusual and people might not have forgotten it.

Since the Romans had arrived in Britannia, the roads had become a lot safer. The patrols the Phantom Army attacked actually had an effect on getting rid of the bandits that used to roam the countryside, preying on travellers. Nevertheless, Huw felt pleased to join another group of merchants heading to the city.

The journey took ten days. It was uneventful and in the mid-afternoon of the tenth day, Huw turned the horse into Treafon. They had hardly crossed the threshold when Gwen spotted them. She dropped the cloth she was carrying and ran to embrace them.

"Ailbert," she said, hugging him. "You're a real man now. How is Awena?" Before Ailbert could answer, she turned to Huw. "How are Dera and the children?"

She called a boy over and told him to take the horse and wagon, and see it was fed and watered. She needed to talk to her brother and Ailbert. They stooped through the doorway into the house. As soon as they were inside, Gwen once again demanded answers to her questions.

"Awena has a baby now," Ailbert told her. "She's hand-fasted to a young man called Rhodri. It's a good match and they're very happy together."

Huw told of his family and how they had lost a baby. Gwen sympathised. She knew what it was like to lose a child. "But what of you, Ailbert? Have you no one you want to handfast?"

Ailbert shook his head. "I'm too busy for that. Perhaps sometime in the future."

Gwen prepared a meal, and they continued talking into the night until Huw said they must go to bed as they needed to be in Londinium as early as possible the next morning.

Just after dawn the next day, they wended their way towards the city. It took a day for the journey and they had to stay the night at an inn before entering the city the next morning.

After the night at the inn, Huw led the oxen to the market and set out his wares under a sunny sky. The people in the city loved the silver and amber jewellery made by the silversmith in Pen Coed, as well as some he had them make from jet; the pair sold out of them very quickly.

Just before the last pieces went, Ailbert spotted a familiar figure: Maeve. He nudged Huw, who looked over at his sister, now a slave. She looked well, if unhappy. The man who had been her husband walked in front of her. The women who had once been her friends smirked as she passed.

Huw banged one fist into another. "If only I could get her out of here. I'd take her to Eberacum with us. Do you think it would be possible, Ailbert?"

Ailbert thought, then said, "Leave it with me, Huw. I'll think of something."

A woman and her daughter passed Maeve, and laughed when they saw her. Ailbert recognised them as Annwyl, his previous owner and her daughter, Claudia, who had owned Awena. He pressed his lips together to prevent himself from saying something to her as they came over to look at the wares.

"Mater," Claudia said, pointing, "do you think I could have this? It's very pretty, even if it is the work of barbarians."

Annwyl smiled. "Yes, Claudia, of course you can." She picked up the jet brooch set in a complex intertwining motif. "It's amazing how the barbarians make things so pretty when they have such little culture of their own."

Ailbert frowned. This woman was a Briton herself, even if she was now also a Roman citizen. Had she forgotten her past? He bit his tongue. He must not allow himself to say anything to this woman. It would make her look at him more closely, and in spite of his dyed hair, he could not risk that.

Annwyl, still looking at the brooch, asked the price. She turned to Claudia and handed it to her. Looking in her purse, she handed the money over with a brief glance at Ailbert. She frowned and paused briefly. Ailbert's heart nearly stopped as he thought she had recognised him, but then she turned away and continued talking to Claudia.

As the pair left, Ailbert heard Annwyl say, "That young man—he reminds me of someone, but I can't think who. We don't know any barbarian merchants, so it must have been my imagination."

"Of course we don't, Mater. I can't think why you think you know him."

"No, of course not, dear. Now, what else did we want?"

The pair disappeared into the crowds, leaving Ailbert a bit shaken, but relieved his disguise had held.

Once he had sold all the goods he had brought along, Huw went to purchase things to take back. He had made a good profit on the amber and jet jewellery, and he decided to try to see if he could get more amber, along with other luxury goods. Ailbert went with him to learn more about the art of bargaining, but all the while he thought of ways to rescue Maeve.

❧ 20 ☙

Ailbert stayed awake most of the night, thinking. They stayed in an inn in Londinium, because the journey back to the village every evening would take far too long. By the beginning of the next day, he had an idea. He told Huw about it, and he agreed it could work, but how could they communicate the plan to Maeve?

Since Maeve could read, Ailbert decided that he would write a note and pass it to her secretly when he thought he would not be seen. It would rely on Maeve coming to the market again though, and the pair resolved to remain in Londinium until they saw her.

As luck would have it, Maeve was in the market the next day. It appeared she was a trusted slave and thus allowed to go into the town alone. She looked as if she were shopping for vegetables today and so Ailbert went to stand by her, pretending to look at the items in front of them.

He held the note firmly in his left hand and when Maeve put her right hand down by her side, he pressed the note into it, whispering, "Say nothing, Maeve. We're here to get you out."

He had not looked away from the stall as he had said this,

but Maeve looked quickly at him and her eyes widened in recognition. She screwed the note up so it would not be seen, and walked away with her purchases.

Ailbert returned to Huw. "Done," he told him. "She's got the note. It simply tells her where to wait and when, but nothing more. She recognised me, though."

"Did she? That doesn't surprise me, really. She was always good at remembering people."

"Do you think she'll betray us?" Ailbert's eyes scanned the marketplace. "I didn't think of her recognising me. After all, no one else has, not even the Domina and Claudia."

"I don't think so, especially after what they did to her."

The next morning, Huw and Ailbert hitched the horse to their wagon and set off back to the village. It would take a full day to get there, and then they had to return for the meeting with Maeve.

They told Gwen, who clapped her hands at the thought that her sister might now be freed, but warned the pair to be careful.

Ailbert and Huw went to the river the next morning. The village had been built on the river Lea and fishing was one of the occupations of the villagers. Here, they hired a boat. It would not take long to get to Londinium on the fast-flowing river, but coming back would be more tricky—they would be rowing against the current, after all.

The pair got into the boat. Huw had grown up in the village and had become proficient at rowing, but Ailbert had not. He vaguely remembered fishing trips on the Rhenus with his father, but he had been too small to do much, if any, of the work. Huw, therefore, had to do most of the rowing.

"You'll need to row some of the way back," Huw advised him. "It'll be hard against the current and we need to get back as quickly as we can. I won't be able to row all the way."

Ailbert decided he would take part in rowing the boat downstream since it would be easier and he could learn a bit about how to do it before having to help on the return trip. Although it was not particularly arduous going with the current, it helped by giving Huw a rest. They arrived at the point where the Lea met the Thamesis in one day.

Darkness started to fall as they neared the confluence of the rivers, and so they slowly manoeuvred the little craft into the Thamesis, to where they had instructed Maeve to meet them. They rowed slowly under a bridge, where they waited until the appointed time for Maeve to arrive. The daylight slowly faded over the river and people went to their homes.

Maeve took the crumpled note and spread it out where she could read it. She had returned to the domus where she now lived in slave quarters with her sons.

She read the note and then read it again. It had indeed been Adelbehrt that she had seen in the market. No, he had a different name now. What was it? Oh yes, Ailbert. Fairly similar. What was he doing here? Suppose someone else had recognised him? He was taking a big risk, especially trying to help free her.

She would go, though. She found it difficult living as a slave in the house she had known as mistress. The note had made no mention of her sons, but she could not leave them behind.

Maeve made a decision to take them with her. If Ailbert and Huw could not, or would not, take them too, then she would not go either. Better to stay here a slave, painful as it was, than to lose her sons. That would prove infinitely more painful.

Waiting until it was dark, Maeve crept into the small room where they kept keys to the house. As the former Domina, she knew where everything was and it did not take her long before she had unlocked the door leading to a small alley running along the side of the domus.

Once she had replaced the keys, she crept to where her sons slept. Opening the door as quietly as she could, she woke the boys, telling them to be quiet and not say a word.

"We're going out of the house," she whispered. "I can't explain just yet, but it's a secret, and we must get out without *anyone* seeing or hearing us."

Her sons dressed quickly, did not put on their sandals, and silently followed their mother to the door leading from the peristylium to the alley that ran down the side of the house. Once out of the domus, Maeve quickly led the children towards the river. The boys were anxious to know what was happening, but Maeve still said nothing. She put her finger to her lips as they crossed a road and found themselves on the riverbank next to a bridge.

Maeve peered around, but could see nothing. Was this the place Ailbert had told her to come? Perhaps the plan had gone wrong and they had been captured? If that were the case, she and the boys had better get back to the domus as quickly as possible before the rest of the house got up and missed them.

A shape appeared from beneath the bridge. Maeve crouched down and made the boys hide behind some bushes. It might be Huw and Ailbert, but it might be someone else. Criminals often used the river.

She heard a whisper. "Maeve, it's us. Ailbert and Huw. Come and get in the boat quickly, and then we can be gone."

Maeve beckoned to her sons, who came out, and the three of them made their way down to the river's edge.

"Maeve," whispered Huw, "we said nothing about anyone else. We're here to rescue you."

Maeve stopped and looked at her brother, hands on hips. Huw knew that if they had not had need of silence, then Maeve would have been shouting at him. As it was, she whispered as loudly as she could. "I'm going *nowhere* without my sons. If you won't take them, then I'm going back."

"It'll be much more dangerous with three of you, Maeve. Anyone seeing this little craft with five people in it will be suspicious. After all, it's not built for five."

"Well, I'm sorry. Thank you for trying to rescue me, but I'd better get back before we're missed." She turned and began to walk up the bank towards the city.

Ailbert leaped out of the boat and ran after her. Before she reached the road, he caught her arm. "Don't be silly, Maeve. You saved me and other slaves in the past. I owe it to you to get you out of this. We'll take you all."

"Did Huw say that?"

"No, *I* said it. I don't think Huw would really leave your boys. He was just surprised. We'd forgotten about them, you see."

She turned and pulled the boys after her as she walked slowly to the boat. All the while, she fixed her eyes on Huw.

He looked down as she approached, afraid to meet her gaze. "I'm sorry, Maeve. I ought not to have queried your decision to bring your sons. Of course you can't leave them."

Ailbert lifted the youngest boy into the boat and the elder scrambled in, followed by his mother and finally Ailbert. Huw pushed the boat away from the bank with an oar and began to row upstream to where the River Lea entered the Thamesis.

Once on the Lea, Huw pulled hard on the oars. The return journey would take them twice as long as the downstream one had taken. They would need to rest often and change rowers frequently. Huw decided they should travel by night, when there was less chance of being seen and so, when daylight began to break, Ailbert searched for a place to pull in. Bushes overhung the river in places and soon he spotted an area where the boat could be almost completely hidden.

They quietly rowed the boat until it lay under the overhanging bushes. Huw tied it to the trunk of one of the bushes while Ailbert made sure nothing of the boat could be viewed from either bank or river.

The two men lay down to sleep while Maeve opened food they had brought with them, and gave some to her sons. The boys, eyes wide with excitement at this adventure, as they saw it, ate the food, but as they had had little sleep the previous night, they fell asleep shortly after eating. Maeve heaved a sigh as they slept. She had not been looking forward to keeping them quiet during the daylight hours. As she sat there, contemplating what her future would now hold, she too slowly drifted off to sleep.

A sound woke Ailbert and he looked around. Everyone still slept. One of the boys made a little snoring noise. Was that what had woken him? Then he heard it again. The sound of someone or something coming towards the water's edge. He froze and held his breath.

He heard a snort and a hairy nose pushed its way through the bushes to sniff the boat. Ailbert grinned when he saw a horse. He almost laughed ... until he realised the horse might have an owner with it. Ailbert gently pushed the animal away, but the horse decided it was having none of it and pushed back.

Ailbert stroked the animal's nose and whispered to it. "Go away, please. We need to stay hidden."

The horse looked at him with big brown eyes and nuzzled him again.

"Oh, you! Please go away. I've nothing for you. We'll need all our food because we've got two more than we expected." He stood up and climbed out of the boat. The horse watched him and Ailbert took it by its forelock and led it away.

It followed obediently.

Huw woke up from his sleep and saw Ailbert had gone. Sitting up, he gazed around and then decided the young man had gone to relieve himself. He lay back, but when Ailbert failed to return after a few minutes, he became concerned. He rose quietly and went ashore.

He quickly spotted the hoof prints of the horse and with them, the footprints of a human being. *A horse? What's Ailbert doing with a horse?*

Then he heard voices and saw Ailbert talking to a man who looked as if he were about to lead the horse away. He slipped into the bushes to listen as he did not want to compromise their situation by rushing up. He had Maeve and the children to think of.

"Yes, we're travelling upstream," Huw heard Ailbert say to the middle-aged man.

"I suppose you've had a hard time of it against the river," the fellow said. "You're bound to be hungry. Why not go and get your companion, and come to eat something with us?"

Ailbert hesitated. "Thank you very much, but we'll be fine."

"That all depends on how far you have to go. Some distance, I'd imagine. You're not from around here or I'd know you."

Ailbert took a breath and gambled. "It's not just me and my uncle. My aunt and her two boys are with us too."

The man scratched his head, then said, "Go and get them, and come for some food." He glanced at the sky. "It's about mid-afternoon. Have you had your mid-day meal?"

"No."

Huw stepped out of the bushes and glared at Ailbert. "I'm

Huw, this young man's uncle. It's very kind of you to offer food, but we ought to be moving on."

The man laughed cheerily. "You won't get very far if you're hungry, pulling against that current."

"We have food," Huw said.

"I bet not enough for all of you, and two hungry lads with you at that. Tell you what. If you don't want to come to my home, then I'll bring some food here for you. I guess you're running away from something, hiding in the bushes like that, and I guess it's something to do with the Romans." He turned to leave, then turned back. "Don't worry about me. I'll not give you away to them Roman dogs, coming here and taking over our country. You've hidden yon boat well. I didn't see it. Only old Meg here found it and that 'cause she was thirsty." With that, he led the horse away, calling back, "Don't go rowing away, now. I'll not be long."

After he had left, Huw rounded on Ailbert. "What did you mean by talking to him like that, and telling him there were more of us in the boat?"

He looked Huw in the eye. "I trusted him. He didn't look as if he'd betray us. You heard what he said about the Romans. He'll not go telling them about us."

"Anyone can say something against the Romans and not mean it. How do we know he's not now running to the nearest Roman and telling him we're here?"

Ailbert thought about what Huw said, then replied, "I don't believe he'll do that, but if you want, we can move the boat a little way and see if he comes back and if he's alone."

Huw shook his head, but then said, "All right then, but I suggest we move the boat quite a long way and you can walk back here to meet your friend."

This they did. In fact, they had not seen much sign of the Romans all the time they had been rowing during the night. They found a spot about half a mile away, where a small stream entered the Lea. Ailbert and Huw manoeuvred the boat into the stream and amongst some reeds, then Ailbert set off back to where they had been previously moored.

Huw and Maeve waited anxiously. Would Ailbert return with food, or would the man have brought Romans?

Time passed very slowly. The boys became impatient and Maeve had to be severe with them in order for them to remain quiet. Then, there came a rustle among the reeds. They froze, then relaxed when Ailbert pushed his way through, carrying a bag.

He threw it in the boat and then climbed in after it. "There's ham and cheese, as well as bread in there," he said.

They ate some of the food the man had given them, and put the rest away to eat another time. Huw estimated it would take them another couple of days—or rather nights he corrected himself—to reach Treafon, and they would need several meals. He concluded that with the food they already had and with that given to them by the kind man, they would have plenty.

"Have you forgiven me for talking to that man, then?" Ailbert asked after they had eaten their fill.

"I suppose so," Huw replied gruffly. "We won't be hungry now, anyway."

The night fell and as soon as it was dark, Ailbert pushed the little craft into the stream and then leaped in. Huw took up the oars and rowed back to the confluence with the River Lea, where he turned the boat back upstream.

It was another fine night and shimmering stars shone down on them as they rowed. It was fortunate it was the dark of the moon and so they could move with the shadows. The river wound its way through the countryside and they passed an occasional farm or small village.

One time, a dog barked as they passed a farm. They held their breaths and Ailbert, who was rowing at the time, redoubled his efforts, but no one came to see what had disturbed the dog.

As Huw had predicted, three days after leaving Londinium, they found themselves nearing Treafon. Both Huw and Ailbert felt exhausted, and both had stiff muscles. They climbed out of the boat and Huw dragged it onto the bank; then, they walked the short distance to the village.

As it was still night, they approached Gwen's home quietly. Huw did not want to waken her and so they sat outside to wait for the dawn. Maeve's boys were tired. They lay on the ground and fell asleep as only the young could do.

Huw yawned and eyed the boys, then the sky. "Shouldn't be long before dawn. Then we can all get some sleep."

After a while, there came a stirring in the houses and people began to emerge. The sun poked its head over the horizon and it promised to be a clear day.

Gwen stepped from her house and saw the five sitting there. She ran to Maeve and threw her arms around her sister. "They succeeded! They got you out of there."

She turned to Huw and Ailbert, and gave them the same treatment. "You must come in and eat something, then get some sleep. You must be very tired. Rowing against that current in the river must have exhausted you."

They trooped into the house, Huw and Ailbert carrying the sleeping boys. When they had put the boys safely into bed, the others ate and then went to bed themselves.

It was mid-day when they woke. Gwen wanted to know all about the rescue and, between them, they provided full details, including the finding of the horse and the man giving them food.

Gwen said, "I want to come with you to Pen Coed. There's nothing here now. The team we used to rescue slaves has been broken up by the Romans. If you're all going to Pen Coed, I'd like to come with you so I can be near my family."

Maeve hugged her sister. "You must come. If you don't, then I'll not see you. I'll be stuck up there and you'll be down here, only hearing of us when Huw comes down to Londinium."

Huw looked at his younger sister. "Gwen, of course we'll take you with us. It'll be a bit of a squash in the wagon with six of us and the trade goods. I think I'll need to buy another wagon."

"Huw, I've enough money for a wagon. I'll buy it and a horse, if you can lend it to me until we get back," Ailbert advised. He smiled merrily. "I could use it to set up some competition to you, too."

Huw punched him on the shoulder in mock anger. "You've some things to learn yet before you can become a successful merchant, lad!"

The pair laughed.

❧❧❧

The next day, Ailbert and Huw went to the gentleman Gwen told them would be the most likely to have a wagon for sale. They bargained hard, and had to pay what Huw felt was too high a price, but he decided they needed it to be able to take Gwen with them.

Ailbert left to try to bargain for a horse to pull the wagon. Huw had said that he thought an ox would suffice, but Ailbert had set his mind on a horse. He loved horses; an ox was no substitute and much slower.

He examined the animals the trader showed him, looking at their eyes, feet and teeth, and settled on a dapple grey mare he got for what he thought was a good price. He led the animal to where Huw had left his cart and oxen, and tethered the mare there before going to Gwen's house.

He found the family preparing to leave. Gwen had been delighted when Huw told her she could bring her loom now they had another wagon, and she was busy packing all her wool.

"We think it would be better to leave tonight, Ailbert," Huw stated. "We're not that far from Londinium and the Romans will come searching here sooner rather than later."

That evening, under a waxing moon, Ailbert and Huw went outside to hitch the horse and oxen to the wagons, and then load them. There seemed to be very little. Maeve did not have much and Gwen took but a few clothes and her loom and wool. They ate a meal, made sure the fire in Gwen's house was out, and settled the children on blankets in the back of Ailbert's wagon.

Maeve climbed onto the driver's seat next to Ailbert, and Huw and Gwen rode in Huw's wagon along with the goods Huw had bought to trade in Eberacum.

Ailbert flicked the reins. "Hup," he said, and the horse that he had named Eira ambled off in the wake of Huw and his wagon.

The wagons rolled along the road. The boys soon fell asleep with the movement and even the adults felt increasingly sleepy. The animals did most of the work; all that Huw and Ailbert had to do was keep them moving and guide them in the right direction. It did not feel at all like rowing the boat, where the men had been thoroughly active.

The night passed and the miles rolled by. The wagons travelled through forests and villages, fields and towns. No one saw them, and if a few dogs woke and barked, they had passed before anyone reacted. When dawn broke, they had travelled thirty miles with a few quick stops.

They now found themselves in an expanse of forest and they drew the wagons off the road and into the cover of the trees. They led the animals in deeper and tetheredthem so t hey would not wander too far..

"No fire," ordered Huw. "We're not far enough from Londinium yet to be safe."

The four adults took turns looking after the boys. It was essential they were entertained and kept quiet, and so they devised a number of games. The adults who were not entertaining the children slept.

The first day on the road passed in this manner until evening, when they reloaded the wagons, hitched the horse and oxen, and set off again.

Before they left, Huw said, "Ailbert, we've been lucky so far. If we meet bandits, though, I want you to take your wagon and gallop away as fast as you can. Gwen and I'll take our chances, but I don't want those two little boys caught."

Ailbert opened his mouth to speak, but Gwen interrupted. "Do as Huw says, Ailbert. Try to get away with the children."

Ailbert nodded, watching the boys climbing into the wagon and lying on the blankets.

Maeve spoke to them and climbed up onto the driver's seat, followed by Ailbert. As he did so, Huw called behind, "After tonight, I think we can probably move by day. If we can find other wagons, we'll travel with them."

Ailbert nodded and clucked to Eira, and the pair of wagons rolled out of the forest and onto the road. They quickly found themselves in the town of Durovigutum, where there was a crossroads.

Huw deemed it safe to enter the town as they were now quite a distance from Londinium. Too far for the news of an escaped slave to reach ... yet. With luck, they might find others who wanted to travel north. They entered the town and found an inn. The animals they left in the inn's stables and then went inside to rest. As previously, the children were not tired because they had slept most of the way, and so Ailbert volunteered to take them out and, at the same time, see if he could find out anything about people travelling north.

Ailbert and the children wandered around the town. The boys constantly remarked on how small it seemed compared to Londinium. Nor did it appear to have all the facilities that Londinium had. They saw the baths, but the boys made scathing remarks about how small they were in comparison to those they had known in Londinium. They saw no theatre either. The forum was tiny, as were the shops. And they were unimpressed with the basilica.

In the forum, Ailbert stopped at a shop and asked if people travelled north from here. The shopkeeper looked at this person dressed in plaid. He looked like a barbarian, but he did know his manners, as did the two boys with him. The man frowned. This young man and the boys had the manners of a Roman and spoke Latin like natives, but the man, at least, wore the clothes of a Briton.

Still, he had decent manners and the shopkeeper decided he would help out. He told the young Briton that he thought a group of traders and travellers would be leaving the town the following morning soon after sunrise, and suggested they arrived in good time to ask if they could travel with them. He watched as the three left the square and made their way back to the inn, wondering if he had done the right thing.

When Ailbert arrived at the inn, Maeve took over the job of looking after the children while Ailbert went to rest. Before he did so, though, he told her what the shopkeeper in the forum had told him, and she promised to tell Huw when he woke.

That afternoon, when they were all up and had eaten, they discussed Ailbert's news and decided in the long run it would be safer to travel with a group rather than alone. They passed the afternoon buying a few provisions to replenish those they had eaten.

Maeve bought the children new sandals as they only had old ones on, having grabbed those when they left in a hurry. "They'll need new clothes soon," she said with a sigh. "They grow so quickly."

"We'll see to that when we get to Pen Coed," Gwen told her. "Once I have somewhere to put my loom, it won't take long to weave cloth and make them new garments." She looked at the boys dressed as young Romans in tunics. "They'll need to look more like Britons once we get there."

The boys looked at her and then at the clothes she and Huw wore. "Mater," said the elder, "do we have to wear those clothes. They look itchy."

"Yes," Maeve replied with a patient smile. "You'll need to look like a Briton."

"But we're Romans," the younger one said with a whimper.

"No. You *were* Romans, but now you're not. Now you're runaway slaves, so you must look like the natives."

"I don't understand," he whined. "Why did we have to leave Londinium and why did Pater no longer want us?"

Maeve knelt by the young lad. "I'm sorry. It's rather complicated, but I did something the Romans thought was wrong, and so they took away my Roman citizenship and made me a slave. This meant you became slaves too … because the children of slaves are automatically slaves."

He rubbed a hand across his eyes. "Why did you do something wrong?"

"I didn't think I did. I still don't think it was wrong. You'll perhaps understand more as you grow up, but in the meantime, you need to wear the same dress as the other Britons." She smiled at the boys before saying, "It's not as itchy as you think. I grew up wearing such clothes. Remember, I was born in the same village as your Aunt Gwen."

The little boy looked confused, but said nothing more. Maeve hoped she had appeased his curiosity, for the time being at any rate. Now was not the time to be providing the details of her trial and slavery.

After a meal and good night 's sleep, Huw and Ailbert drove their wagons into the forum where they saw a gathering of four other wagons and a half-dozen armed guards.

Huw guided his wagon towards them. "May we join forces with you? We understand you're travelling towards Eberacum and as that is our destination too, we wondered if you'd accept our company?"

One tall, slender man stepped forward and looked Huw up and down before replying. "If you'd be willing to pay part of the hire of these guards, you can travel with us. I hear there are bandits further north. They're calling them 'The Phantom Raiders' or some such. I haven't heard they've attacked any travellers yet, just Roman patrols, but it's only a matter of time before they start."

Ailbert smiled inwardly as he heard this. They were not in any danger from the Phantom Raiders, nor would be, but it seemed his little band was spreading fear around the country. He listened closely to what the trader told Huw.

"There seem to be a lot of them. Several groups, I'd say. The attacks are all in different places, you see. Yes, it'd be wise for you to join us."

Huw thanked him and went off with him to find out how much he needed to pay towards the guards. Once he had done that, and money was returned to the other travellers, they set off.

The man to whom they had spoken, Severus by name, led the way; Huw and Ailbert brought up the rear. The guards spread themselves down each side, riding with drawn swords, even through the town. They did not meet the Phantom Raiders, nor any other bandits. It looked as if the Romans had rid this area of them.

Maeve and her boys travelled with Ailbert as before. After a few hours, he looked at her and asked, "Why did you rescue us? You knew we weren't Britons."

Maeve stared ahead, thinking. Then she said, "When I first met you, you were a little boy. A pet for Annwyl. You were a beautiful child, as was Avelina, and unusual with your almost white hair."

He had never understood why the rescue group had chosen to help them. He turned to her, listening carefully.

"You were a pampered pet, and Avelina was more a friend to Claudia than a slave. Then you began to grow up. You lost your attraction for Annwyl. You were no longer a pretty little boy and she sent for you less and less."

Ailbert nodded. "I remember that time. I wondered if I'd done something wrong. I'd always been in her company when she had friends visiting, but then she began to see her friends without me."

Maeve smiled. "The only thing you did wrong was to grow up. You were, and still are, a good-looking young man, but not cute anymore. That was why Annwyl stopped sending for you. Also, the novelty of having such a pretty, little slave had worn off. Annwyl needed something to impress her Roman friends, and you were no longer it."

Maeve ran her fingers through her hair and looked away. "Did you know they were planning to sell you?" she murmured.

Ailbert took his eyes off the road. Eira took the chance to veer off the road towards the grass and bent her head to eat. Ailbert ignored her. "What did you say? I thought I heard you say they were planning to sell me."

"Yes. They were going to send you to the next slave market." Her voice remained quiet. "Fortunately, Marcus heard about it and suggested to Lucius that he teach you to write and figure so you could take over from him in his old age."

Ailbert, noticing Eira had strayed, pulled her back to the road and clucked at her; she went into a brisk trot to catch up with the others.

They did not speak until they were safely behind Huw's wagon again, then Ailbert said, "I'm even more grateful to Marcus than I thought I might be. If I'd been sold, I'd have lost Awena."

Maeve said nothing for a while, then Ailbert burst out with, "How could they treat someone like that?. I was a pet and a favourite. As soon as I was no longer suitable as a pet, they were going to sell me and separate me from my sister. I'd promised my mother I'd look after her. They knew that. I talked about it, but it meant nothing. I hate the Romans."

He went on to list all the things that made him hate the Romans—from the crucifixion of his father to the planned sale of himself.

Maeve allowed him his rant, then placed a hand on his arm. "To answer your original question, I decided to rescue you because I liked you and thought you were being treated unfairly. Then, when they sent Avelina, Awena as you now call her, to that brothel, it was too much for me. I decided I'd make an exception and rescue you."

"Thank you, Maeve. I never did really thank you, did I?"

"You have now, by rescuing me in your turn."

Ailbert turned to the woman and smiled cheerfully. "Yes, I suppose I have."

An inn appeared on the road and Severus decided to stop there for the night.

The next morning, after they set off again, Maeve resumed her conversation with Ailbert. "You said you hate Romans. All Romans aren't bad, you know."

He looked at her and huffed. "I've not come across many good ones."

"My husband was a good man."

"And yet he let you be made a slave." Ailbert turned to study her.

Maeve looked sad. "I married him because he wanted me, and I thought it would be a good way to get someone into Londinium to find out about Britons who were slaves. I didn't love him, but I came to respect him, and I liked him. He had no choice about me becoming a slave. I was tried and found guilty. I *was* guilty."

"But his sons. They became slaves too. He did nothing about that. Didn't he love them?"

"He loved his sons, but again, he could do nothing, The children of slaves are slaves. I'm sure he's devastated now we're gone, but the law is the law."

Ailbert huffed again, but Maeve continued. "You object to slavery, Ailbert, but we Britons have slaves too."

"People taken in battle. That's different from children ripped from their mother's side. I was only little, but I'll never forget her screams as the soldiers dragged us away."

"I became a Roman citizen when I married. Many of the Roman citizens are in fact not born and bred Romans."

"It's the systems I object to, and the way they think they can march into someone's country and impose their way of life. It's not right. The people of Britannia are not free to live as they wish any more. The druids are persecuted, and the religion barely tolerated. They think that by saying anyone can become a Roman Citizen they are giving a great gift. I disagree. I don't want to be a Roman."

"What do you want then? The Romans are here, like it or not."

Ailbert's eyes blazed. "I want to drive them out. I want them to think it's not worth their while staying here. I want to make their stay here so uncomfortable that they decide to go back to Rome."

"What about those who've become Roman citizens but are Britons? What about those Britons who like, and perhaps prefer, Roman things like baths, sewers, paved roads, theatres —all those things the Romans brought here?"

"They don't need to keep their soldiers here. They're only here to keep the people down."

"Look, Ailbert,' Maeve said patiently, "I understand you. I understand why you hate the Romans, but what I'm trying to tell you is that not *all* Romans are bad. There are some bad ones, yes, just as there are some bad Britons. But there are many good Romans who try to help others and live a good life. Think about that won't you before you go raiding again?"

Ailbert turned to her sharply. "What do you know about the raids?"

"Oh, Ailbert, anyone who feels as you do about the Romans is bound to try to do something. I guessed you had something to do with those Phantom Raiders long ago. They come from near Pen Coed and while you've been with us, there have been no reported raids. I made a wild guess. Seems my guess was right."

They travelled for another three days, until they were almost at Eberacum. Huw called to Severus and told him this was the place where they would leave them to travel the short distance to Pen Coed. The two men shook hands and Huw and Ailbert turned their horses homeward. They drove into the village and handed the wagons to a boy to take care of the horses, then made their way to Huw and Dera's house.

Dera sat outside spinning some wool that had been sheared from the sheep when she saw them. She leaped up and rushed over. She did not know who to embrace first. Her excitement knew no bounds as she hugged first Huw, then his two sisters. The boys she nearly smothered, and then she turned to Ailbert and gave him a hug too.

"What's this? You've rescued Maeve and brought Gwen? How wonderful! Now we're all together again. How did you do it? No, come in and have something to eat first, and then tell me all about it."

Dera bustled about getting food. She was convinced they must have starved on the journey, despite their protestations to the contrary. Once she had them eating, she sat down to hear about their adventures.

Ailbert decided to leave them to their storytelling and went to see Awena. He crept into her house to find her feeding the baby. She grinned when she saw him, but did not jump up as she once would have done. She would not disturb her child's feeding.

"Ailbert, I'm so pleased to see you." She removed the baby

from her breast and held him over her shoulder to burp. "Did you have a successful trip?"

"More than you could guess, Awena. Not only have we a wagon full of luxury goods, but we've also got Maeve, her children and Gwen."

Awena gave a little squeal. "You rescued *Maeve*? How is she? Is she well? And Gwen! She came with you too? I can't wait to see her! She was so kind to us."

Ailbert laughed at his sister's exuberance.

"As soon as I've finished feeding Bran, I'll go and see them both. What about Maeve's children?"

"They're here as well, and Gwen's loom, which took up a big part of my wagon."

Awena frowned. "*Your* wagon?"

Ailbert told her how he had bought a wagon and a horse in order for Gwen to be able to accompany them north.

"I hope you've not spent too much money, Ailbert. One day you'll marry and need that money."

Ailbert laughed again. "There's no one I want to marry, sister. I'm just happy to have a horse and wagon of my own. I'll be able to set up as a trader myself one day."

Maeve lay in bed that night with her mind racing. She had talked to Ailbert about how all Romans were not bad, and that some were actually good. She was unsure how her words had gone down with the young man though. She had felt his hatred for the Romans as a palpable thing and she knew how such hatred could affect a person. Negative emotions were always bad.

Even she had hated the Romans at first. Her marriage was one of convenience, although her husband had not known that. She married him, as she had told Ailbert, to ease the rescue of Britons from slavery.

Her marriage had brought her into close proximity to many Romans and she had quickly learned there were a lot of good ones. Oh, they could not get away from their upbringing, but within that framework, there were many good people.

As she lay thinking, she considered those Britons who had become Roman citizens. She would not have joined them if she had not been a part of the group that freed the slaves. Most of those that did become citizens, did so because it offered what they considered a better and safer life. Certainly many of the things the Romans brought with them improved life. That she could not deny.

Would what she told Ailbert have any effect? Would it make him think about how his hatred was eating away at his soul? If he did not stop these raids, he and his companions would be caught sooner or later, or killed. But youth is hot-headed, especially young males.

She turned over. At least I tried, she thought as she fell asleep.

The next morning Ailbert woke well rested. He and Huw agreed to sort through the goods they had bought before doing anything else. Ailbert had kept a record of everything and so it would not be too arduous a task.

On his way to meet Huw, Rees ran over to him. "I'm glad you're back, Ailbert. It's been too long since the last raid of the Phantoms. When can we do another? I've heard there is a group forming in Blaenafon, hoping to do the same sort of thing we're doing … driving the Romans out."

Ailbert eyed the young man. "Rees, please let me do my job. I need to sort the goods we bought before anything else. Huw will have me strung up if I don't get there to help him with the accounts."

A sigh escaped Rees. "All right, then. But can we have a meeting soon?"

"I'll see about arranging one," Ailbert promised and continued to where the wagons were standing.

"Didn't know you were so friendly with Rees," Huw said as Ailbert approached.

"I'm not," Ailbert replied flatly.

"He seemed anxious to greet you though."

Ailbert shrugged. "He wants me to do something I've not got time for yet."

"Like organise a new raid, I don't doubt," Huw replied with a shake of his head.

Ailbert said nothing, but began to check through the goods.

Later that day, when they had stacked the goods, Ailbert went to see Rhodri and Awena. They were outside, playing with their son in the bright sunshine. The little boy gurgled with laughter as Rhodri tickled him.

"Ailbert," Rhodri called. "Rees told me you were back. I understand you've brought more than goods this time."

Ailbert grinned at his friend. "Huw's two sisters and nephews, no less," he said. "Maeve we rescued from slavery and Gwen wanted to come with us. There's nothing left for her down there if all her family are up here, so she asked if she could come too."

"It'll be a bit crowded in Huw and Dera's house now, until we can build houses for them, so why don't you come and stay with us?" Awena asked. "That 'd be all right, wouldn't it, Rhodri?"

Rhodri put the baby down and hugged his wife. "Of course it would. I'd love to have Ailbert stay." He turned to his friend and his expression turned serious. "Rees is anxious to start raiding again."

"I know. He approached me first thing this morning. I said I'd call a meeting soon."

Ailbert did not call the meeting that day, nor the next. Maeve's words went round and round in his head. He kept seeing Flavius helping him when he broke his leg. Not only helping him, but keeping him at his house and paying for the doctor. No doubt, this act saved him from being a cripple for the rest of his life.

He thought about the fun he had with Sylvia and Quintus, and the talks he and she had. She seemed like a normal girl. Then he remembered the hostility of Octavia and Laurentius, and his anger grew again.

"All Romans aren't bad." He heard Maeve's voice in his head and frowned. He had directed such hatred towards the Romans all his life, yet he was now feeling ambivalent.

The Roman soldiers had caused the death of his father and his removal from his family and friends, and he had thought of them as being the worst of the lot. Yet here was a Roman soldier being kind and caring for a total stranger, and one he considered a barbarian, too.

Fortunately, for him, Huw had decided to go to Eberacum before he had been able to arrange a meeting. He knew it was just putting off things, but he felt glad all the same.

"I think I'll take a gift for Sylvia and Octavia as thanks for what they did for me last winter," he told Huw. "Also for Flavius. It was because of him that I got treatment to heal a broken leg; I might have become a cripple otherwise. Quintus and Laurentius too. What do you have that I can buy from you?"

Huw protested that Ailbert did not need to buy the goods, but Ailbert insisted. He did not want to eat into Huw's profits and so they agreed on cost price. He bought wine for Flavius, perfume for Octavia, jewellery for Sylvia, and a couple of small hunting bows for Quintus and Laurentius.

The two set off for Eberacum without a planned meeting

of the Phantom Raiders, much to the disgust of Rees. The others understood the need for work to come first, but Rees went away scowling.

"I hope there's not going to be trouble from him," Ailbert said anxiously to Gareth just before he left.

"I'll keep an eye on him," promised the young man.

With that, Ailbert and Huw left for the city.

❧ 21 ❧

When Ailbert and Huw reached Eberacum, Huw told Ailbert he ought to give his thank-you gifts immediately.

Ailbert expressed confusion as to which entrance he should use. He was, after all, a trader so felt he ought to use the trader's entrance.

"Don't be silly, boy," Huw told him. "You are not selling or delivering things. You were taken in as a guest and you are returning as a guest, with presents as thanks. You should use the vestibulum, as befits your status as a guest."

Ailbert shrugged, but set off to Flavius' domus. As he walked, he grew more and more nervous. What if Octavia still felt the same way she had when he stayed there and refused his gift? What if Sylvia had been influenced by her mother and also refused his gift? He wanted to see Sylvia. They had got on very well when he had stayed there.

Shortly, he found himself standing in front of the domus. He knocked on the door and a slave he did not remember seeing before quickly answered.

"I've come to see the Dominus and Domina," he told him. "I have gifts for them."

The slave stood back to allow Ailbert room to enter, then said, "I'll go and see if the Domina will see you." He disappeared, leaving Ailbert standing in the vestibulum.

Octavia soon appeared. She gave a stiff smile and told Ailbert to follow her into the atrium. She indicated a seat for him to take and then sat on another.

"I came to thank you for your kindness last winter when I broke my leg," Ailbert said, smiling. "I've brought gifts to show my appreciation. Something for each of you—you, Flavius, and your children."

"That's very kind of you," said Octavia, but offered no smile. "My husband insisted you stay so the doctor could set your leg properly. I trust it's better now." She looked at his leg as she said this, but as it was encased in breeches, she could see nothing.

"Yes, thank you. My leg has set straight and I have no trouble with it. All thanks to your husband and the doctor. I could not allow such kindness to pass without showing my thanks." He reached into the bag he carried and pulled out the container of perfume he had bought for Octavia. It was in a beautiful blue glass bottle, the bottle alone was worth a lot of money.

He handed it to Octavia, who pulled out the stopper and sniffed. "Why, it's a lovely scent." Her eyes widened as she looked at Ailbert. "And the bottle is beautiful. Such fine glass … I've not seen any like this in Eberacum."

"It came from Londinium and was made in Rome as I understand it."

Just then, a door opened and Sylvia came out. She saw Ailbert and came over to greet him.

Ailbert's stomach turned as he watched her approach. What should he say?

Octavia saved him by turning to her daughter and telling her of the presents Ailbert had brought.

Sylvia smiled at the young man. "Presents? Why have you brought us presents?"

Octavia replied before Ailbert could regain his composure. "Ailbert has come to thank us for our help last winter. You remember him, don't you? The young man with the broken leg who stayed here?"

Sylvia's eyes twinkled. "Of course, Mater. He was here for several weeks."

Ailbert reached into the bag and brought out a small box, and handed it to Sylvia, who opened it with an exclamation of delight.

"It's beautiful, Ailbert." She lifted a silver and amber bracelet from the box.

"Let me put it on for you," Ailbert said, and she passed the bracelet to him and held out her arm. "It looks beautiful on you. I'm glad I chose that one. It's delicate, just like you."

Octavia cleared her throat and broke the spell that had begun to encircle the young people. They became aware of the world once more, and Sylvia sat down next to her mother and studied the bracelet on her arm.

"I'll go and get the boys," Octavia said, rising. "You can give them their presents as well. I'm afraid my husband is not here at present to receive his. You can give it to one of the slaves. I take it the wine is for him?"

Ailbert nodded as she called a slave and he handed over the wine. The slave left with the wine through to the peristylium where they kept the store. Octavia left as well to find the two boys.

She returned with the them far too quickly for Ailbert's liking. He had been unable to say much more to Sylvia than a polite enquiry as to her health.

Ailbert handed over the hunting bows. Even Laurentius was delighted. Both boys rushed away to try them out.

"You need to practice hard," Ailbert called after them.

"Will you come and help us?" Quintus asked, stopping and turning round.

"I'm afraid I have to go and help Huw in the market," he replied, "so I can't come now. Perhaps another time?" Ailbert looked at Octavia for confirmation that this would be all right.

The Domina nodded her agreement and Ailbert rose to go. He took his leave of the two women, and his hand lingered a little longer on Sylvia's as they shook hands.

She gave him a lovely smile and said, "I hope I see you when you return to help Quintus and Laurentius with their bow practice. I enjoyed our talks last winter."

Ailbert returned her smile. "So did I." With that, he left to make his way back to Huw in the marketplace.

"You were long enough," Huw commented.

"I had a brief chat with them all, except for Flavius. He wasn't there."

"How did Octavia react?"

"She was a bit cool at first, but she liked the perfume and it seemed to thaw her. Sylvia was her usual, delightful self. She really is a very pretty girl."

Huw stopped setting out his wares to glance sharply at Ailbert. He hoped the young man was not falling for this Roman girl. With her mother being so certain of the inferiority of 'barbarians', he was sure nothing good could come of it.

His thoughts on that matter stopped when people started to shop. There were many customers this morning and trade was brisk. The olive oil and wine, in particular, were in great demand and so it was not until much later that he had a chance to talk to Ailbert.

"This girl," he said casually. "I'm afraid you might be in for a disappointment if you allow your admiration to continue."

Ailbert looked at him in surprise. "She's a Roman. She's a pretty girl and I like to look at pretty girls, but she's a Roman.

You know I hate the Romans. She's not even a Romanised Briton, but from Rome itself."

Huw looked at him disbelievingly, but let the matter drop. Ailbert's answer did not stop his anxiety though. He recognised the look in the young man's eyes when he mentioned Sylvia. He had been there himself when he first met Dera. Still, it was none of his business.

They had a successful day but, even so, Huw had not sold all his goods. He decided they would stay until the next day.

"If it's anything near as good as today," he told Ailbert, "we'll make an excellent profit. Enough to fill your wagon as well as mine when we next go to Londinium. We're on the way up, young man."

The next morning, soon after they had set out the stall, Sylvia walked by. She had a slave boy with her to carry her purchases. Ailbert glanced round but could see no sign of Octavia. Sylvia turned to look at the wares on the stall, then looked up and saw Ailbert. Her eyes opened wide as she feigned surprise upon seeing him there. He noticed she still wore the bracelet he gave her.

She fingered it as she eyed the wares on display. "I didn't know you were still here," she said softly, looking away and not meeting his eyes.

Ailbert felt familiar butterfly wings fluttering in his stomach as she spoke.

"We hadn't sold everything so we decided to stay another day," he told her, drinking in how the sunlight played with the auburn highlights in her luxurious hair.

"Mother loves the perfume you gave her," she said, picking up a string of amber beads. "And Quintus and Laurentius are most anxious that you come to show them how to use their bows properly." She laughed and met his eyes for the first time. "They've been frightening the slaves because of the way their arrows fly in random directions."

On hearing her laughter, Ailbert's heart did a flip. It

sounded like the tinkling of a brook over stones. "I'll try to get away later and come and give them a lesson," he promised. 'If that will be alright with your mother, that is."

"I'm sure Mater will be delighted if you can teach them to shoot straight."

"Excuse me, are you serving?"

The voice brought the two young people back to the present. Ailbert had felt as if the world had shrunk to include just the two of them.

"I'll perhaps see you later then, when I come to train your brothers," he said with hope in his heart.

"I hope so," Sylvia responded and disappeared into the crowd.

"Now, what can I do for you, sir?" Ailbert asked.

Late in the afternoon, Huw had sold all his goods. He decided it was too late to go back to Pen Coed that evening and so he and Ailbert booked into the inn for another night. Ailbert told Huw he had agreed to give Sylvia's brothers their first lesson in using the bow.

Arriving at the domus, Ailbert knocked on the door. The same slave as the previous day opened it and bade him to enter.

As he entered the atrium, Quintus saw him and ran over. "Have you come to teach us how to use the bows?"

Ailbert smiled at the young lad. "Yes, I have. Do you have time now?"

"Oh, yes. I'll go and find Laurentius. Wait here. I won't be long."

Ailbert stood by the impluvium, gazing into the water when he noticed another figure reflected in the pool. He looked up and saw Sylvia standing next to him.

"So you've come to give the boys a lesson," she said, sitting on the edge of the impluvium and trailing her fingers in the water.

Ailbert regarded her intently. She focused her gaze on the water and refused to look at him. Had he done something to upset her?

She took her fingers out of the water and turned her eyes up to meet his. "I would like to talk with you after the lesson. I've missed the conversations we had when you stayed here."

"I would like that very much," Ailbert affirmed.

Further conversation ended when Quintus and Laurentius came rushing across the atrium, clutching their bows.

"We're ready, Ailbert," Laurentius called, his original hostility forgotten. "Where's the best place for us to practice?"

Ailbert tore himself away from Sylvia and went over to the boys. She rose and followed.

"We ought to go somewhere where there's no danger of a stray arrow hitting someone," Ailbert told them.

They ended up in the peristylium. Sylvia trailed them and warned the slaves to stay clear of the area where they were about to practise.

All the time the boys practised their archery, Ailbert was aware of Sylvia watching. The boys made some progress but after an hour, Ailbert told them they had done enough for one day. They packed their bows away and disappeared, chatting about how they would become the best hunters in Britannia.

Ailbert turned to Sylvia and sat beside her. "They did very well for a first time."

"You're a very good teacher. You showed extreme patience. I'd never have been able to keep cool like you did when they kept making mistakes."

"Losing my temper with them would have made them make more mistakes … out of anxiety."

Ailbert and Sylvia talked for a long time. If anyone asked Ailbert later what they had talked about, he would not have been able to tell them, but he enjoyed Sylvia's company so much, it wouldn't have mattered what the conversation was about, just that it continued.

Eventually though, Ailbert noticed it had started to get dark and he left to return to the inn and Huw.

⚜

Huw and Ailbert left Eberacum for Pen Coed the following morning. Ailbert looked to see if Sylvia came to the market again, but he was disappointed. He could see no sign of the girl. He had one last look around the forum, then took his place next to Huw.

They arrived back home and unhitched the oxen, and fed and watered them. When they had finished, Ailbert checked that Eira had been looked after properly; he had asked Gareth to see to her while he was away.

Gareth spotted him and came ove.

"How's Eira?" Ailbert asked.

"She's just fine," replied his friend cheerily. "Come and see for yourself."

Eira trotted over when they approached, followed closely by the chestnut stallion, Tân; seeing Ailbert, he hoped for a titbit.

Ailbert reached into his pocket and pulled out a shrunken pair of apples. They were the only ones left from last year's store. He held one out to each of the horses and they ate them with gusto. He patted both and turned to Gareth. "So, what's been happening here in the last few days?"

"Not much. Work, hunting, the usual sort of things. Rhodri's taken up with Awena and the baby, Rees is still agitating for more raids on the Romans, all that sort of thing."

"Rees again," Ailbert murmured, his eyes narrowing. "He's so keen to kill Romans, I could almost believe he's been through the same sort of thing I went through."

"No, he's just a hot-head."

Ailbert decided he would call another meeting of the Phantom Raiders for the following evening and see about planning the next raid.

ॐ

As the sun went down the following day, the eight remaining raiders met in the usual clearing in the forest.

"About time you got round to talking about another raid, Ailbert," Rees said irritably. "Some of us have been thinking you'd got cold feet about it."

"As you should realise, Rees," Ailbert replied, "there's work to do as well as raiding. And if we raid too regularly, the Romans will anticipate our attacks. As it is, they don't know if we're going to pull one or if we've given up. That confusion works to our advantage."

Rees snorted, but remained silent while Ailbert told them of the next attack. He had planned this one before he and Huw went to Londinium, and he discovered, while in Eberacum, that the place he thought would be an excellent ambush was on the route of the next day's patrol.

Having had the details of the plan explained to them, the group parted company to meet again the next morning to go to the ambush point.

Soon after dawn, the Raiders approached the designated area. Ailbert set them up in their allotted places and waited. Soon, he heard the familiar sound of marching feet. The patrol was coming. Up trees and behind rocks, the eight young men waited patiently. Each had his bow at the ready, with an arrow nocked.

The patrol marched into view. It seemed a smaller one than those Ailbert had seen leaving Eberacum recently. Perhaps the Romans had decided there would be no more raids. It had certainly been a long time since they had attacked a patrol.

As they came within shooting range, Ailbert drew the string of his bow back to his ear and trained it on one of the men. Each of the Raiders had been instructed which man to target so that they would not all end up shooting the same man.

Now came the time to release. His arrow flew through the air, followed immediately by seven others. Every one struck true and eight men fell.

Ailbert grinned. They had practised during every spare minute and now they were deadly accurate with their shots. He did not waste time thinking, though. Immediately, he strung another arrow and let it fly before the Romans could form their testudo. Eight more men, including the leader, fell. Sixteen men dead or seriously injured.

This patrol had only been two contubernia, half the size expected, and Ailbert and his men had downed them all. *Sixteen men.* He rubbed his hands gleefully and prepared to loot the downed soldiers. They would not take the soldiers' clothing, as that would lead to them being eventually caught. No one could get rid of Roman army uniforms without having questions asked.

When Ailbert arrived at the patrol, he found Rees carefully killing the men that had been alive.

"Stop!" Ailbert ordered. "We don't kill helpless men. If they die before help gets here, that's one thing, but we don't kill for the sake of killing."

"Isn't that what this is about?" Rees drew himself up to his full height, facing Ailbert. "*Killing* Romans?"

"Yes, but not in cold blood. We attack armed men who can defend themselves."

Rees reluctantly sheathed his dagger and began to search the bodies.

Ailbert went to the leader and turned him over. He was still alive, but wounded. He had taken an arrow in the thigh. Ailbert removed the man's helmet. He was not sure why he did this. He was not going to take it, but when he looked at the injured man, he realised he knew him. It was none other than Flavius, the Roman who had helped him the previous winter, and whose daughter he found so attractive.

Flavius had not seen him. He had his eyes closed in pain. Ailbert stood and backed away before Flavius opened them.

"Go. Disappear," he told his men. "I'll see you back at the village."

The men melted into the landscape and Ailbert stood out of sight, wondering what to do. He owed Flavius for his kindness and help when he had broken his leg. If it had not been for the Roman, he would have likely been a cripple, but how could he help the man without giving himself away as a member of the Phantom Raiders?

Then he had an idea. Pen Coed was only a half hour's walk directly over the hills, so he set off as quickly as he could.

Once there, he found he had arrived before his men, much to his relief. He did not want to explain himself to them just yet.

He hitched Eira to his wagon and started back towards where they had ambushed the patrol. Once out of the village, he urged Eira into a trot; although the way was slightly farther along the roads, he made good progress.

A mile or two before the place where he had left the dead and injured, he spotted two soldiers hobbling along. They were two whom he had left at the scene, alive but injured.

When he got alongside of them, he asked, "What happened to you?"

"Those blasted Phantom Raiders," replied one man grimly. "There must have been at least a couple of dozen of them. They attacked our patrol and killed most of us."

The second man, who now leaned on the wagon, continued. "There are only four of us left alive. The bastards were killing those they'd downed. Cowards to kill helpless men. Then, suddenly they all disappeared. Don't know why."

Ailbert looked from one to the other. The men did not look too badly injured. They were tired from loss of blood, but their injuries would mend.

"You said there were four of you alive. Where are the other two?"

The first man sank onto the ground. "One is our commander. He gave us orders to leave them and take the news back to Eberacum. They'll send help. We left them some water. I hope it'll be enough."

The second man coughed, then said, "The commander's a good man. Never asks his men to do something he wouldn't do himself. I'll be sorry if he doesn't make it."

The first soldier nodded his agreement.

"I'm going that way," Ailbert told them. "I'll see what I can do for them when I get there. I've stuff in my wagon I can use for bandages."

The soldiers thanked Ailbert and continued limping towards Eberacum. Ailbert shook the reins clucked to Eira, and set off again at a trot.

Soon he saw bodies in the road ahead. When he drew near, he pulled Eira to a halt and got down from the driving seat. He ran to where he had left Flavius. He was not there, but the young man looked round and saw him sitting at the side of the road, with the arrow still sticking out of his thigh.

Ailbert ran to him and feigned surprise. "Flavius, it's you!"

Flavius opened his eyes, which widened when he saw Ailbert in front of him. "Are you real, or are you in my dying imagination?"

Ailbert ran back to his wagon where he retrieved bandages. When he returned, he replied to Flavius' question. "I'm real, Flavius. I happened to be travelling this way. I saw your men down the road and they told me what had happened. I've things in my wagon I can use as bandages."

Flavius began to squirm as Ailbert tried to bandage the

wound as best he could; he found this difficult due to the arrow still lodged in Flavius's thigh. "Hold still."

"Take that blasted arrow out," Flavius snapped as Ailbert knocked it. "You'll find it easier to bind the wound."

"Sorry, Flavius," Ailbert replied firmly. "I daren't do that. The arrow might have penetrated a blood vessel and if I remove it, you could bleed to death. Anyway, some hunting arrows are barbed and if I pull it out, it'll tear your muscle at the very least."

When he had finished the binding, Ailbert looked around at the other men. None moved. "Your men said one of the others was still alive."

"Yes, young Maximus was alive when they left, but he died not long ago. There's only me here now."

Ailbert brought his wagon close to the commander and knelt down beside Flavius. He put his arm under that of the older man and managed to heave him up onto the wagon bed.

"It won't be a comfortable journey," he advised the man, "but I'll get you to a place where someone can tend you better than I can."

He climbed onto the driving seat and turned Eira back towards Pen Coed. He considered taking Flavius to Eberacum, but decided against it. It was a much longer journey, and Ailbert thought the man needed tending as soon as possible. There were healers in Pen Coed who could at least start the healing process.

It was a bumpy journey and when they arrived at the village, Flavius had lost consciousness. Ailbert pulled his wagon up before Awena and Rhodri's home. He got down and entered. The sun had started setting and so Rhodri was home.

"I've a wounded man in my wagon. Can I bring him in here?" he asked.

"Of course," Awena replied. "Rhodri, go and help Ailbert bring him in."

Between them, the two young men carried Flavius into the house. When she saw a Roman soldier, Awena gasped. "Why a Roman, Ailbert? I thought it would be one of our men, not a Roman."

Ailbert explained to her who this particular Roman was. "I owe him, Awena. If it hadn't been for him and his kindness, I might be a cripple today."

"I'll go and get Dera," the girl stated. "She'll know what to do. She's good with wounds." She ducked out of the house, leaving Ailbert with Rhodri.

"A Roman, Ailbert? You hate Romans, especially soldiers."

Ailbert sat down and put his head in his hands. "I know, but this man's different. He's not a typical Roman. He's more like us."

Just then, the baby began to cry and Rhodri went to pick him up. "He's hungry. I hope Awena's not too long."

As he said this, Awena and Dera appeared in the doorway, Dera carrying a bag with her.

She looked around and saw Flavius. "This is the man, I take it?" She knelt and opened her bag, and pulled out several smaller bags, each filled with various herbal preparations. Dera then carefully removed the bandage Ailbert had put on. It had become soaked with blood and she passed it to Ailbert with instructions to throw it on the fire.

Dera looked at the arrow, then at Ailbert. She knew where the arrow had come from. "Is this arrow barbed?"

Ailbert nodded. Dera looked at Flavius. He had regained consciousness and was looking at her.

"This is going to hurt," she advised him. "I need to push the arrow through to the other side of your thigh. I daren't pull it out as the barbs would tear the muscle, and you would likely not be able to use your leg properly again."

Flavius grunted. "Get on with it then. The sooner the better."

Dera turned to Ailbert. "I want you to boil some water

and make this into a tea." She handed him a bag containing some kind of bark.

Ailbert looked at it and his brow puckered.

"It's willow bark," she told him. "It'll help with the pain."

Ailbert boiled water and poured it onto the bark. He left it to steep for a while and when it had cooled, he handed it to Flavius to drink.

In the meantime, Dera examined the wound. When she thought it had been long enough since Flavius had drunk the willow-bark tea, she proceeded to push the arrow. Even with the willow, Flavius winced in pain, and once cried out, but he managed to keep still throughout the ordeal.

A brave man, thought Ailbert favourably.

Once the head of the arrow appeared, Dera cut it off and pulled the shaft back out the way it had entered.

The wound bled profusely. Dera mopped it up as much as she could and put on a poultice of yarrow leaves. Then she bandaged it again.

She turned to Flavius. "You did well. I've put on a poultice to stop the bleeding, but you must stay here for a few days. I need to change it until it's stopped, and to make sure no infection gets in or you'll lose your leg."

Flavius flopped back. "Ailbert, will you go to tell my family where I am? Octavia will worry, especially when the men get there and she hears what happened."

Ailbert nodded and left the house. He got Eira and mounted her, calling to Huw, who appeared in the doorway of his house; he told him he had to go to Eberacum to tell Flavius's family what had happened. Then he kicked Eira into a canter and set off for Eberacum, thinking how strange fate was. He had needed to stay in Flavius's home because of an injured leg, and now Flavius needed his help in the same way.

❧ 2 2 ❧

Ailbert pulled Eira up outside the domus where Flavius lived. He had stopped cantering after a while because he did not want to hurt his horse and thus, he continued at a trot and walk, interspersed with the occasional canter. Darkness had fallen by the time he arrived and he took Eira round to the back of the domus, where he handed her to a slave before going back to the front to knock on the door.

The same slave as before opened the door and stood back to let Ailbert enter, recognising the young man. As Ailbert entered the atrium, Quintus saw him and ran over.

"Ailbert, what are you doing here? It's too dark for an archery lesson."

"I came to see your Mater. Is she here?"

Quintus called to a passing slave to find his mother, and continued to question Ailbert. "You can't be here for the market at this time of night. What do you want to see Mater about? Pater will be back soon. Do you want to talk to him too?"

"Quintus," Ailbert told the boy patiently, "what I have to say is for your mother."

As Ailbert began to field off another barrage of questions,

Octavia appeared and sent the boy away. She led Ailbert into the tablinum and indicated he sit on one of the chairs.

She sat in the other, facing him. "What do you want to see me about, Ailbert?" She held herself rigid as she spoke.

Ailbert ignored her attitude. "I don't quite know how to put this, but I was driving my wagon along the road this morning when I met two soldiers. They were from a patrol of two contubernia. They told me they had been attacked."

Octavia's rigid stance disappeared as her hand went to her mouth and her eyes widened. "Flavius?" she whispered.

"The men told me he was alive but wounded. I went on and found him. I managed to get him into my wagon. He was the only one left alive and he'd told the soldiers to go back to Eboracum to tell of the attack. I took Flavius to Pen Coed, where I live, and our healer Dera tended him. He asked me to come and tell you."

"How badly is he hurt?" Octavia asked as she moved her hand from her mouth.

"The arrow went through his thigh. There's a lot of muscle damage, but nothing major. It missed the main blood vessels."

"Your healer has tended him, you say? I expect he's bandaged up. Can you bring him home tomorrow? You can stay here tonight and leave first thing."

"I'm sorry," Ailbert replied, "but Dera said he can't be moved for a while. Moving him might aggravate things and make it worse. I'm sorry to have been the bringer of such difficult news."

Octavia drew herself up straighter. "I am the wife of a soldier. I've lived with the possibility of Flavius being injured or killed all my married life. Risking his life is what he does. I can do no less than accept his injury. At least he's still alive."

Ailbert's eyes grew dark as she said this. How dare she imply Dera was not good enough? He managed to keep his temper though and followed the slave to the room assigned to him.

He lay in bed thinking of how close he was to Sylvia. He wanted to see her before he left the next morning and was not looking forward to travelling with Octavia.

Early the next morning, Ailbert mounted Eira alongside the carriage that would carry Octavia. A slave harnessed two horses to it and they waited for the Domina to emerge.

Octavia came out accompanied by Sylvia. The girl smiled at Ailbert and, to his surprise, entered the carriage alongside her mother. Octavia gave the order to move off and Ailbert kicked Eira to follow behind.

It would take most of the day to travel to Pen Coed. It had only taken Ailbert half a day to get to Eberacum, travelling as fast as he could and pushing Eira as much as he dared, but the carruca, as the carriage was called, would take nearly twice as long.

As Ailbert had thought, it was dusk when they pulled through the gates of Pen Coed. He found someone to look after the horses and then escorted Octavia and Sylvia into the house where Flavius lay.

On entering, Octavia coughed and took out a handkerchief, which she held to her mouth. She looked at the firepit burning in the middle of the house and wrinkled her nose, but , she said nothing.

She hurried across to where Flavius lay. "Flavius, how are they treating you? I asked Ailbert to let you come home with us, but he tells me the healer here said you must not be moved. We've brought the carruca and can easily fit you in."

"You didn't need to come all this way, Octavia. I'm being treated very well. These people know quite a lot about medicine. Dera has given me tea made from some bark or other, and it's marvellous for pain. I have every confidence her other treatments will work just as well."

"Oh, Flavius, dear," Octavia said , "surely you don't think

they can be as good as our own doctors? Sylvia, come and help me tell your father he should come back with us."

Sylvia had been standing near the door, watching Ailbert. He, on his part, had been watching her. If either of them caught the other looking, they quickly glanced away. She turned her attention to her parents, and Ailbert left the family to themselves.

"Pater," said Sylvia, bending and kissing her father on the cheek, "Ailbert tells me the healer here has been treating you. Don't you think you ought to return to Eberacum, where you can be tended by a Roman doctor?"

"Sylvia, dearest," Flavius replied, "the healer has told me that if I'm moved, it might start the bleeding again." He hitched himself up in the bed and winced. "The treatment Dera has given me so far has stopped the bleeding, and quicker than I would have thought. I trust her judgement when she says moving me would start it off again. No, I'll stay here until the wound begins to heal."

"But, Flavius," Octavia began.

"Don't try to persuade me,. My mind is made up. I will do as Dera instructed and stay still. It makes sense to me. I've learned a little from watching the army doctors and they say the same. Men have died because we moved them against the doctor's orders."

Octavia took a deep breath. "As you wish, Flavius, but I still think our own doctors would do a better job than these barbarians."

Ailbert came back in and spoke to Octavia. "We've been building a house for two people who have just moved here. It's nearly completed and my sister and her family have agreed to move in there for tonight so you can stay here." He looked at Sylvia who looked back and did not look away this time. "The house is complete, except for the firepit. We'll be quite comfortable there; it's not a cold night. I'll escort you to Eberacum in the morning."

"Thank you." Octavia began to cough. "But can we not go to the new house? All this smoke is making my eyes sting and making me cough. And I'm sure Flavius would be more comfortable out of this smoky atmosphere. Really, how you live in it I don't know."

Ailbert regarded the older woman and remembered how he had felt on first entering a Briton's house. Yes, he had hated it too. Since then, however, he had become so used to it he no longer gave it a second thought, but a woman like Octavia would hate it even more than he had. He agreed to the proposal, but not to the suggestion that they take Flavius too.

"Dera said Flavius must not be moved," To his surprise, Sylvia agreed and so, outvoted, Octavia reluctantly agreed, with murmurs about smoky, hot places.

The following morning, Octavia bid farewell to Flavius. She still muttered about how he would be better off in Roman hands, but she entered the carruca along with Sylvia and they set off back to Eberacum, with Ailbert accompanying them to ensure their safety.

Ailbert had to stay the night again because, by the time they arrived in Eberacum, the sun was low in the sky. He ate with the family. It was strange as he was not used to eating while reclining on a couch. He had seen this many times while a slave boy in Londinium, though, and he persevered.

After the meal and before bedtime, Sylvia and Ailbert found time to talk. They rediscovered the pleasure in each other's company, and Sylvia became bold enough to say she felt glad Ailbert would come to visit, even if only to provide updates on her father's condition and to give archery lessons to her brothers.

Bedtime came all too soon for Ailbert's liking. The next

morning he would be leaving early and he felt disappointed he could not spend longer in Sylvia's company.

❦

On arriving back at Pen Coed, Ailbert went straight to see Flavius. "Your wife wanted me to spend my time galloping backwards and forwards to Eberacum with news of your progress," Ailbert informed him.

"I hope you told her you have work to do here," Flavius replied. "You can't spend all your time on our business. You have your own to consider."

"Yes, I did. She was none too pleased, either. I think she considers me one step above the slaves, and I should do her bidding just like them."

"Don't blame her, Ailbert. She's had little to do with people other than Romans. I'm afraid she thinks of all others as barbarians."

"Yet you don't, Flavius."

"I've been with the army for many years. In the army, there are men from all over the empire. I've learned people are the same the world over, and those we call 'barbarians' have their own civilisations."

"I'll try not to judge her … but perhaps this meeting of our culture with hers will help enlighten her." Ailbert went out to help complete the building of the house for Gwen, Maeve and her boys, and did not speak to Flavius again that day.

❦

A few days later, Ailbert sat in the house he shared with Awena and Rhodri. As he chatted to Flavius about how their cultures differed, and in what respects they were similar, Dera came in to change his bandages.

"Go over there," she ordered Ailbert. "Give me room to see."

Ailbert complied and sat by the fire, although it was a warm day. He waited while Dera finished, but she called him over. "Look at that, Ailbert. I'm not happy with the look of that wound."

Sure enough, as Ailbert peered at Flavius's leg, he saw the edges of the wound were inflamed and there was pus oozing out.

"There's some infection there," Dera said, frowning. "I could do with wild garlic leaves and roots, but I've run out. There's a jar of honey in the store in my house. Would you get it for me please?"

Ailbert worried as he ran from his sister's house to Dera's. Infection was the worst thing now the haemorrhaging had stopped. If the infection could not be stopped, the best thing Flavius could hope for was amputation of the leg. In spite of himself, Ailbert had come to like the Roman, telling himself that Flavius was not like other Romans.

When he returned with the honey, Dera smeared it onto Flavius' leg wound before binding it again. She called Ailbert as she started to leave. "He feels as if his temperature is up. That's not a good sign. Watch him carefully and if he seems to get worse, or becomes delirious, call me immediately."

That night, when he went to bed, Ailbert worried about Flavius. He liked the man, in spite of his being a Roman, and a soldier at that. He was kind and thoughtful. Then he remembered his talks with Maeve on the way from Londinium. In spite of her treatment, she did not hate Romans. His confusion grew as he thought of Sylvia. He liked her … perhaps even more than liked. Her mother, however, was more like what he had always thought of Romans— thinking everyone not a Roman was inferior and could be treated however the Romans wished. It took him a long while to get to sleep that night and, for the first time since his capture all those years ago, he forgot to chant his litany of hate.

The next morning, Dera stopped by again. She examined Flavius, feeling his forehead for fever, then looking at the wound again.

Ailbert thought that perhaps the inflammation appeared a little less red, but Dera clucked and spread on more honey before re-binding it. She took the old bandages away to be washed as she had each time she changed them.

The world went on, though, and Ailbert did Huw's accounts as normal, and went to see if the silversmith had finished making the jewellery with the amber they had brought back from Londinium and the jet from Eberacum.

The merchants in Eberacum had told him the black stone could be found on the coast not too far away. Ailbert determined to find the place and gather some himself. That would save the cost of buying it from the merchants in Eberacum.

The silversmith needed a bit more time. Just a few more hours, he told Ailbert, and so the young man fed Eira and gave Tân a titbit. Gareth appeared and the chestnut horse pulled back his ears at his approach.

"You should buy that horse." Gareth laughed as the horse snapped at him. "You're the only one he responds to."

Ailbert patted the stallion and turned to his friend. "I'd love to, but I can't afford him. At least, not yet."

"He's no use to anyone else. He'll only work for you."

"Did you want me for something?" Ailbert asked, climbing from the fence where he had been sitting while watching the animals.

"It's Rees," Gareth said somberly. "He's saying all sorts of things about you. He says you've gone soft, bringing that Roman soldier here to look after. Worse things, too. He's implied you're a traitor. He's not actually said anything in so many words, but I think it's only a matter of time."

Ailbert ran tense fingers through his ash-blonde hair. "You don't think that, do you, Gareth?"

"No, and nor do any of the other Raiders. It's the young-sters who listen to him. I keep telling them you owe this man a debt and that you're repaying it by tending him as he tended you last winter."

"I'll speak to Rees."

"He's going on about another raid, you know. I think he might try to take the youngsters on one."

Ailbert swung away from Gareth and began to march back to the village, fists clenched. Gareth ran to catch him up.

"He can't take those kids," Ailbert declared angrily. "Look at how long it took us to get good enough to raid! They aren't trained. They'll get killed."

Gareth grabbed Ailbert's arm and swung him round. "It's no good going to talk to him in anger, Ailbert. That'll only put his back up. Calm down and *then* talk to him reasonably. I agree with you that he mustn't take the kids. He already got one man killed with his poor planning."

Ailbert took Gareth's advice and did not go to seek out Rees immediately. He did Huw's books for him and then visited the village silversmith to pick up the jewellery he had now finished. Ailbert also bought more pieces from him, in the typical complex Celtic designs. He took them back to Huw. It was not until he had finished these tasks that he went to search for Rees, who was working on the finishing touches to the house that the villagers were building for Maeve and Gwen.

He stopped when he saw Ailbert approaching. "So, you've managed to tear yourself away from your pet Roman have you?"

Ailbert did not rise to the taunt, but said in a quiet voice, "I hear you've been saying I've lost my nerve, Rees."

Rees stiffened. "Well, haven't you? You seem to be

consorting with the Romans these days, and you've not suggested a raid for a while now."

"A few days, Rees; it's only been a few days since the last one. You know we can't raid frequently or on a regular basis, or we'll end up being wiped out. The Romans will know what to expect and where."

"So why do you have that soldier in your home?"

"He's not just any soldier, and you know it. You know how I was helped last winter when I broke my leg. It was this very soldier who helped me." He raised his voice, anger getting the better of him. "For goodness sake, if it weren't for him, I'd probably be a cripple now and there would be no raids at all. I owe him."

Rees scowled, but said nothing.

Ailbert continued. "It has also come to my ears you're talking to the young lads."

"So what? They'd be going to war with other tribes in the old days. They're old enough to fight."

"And get killed?"

"Look, Ailbert, you aren't one of us. You came here from Londinium, and not so long ago at that. I don't know what you did that made you need to leave, but you're still an outsider here." Rees scowled again and continued. "They're eager to fight ... more eager than you, it seems. Some are wondering if you're a spy for the Romans."

Ailbert grabbed Rees by his jerkin and pulled him forward. "I suppose you've been feeding those lies to them, haven't you? You never liked me, especially when my ideas proved better than yours."

He pushed Rees and the man fell to the floor. Ailbert turned to walk away, but then turned back. "I've never lost a man, Rees, unlike you."

Rees lay sprawled in the dust. Others had been watching, including Rhodri, who came over and walked with Ailbert.

"I shouldn't have done that, Rhodri," Ailbert said, not turning to look at his friend.

"He had it coming. If you hadn't done it, then I'd have hit him, not just pushed him down."

"How much damage has he done with the youngsters?" Ailbert asked anxiously.

"I don't know. They haven't said anything to me, but then they wouldn't, knowing we're family. Ask Gareth. He can probably find out more."

Ailbert sat on a log outside the house door and Rhodri sat beside him just as Awena came out. She had wool with her and was about to begin weaving on the loom Rhodri had built for her. She was becoming quite proficient at the task, especially now Gwen had arrived to give her advice.

She sat at the loom and began to weave. As she did so, she asked, "Why are you two here?"

The pair looked at each other and an understanding passed between them.

"The house is about ready for Maeve and Gwen to move in," Rhodri told her, "so we decided there were enough people there to finish it and came home."

Awena knew when her husband lied, but she just gave him a long, searching look before saying, "Well in that case, go and see if Bran's alright. You can look after him until his next feed. And stir the pot over the fire while you're in there."

🌿 23 🌿

"I think you should go and see Octavia," Dera said the next day, "and tell her the wound has become infected. I don't think it's too bad, but she should know ... just in case it gets worse."

Huw had planned to go to the market that day, but Ailbert rode to Eberacum and arrived just after noon, the journey being quicker on horseback than with a wagon pulled by oxen.

Octavia frowned when Ailbert told her the news. "I knew we should have brought him back with us. This would never have happened if we'd insisted."

"The wound is a little less inflamed since Dera used honey on it. Honey seems to help to kill the infection."

"I suppose you barbarians have learned something of treating wounds," Octavia grudgingly admitted. "After all, you were always at war with one another before we came to civilise you."

She really believes we were uncivilised before they came, and his hands clenched into fists by his side.

Sylvia appeared in the atrium and her mother told her the

news Ailbert had brought. The pair had no time for talk, as Ailbert had to return to Huw in the marketplace.

Not long afterwards, while he showed a customer a pewter tankard, Ailbert spotted Sylvia strolling across the square towards him.

"Can you spare some time?" she asked. "I'd like to talk to you about Pater."

Ailbert looked at Huw, who nodded, and he walked away with Sylvia.

"Let's go out of the city," the girl said. "I'm tired of the noise and dust. A walk in the woods would be pleasant."

The pair made their way to the forest just outside the city walls.

"Your father has an infection in the wound," Ailbert said once they arrived in the wooded area. "I told your Mater because I promised to keep her updated. I don't think it's going to be a problem. Dera has been treating it with honey."

Sylvia laughed, surprising Ailbert. "I know all that, Mater told me."

"Then why …?"

"I wanted your company. It's been ages since I saw you and I like talking to you."

"Your Mater knows you're with me?"

She laughed again. "Mater thinks you're a barbarian, even if you are fairly civilised for one."

"And you?"

"You're asking a lot of questions today, Ailbert. No, I don't think you're a barbarian. Your people have a culture, a religion, and make wonderful metalwork. Those are things of civilisation. It's just a different civilisation from ours."

The pair walked and talked for what seemed a short time, but when they returned to the city they realised they had been away much longer than they thought.

"Mater will be so angry," Sylvia said worriedly. "I'd told

her I'd be back soon." She saw consternation on Ailbert's face. "Don't worry, I'll think of a good reason why I was so long. Goodbye."

She turned to leave, but Ailbert caught her arm and turned her towards him. "Before you go ... I know this is probably not a suitable question, but can we do this again? Soon?"

Sylvia laughed her tinkling laugh. "I thought you'd never ask. Tomorrow, at the same time? You'll still be here, won't you?"

From that day onwards, every time Huw came to Eberacum, Ailbert met Sylvia to walk and talk.

Ailbert saw Sylvia in the domus whenever he came to provide a report on Flavius' progress and give the boys their archery lessons, but they had little opportunity of engaging in much talk.

Flavius stayed in Pen Coed for several weeks, until Dera decided he could be moved back to Eberacum without any danger. Octavia came with the carruca, and helped Flavius into it. The man could now walk a short distance with a stick.

Flavius thanked Ailbert and Dera for their help.

"Without what you did for me, I would be a cripple at the very least," he told Dera. "And Ailbert, if you hadn't come along and brought me back here, then I would probably have been dead. I cannot thank you enough."

Ailbert gazed steadfastly at the Roman soldier, now his friend. "Flavius, you took me in and tended me last winter. To do the same for you was the least I could do. No thanks are necessary."

Ailbert thought long and hard about his relationship to the family after Flavius departed. He liked them all. Octavia had thawed towards him somewhat and Laurentius was now as friendly as Quintus.

He finally admitted his love for Sylvia. He thought about her and decided he would have to tell her how he felt.

After his decision, Ailbert felt better. At least about Sylvia, but it did not help his relationship with the Phantom Raiders. He learned during his time with Flavius and his family that the Romans were no different from the Britons. It was as Sylvia had said. Both were civilised; it was just that their civilisations were different. He could no longer go on killing Roman soldiers.

He sat in the house he shared with Awena and Rhodri, his head in his hands.

"What's wrong?" his sister asked him.

He looked up and saw the worry in her eyes as she stirred the pot over the fire. "I don't think I can go on killing Romans, that's all."

"That's a big change of heart." Awena stopped stirring and turned her gaze on her brother. "Your whole life has been dedicated to ridding Britannia of the Romans. Your whole life you've hated them."

"Let's just say I've learned that hating is not the way."

"It's Sylvia, isn't it? Flavius's daughter. I like Flavius, but I didn't like Octavia much."

"It's what I've learned from them as much as what I feel for Sylvia. Flavius, Sylvia and Quintus take people as they are and don't judge them by their background. There are Romans who are bigoted, just as there are Britons who are bigoted."

Awena put the spoon down and went to pick up Bran, who had begun to whimper. She sat next to Ailbert and put the baby to her breast. The little boy quieted immediately.

"I know what you mean," she said. "I don't like Rees at all. He's worse than you were. Rhodri tells me he's planning on taking the youngsters on a raid."

Ailbert jumped up, angry. "Even after I told him he wasn't to? I'll go and sort him out once and for all!"

He strode from the house towards the one occupied by Rees and the young woman he had recently handfasted. He did not wait to be invited in, but burst through the door.

Rees's woman screamed, then recognising Ailbert, said, "What do *you* want?"

Ailbert's eyes blazed. "Where's Rees?"

"I don't know." The woman scowled. "And if I did, I wouldn't tell you. You threw him down into the dirt in your temper."

Ailbert could see he would get nothing out of the girl so he turned on his heel and strode out of the house. He asked all over the village, but no one seemed to have seen Rees nor know where he had gone. At least not until he asked one of the old men sitting outside a house near the gate.

"Saw the young whippersnapper going off in that direction." he pointed to the east. "Had a bunch of lads with him. Suppose they've gone hunting."

Ailbert swore.

The old man looked at him. "No need for that, now. Gone without you, have they? If you hurry, you might catch them, but they've been gone some time."

Ailbert walked slowly across the village, back to where Maeve and Gwen lived. Gwen sat weaving outside, as it was a warm day. He wondered if he could catch them and stop them if he ran very quickly, but decided he could not, and so he sat wearily down beside Gwen.

The older woman looked up from her weaving. "What's the matter?"

Ailbert shrugged.

"Come on, now. Something's wrong. Is it a girl?"

"No." Ailbert shook his head. "Not a girl. Something perhaps more serious."

Gwen smiled. "I didn't think there was anything more serious than that for a young man of your age."

Ailbert did not reply for a short while, then turned to her and said, "It's Rees. It seems he's taken some of the young lads and gone to ambush a Roman patrol. I'm afraid he's going to get them killed."

Gwen stopped weaving and looked hard at Ailbert. "And you're feeling responsible because of your involvement previously." It was a statement, not a question.

"Did Huw tell you?"

"No, but I've got eyes in my head. I've noticed how you young men have gone out hunting … and shortly afterwards there has been a report of an attack by the Phantom Raiders."

"Yes, I suppose there is some element of guilt about it. If I hadn't nurtured my hatred of the Romans all those years and put it into practice here, then this wouldn't have happened."

Gwen sat beside Ailbert and put her hand on the young man's arm. "Look … did *you* instigate the initial rebellion?"

Ailbert looked hard at her. "No. In fact, at first they didn't want me to join. We'd not been here long and they didn't trust me."

"Well then, they would have raided with or without you. What you did, by planning properly, was to save the lives of probably all those young men. You only lost one, I think."

"No, I didn't lose any." Ailbert looked away. "The one who died was on a raid with Rees. I had nothing to do with that one. Rees did it off his own bat."

"Then you have nothing to feel guilty about. This raid is *not* your responsibility."

He returned his gaze to the older woman. "I know, Gwen, but I feel bad for those youngsters in danger. They have all their lives in front of them, and the village needs them too."

"Ailbert, you and the others who have been a part of the Phantom Raiders are also young."

He stood to leave, but turned back. "We may still be young, but we're old enough to know what we're doing. Those kids aren't." He strode off through the gate, towards where Eira and the other horses grazed.

He called his horse over and as soon as he had her saddled, he galloped in the direction the old man told him Rees had gone.

He had only travelled about thirty minutes when he saw three figures approaching, carrying something. He reined in Eira and jumped off. It was, as he thought, three of the youngsters carrying a fourth.

Ailbert quickly assessed the situation. "Put him on Eira," he commanded.

The young men did as Ailbert told them, and the injured youngster, a boy of thirteen summers, groaned as they hoisted him up. Ailbert made a quick estimation of his wounds. They did not seem too serious.

"How many of you went?" he demanded, "and where are the others? More to the point, where's Rees?"

The boys looked at one another. "Cedric's dead," one said and they all looked down at the ground. "Glyn, Tristin and Rees are prisoners. I don't know what happened to Owen."

"Ten of you set out and only four are returning." Ailbert scowled. "What did you think was going to happen? No, don't answer that! You all had thoughts of glory put into your heads by Rees."

He grabbed Eira's reins, making her shy. She nearly deposited her burden on the ground.

"Come on. We need to get Floyd back and treated. Then you need to go to Adair and tell him what has happened, and to Cedric's mother and tell her too."

The three looked up and quailed when they saw Ailbert's face. "Do we have to?" asked the smallest boy.

"Yes. You tried to be men, now you must act like men and take responsibility for your actions."

The sad little party wended its way back to Pen Coed where the villagers met them with wailing and tears. Adair questioned the boys and learned that Rees, Glyn and Tristin had been taken prisoner by the Romans.

"What will happen to them?" Brianne whispered.

"I don't know," Adair replied glumly. "They could be enslaved … but they could equally well be put to death."

⚜

Later that day, Ailbert discussed the situation with Huw. He had gone to the older man to ask his advice as to what to do about those the Romans had taken prisoner.

"Ailbert," Huw said grimly, "I don't think there's much we can do. We don't want to bring the anger of Rome down on Pen Coed. That would mean the deaths of many more."

"I feel guilty about it, Huw," Ailbert replied, looking into the distance. *I know all about Roman reprisals for attacking them.*

"You don't need to. It wasn't anything to do with you. You neither ordered nor planned it."

"I know, but I want to do something to help those boys."

They discussed possibilities far into the night, until Dera got annoyed and called Huw in to come to bed, but by then they had the beginning of a plan.

⚜

The next morning, Huw told Dera he was going to the market in Eberacum.

"But you've not got much to sell," his wife replied.

"I have other business there," Huw murmured, not looking at his wife. "There are things I might buy to trade in Londinium."

Dera knew that look in Huw's eyes. She knew that she would not succeed in changing his mind and shook her head as she watched her husband and Ailbert trot out of the gate to the city, wondering what he was up to now.

The pair arrived in Eberacum towards evening and went immediately to the inn where they usually stayed. Huw asked about news in the city and was rewarded by the innkeeper telling him of the successful fight of the patrols against the Phantom Raiders.

"Not so 'phantom' this time," he told them. "The patrol killed two of them, injured at least one other, and captured three."

"What's going to happen to those they captured?" Ailbert asked casually.

The innkeeper shrugged. "Dunno, really. I think the two youngsters'll probably be sold as slaves. They're young and strong. Pity to waste them and the profit they'll make. The other, who seems to be the leader of the Raiders, will probably be killed in one form or another. I hope they send him to the arena. He'll make a good spectacle." He grinned.

Ailbert paled at the thought. The arena? There was no way Rees could fight either gladiators or wild beasts. If that were to be his fate, then they would need to act swiftly if they were to effect a rescue.

Huw asked the innkeeper, "When will their fates be decided?"

"In the next day or so I'd think. There's a slave market in three days, so they'll want to sell the boys there if they're to be sold."

❦

Ailbert and Huw discussed what they should do and hatched a plan. The pair spent an anxious three days, but eventually the day of the sale arrived and they went with many affluent Roman citizens to the slave market.

When they arrived, they found the slaves standing on

wooden platforms. Every slave was surrounded by a large group of potential buyers, poking and prodding the 'goods', and asking questions of the traders.

The slaves also had boards around their necks, with details of education, whether or not they were a risk of running away or suicide, and other such things. Ailbert closed his eyes at the sight of the boards. *I had one just like those.* He tried to banish the memory. His stomach turned as he watched the Romans treating the slaves like animals to be bought. They looked into their eyes, pulling eyelids down, opening their mouths and examining their teeth. They felt their muscles and scrutinised their skin for signs of disease.

The Romans don't think of them as human. I was treated like a pet until I grew out of my prettiness. Then they were going to sell me, just like a puppy that had become too big.

His anger began to rise and his fists clenched. He pressed his lips together.

Eventually, Ailbert spotted Tristan and Glyn. He indicated to Huw where the boys stood, but did not approach them. They did not want Tristan or Glyn to know they were there in case they gave an indication they knew the two men.

It seemed a long time to Ailbert before the slave trader brought Tristan to the attention of the market. By this time, many of the buyers had left, all the best slaves having been bought. Only a few still stood around, some out of simple curiosity and others believing they could get a bargain. After all, these boys had attacked a Roman patrol. They would likely make difficult slaves.

The bidding started and Ailbert raised his hand after the initial bid had been placed. The people around him expressed surprise that a barbarian should be bidding for a slave, but the bidding went on.

Tristan was small for his age and not a very attractive looking boy, and so the bidding quickly slowed. Ailbert managed to buy him for a reasonable price. The trader indicated to the guards to remove the boy and take him away to where his new owner could pick him up at the end of the market. Then he began the sale of Glyn.

Glyn stood looking defiantly at the crowd in front of him. He seemed much more the rebel than Tristan. He gazed straight at the Romans crowding around and he stood tall, hands at his sides. Earlier, he had received a beating for biting a customer who had been looking at his teeth. This fact soon travelled round the crowd, and when it came his turn to be sold, few buyers remained.

Of those few buyers, though, one man seemed anxious to buy the young rebel. Ailbert could not understand why. Glyn would give trouble and most certainly try to escape. Ailbert remembered the lad as a bit of a troublemaker in the village. Whenever something went wrong, people always looked for Glyn and his friends.

The bidding continued and Ailbert looked at his purse. This attempt at rescuing the young man was costing him nearly all his money and that lent to him by Huw. This would have to be his last bid. Then his opponent threw up his hands and walked away. Glyn was his. He looked at the boy to see if he had noticed who bid for him, but the boy was now in tears, his defiance having melted away when he realised he was truly a slave.

Ailbert asked the slave trader to bind the boys' hands and feet, and also to blindfold them before loading them into his wagon. He decided it would be safer not to risk the boys' reaction when they saw who had bought them.

With the two slaves safely in the back of the wagon, Ailbert clucked to Eira and they left Eberacum immediately even though it would mean they would arrive in Pen Coed long after dark. They waited until they had travelled about an hour before stopping and releasing the boys from their bonds.

"Ailbert, Huw," Glyn exclaimed and grinned.

Tristan broke down into tears. "We're your slaves. You

bought us, so we're your slaves. That will be humiliating back at home."

Huw put an arm round the young man. "We've not bought you to be slaves, but to rescue you from that very fate. When we get back to Pen Coed, you will be free to return to your families and take up your lives again."

"Thank you, Ailbert and Huw," the boys said in unison.

Ailbert said, "Just one thing. You must promise not to do such a foolish thing again. You weren't ready and Rees shouldn't have made you think you were."

"We understand," Glyn said thankfully. "Rees said you'd lost your nerve, and the others, too. He made it all sound so exciting, and told us how easy it is to attack the patrols."

"It's not easy, though," Tristan whispered, head bent, looking at the bed of the wagon. "It was hard, and frightening. When it came to shooting, I couldn't do it. I couldn't kill a man."

When they arrived in Pen Coed, the boys were fast asleep on the wagon. "Leave them sleeping," Huw said as they tiptoed away. "They've been through a terrifying experience and tomorrow will be soon enough to reunite them with their families."

Ailbert and Huw crept back to their homes and silently entered.

The next morning, when they awoke, it was to cries of joy as Glyn and Tristan found their families. The parents of the boys smothered the two men with praise and thanks. They could not have been more grateful.

Not so the parents of the missing boys, nor Rees' parents and wife. They turned their backs on Ailbert and Huw. Ailbert heard the murmurings.

"We should not have allowed strangers to settle here. Look what's happened. It was peaceful before. They stirred it up and got some of our young men killed." Rees's fatherbanged his fist on the side of his house..

"I don't like the Romans," the mother of one of the missing boys said, "but at least it's peaceful. These strangers have made our young men rebels."

Rhodri tried to placate them by telling them the raiding was all his idea. All Ailbert did was ensure the plans were such that they did not get killed. The boys that went with Rees had nothing to do with Ailbert. Rees had been acting on his own. It had no effect, though. Those families shunned Ailbert.

✣ 24 ✣

Ailbert was now in debt to Huw. He had borrowed a lot of money in order to assuage his conscience and free the lads. He needed to make more than he did working for Huw. He lay in bed, sleepless, for many nights; he needed to get so many things clear in his head.

First, there was the debt to Huw. He must pay it back as quickly as he could. He had plans to make and he could not do what he wished as long as he had that debt.

Second, there were his guilty feelings about the deaths and loss of the boys who had gone with Rees. And then Rees himself. Could he have done more to prevent Rees from having taken the raiding into his own hands? If he had managed that, those boys would not be dead or missing, and Rees would be alive too.

On a subsequent visit to Eberacum, not long after the rescue of the two boys, they heard that Rees had been thrown into the arena to face wild animals and had met a grizzly death. The gruesome picture in his mind haunted Ailbert. That he might have done something to prevent Rees from taking the actions he had—that resulted in his horrific death —added to his sleepless nights.

There was also his hatred of the Romans. He had nursed his hatred for what seemed like the whole of his life. He had nurtured it and fed it. Now, he did not feel so strongly about them.

This was largely due to his contact with Flavius and family. He understood that Roman people were no different from Britons. They loved and hated, were generous and mean, and laughed and cried just like Britons. Men like Flavius came here because they had been told not to deliberately persecute the people, and his family had come with him.

He went to talk to Maeve.

"You're right, Ailbert," she told him when he explained his confusion. "Roman people are just that: people like us—it's not the people who are bad, but the system."

"Their punishment system in particular," he said with a frown. "So barbaric. I can't get the picture of Rees being torn to pieces by animals out of my head."

Maeve shook her head as though to dislodge something. "Yes," she said, almost whispering the words. . "That is something unpleasant … and Romans go to watch and enjoy it. In that I'm with you about the people being bad." She looked at him and shrugged. "But it's what they've been told is entertainment. It's hard to resist accepting what you've grown up with as normal."

"And it's how they think they should conquer other people's countries too."

"Let me tell you a bit of history, Ailbert. Long ago, there was a man called Julius Caesar. He wanted power in Rome, but had fallen out of favour. He decided to gain that favour by conquest." She brushed a lock of hair from her eyes and continued. "This Julius Caesar was a brilliant general. He managed to conquer Gaul and to invade Britannia." She laughed lightly. "He went back to Rome, having been beaten by the Britons, but he didn't say so. He put it about that he'd won a great battle. No one tried to conquer us for nearly a hundred years after that, so did *he* win?"

Ailbert smiled at the thought of the Britons beating the great Julius Caesar.

With a fleeting smile, she continued. "Under Emperor Claudius, they came again and were more successful, as we can see now. However, they do allow our chiefs to maintain their autonomy and even give them jobs in exchange for tribute. They give us Roman citizenship too, if we want it. I got to be a citizen by marrying a citizen, but it was stripped from me, as you know."

Ailbert thought for a short while, then said, "They're very clever, these Romans. They let us think we're ruling ourselves by allowing our previous rulers to continue. They also make us dependant on them by showing us such things as theatres and baths."

"Right, but does that make them all bad?"

"No, I suppose not. Certainly Flavius and most of his family are good people."

"Most?"

"I don't like Octavia very much, and she doesn't like me, solely because I'm not a Roman."

"You find bigoted people everywhere, Ailbert."

Ailbert thought for a moment, then looked away, saying, "That was me, wasn't it? I was just like Octavia, only worse. I actually took my hatred and let it feed on itself. It led me to killing people, and ultimately the death of those boys and Rees." He stood and walked away.

Maeve's eyes followed him and she smiled. He was *almost* healed.

❦ 25 ❦

A ilbert thought long and hard. He had plans for his future and, sooner or later, he would have to put them to Huw. He arrived at Huw and Dera's home and found Huw sorting cloth to take to the market in Eberacum.

"I need to talk to you," he said.

Huw stopped what he was doing and looked at the young man. "Well, what do you want to say?"

"I know I owe you a lot of money for buying back those two boys. It will take me a long time working for you, so I propose that I set up on my own as a trader."

Huw put his hands on his hips and looked at Ailbert. "It's not an easy life, you know? You need to be away from home quite a bit."

Ailbert looked at the ground and nodded solemnly. "I know. I've been travelling around with you long enough to understand that ... but travelling around Britannia to trade doesn't take so long. It's not like travelling across Europa."

"It's not as if you're married, I don't suppose. Well, good luck to you, Ailbert. Just as long as you don't offer me too much competition." He laughed and clapped Ailbert on the back.

Ailbert heaved a sigh of relief. Huw had not been annoyed that he planned on becoming a rival. He would need to work hard, though, before he became a serious threat to Huw's business.

They planned on leaving in the next few days for Londinium. Ailbert said he would take his wagon and buy a few things to bring back to Eberacum to trade. Gwen gave him some cloth she had woven; he thought it would bring a good price. Maeve provided woollen cloaks she had made from Gwen's cloth and Awena furs that had come from the animals Rhodri had hunted.

After visiting Londinium, Ailbert returned with olives and figs, as well as an amphora of wine. It was a small start, but a start it was and he anxiously awaited the market in Eberacum.

Before the market, he managed to buy flour from a miller in the village that he hoped to sell to a baker in Eberacum; then he settled down to his accounts. He should make some profit from this journey, and he intended to plough it all back and buy more things next time.

He had other plans too that did not involve trading, like seeing and walking with Sylvia, which he very much looked forward to.

࿇

The day came when he and Huw set off for the town. They arrived in the late afternoon and stayed at the usual inn. Early the next morning, Ailbert went to visit Flavius' family. He made the excuse that he would come to give the boys their archery lesson later that evening but, in reality, he hoped to see Sylvia.

She did not appear, much to his disappointment. He hoped she would hear of his arrival and come to visit him at his stall.

All day he worked in the forum, selling goods. He did well

and, by mid-afternoon, he had sold everything. Sylvia had still not arrived. He sat under the shade of the portico that ran round three sides of the forum and gazed at the crowds passing by.

Then he saw her. She paused at Huw's stall and looked at some of his goods, especially a glass cosmetic container Huw had purchased in Londinium. The container had been made in the shape of a bird's head and had come all the way from Hispania. Sylvia examined it, then brought out her purse to pay. She looked around and Ailbert saw her speak to Huw. He pointed in Ailbert's direction and, after passing her purchase to the slave who carried her parcels, she crossed the forum towards him.

Ailbert watched her and the boy carrying her parcels. He was momentarily reminded of the days when he had done the same job and his fists clenched. Then Sylvia was standing in front of him and he forgot all about his days as a slave.

He smiled. "Shall we walk?"

She smiled back. "Have you finished here?"

Ailbert nodded and Sylvia told the boy to take the goods she had bought back to the domus. If anyone asked, he was to say she had met an old friend and was going for a walk.

The pair followed their usual route through the gates and into the woodland. Neither of them spoke until they were in the clearing they had found some months before. There was a fallen tree by the side of a stream and the sun shone down through the space the tree had left. The little brook sparkled under its light.

Sylvia sat on the tree trunk and patted it for Ailbert to sit next to her. "This has been my favourite place," Sylvia told him, "ever since we found it. I love the brook and the way the breeze makes the leaves rustle."

"It'll soon be autumn," Ailbert said, looking at the water as it burbled past, "then the leaves will have gone."

"Don't say that, Ailbert. When it gets too cold, we won't be able to take our walks."

Ailbert turned to her. "Sylvia," he began, then paused and looked away. Drawing a deep breath, he tried again. "I've enjoyed our walks, too. And the talks we've had. I don't want them to stop for winter."

Sylvia opened her mouth to speak, but Ailbert interrupted. "Don't stop me. This is hard. I don't want to stop seeing you over the winter." He turned away, coughed, and turned back. "What I'm trying to say, Sylvia, is … that I love you."

Sylvia 's eyes opened wide at the announcement, then she lowered them. "I love you too, Ailbert. I didn't think my feelings were reciprocated. Oh, I know you like me and enjoy my company, but I had no idea it was more than friendship."

"Then we should get married."

Sylvia burst into tears and Ailbert took her in his arms. It was the first time he had done so, although he had dreamed of it so many times.

"We can't get married, Ailbert," she sobbed into his shoulder.

"Sylvia, I know your mother will object because I'm not a Roman, but I can become one. I'll become a Roman citizen for you and live in Eberacum."

"Oh, who gives a fig about what Mater thinks." Sylvia dried her eyes with the back of her hand.

Ailbert frowned. "Then what …?"

"Pater's the one who'll decide. Mater will have to do what he says, and so will I. Only Pater has the power to decide the future of any member of the family."

"Then why are you crying?"

"Pater has betrothed me to the son of a friend of his. I was betrothed when I was twelve years old, and am going to be married next summer."

Sylvia began to weep again and Ailbert did his best to

comfort her and persuade her she could break off this betrothal. They could go to Pen Coed and have a handfasting.

Sylvia was adamant that the betrothal could not be broken and the pair walked sadly back to the gates, hand in hand for the first and last time.

AFTERWORD

After this, Ailbert threw himself into his work, building up his merchant business. He became successful and travelled all over Europe, searching for rare and valuable goods to trade. He went back to the Rhinelands, but he could not remember enough to be able to find his home village, and no one recognised the ash-blonde young man as the pale-haired six-year-old who had been taken as a slave all those years ago.

He married a girl from a nearby village and had eight children, five of whom grew to adulthood. As he became more successful, he moved his family to Eberacum and became a Roman citizen.

He sometimes saw Sylvia and her husband, and had the occasional few words with her. He never lost his love for her, even when she became old, but he hid it from his wife, of whom he was fond and would not have wanted to hurt.

He died in the year 136 AD a wealthy and respected Roman.

Dear reader,

We hope you enjoyed reading *Vengeance of a Slave*. Please take a moment to leave a review in Amazon, even if it's a short one. Your opinion is important to us.

Discover more books by V.M. Sang at: https://www.nextchapter.pub/authors/vm-sang

Want to know when one of our books is free or discounted for Kindle? Join the newsletter at http://eepurl.com/bqqB3H

Best regards,

V.M. Sang and the Next Chapter Team

GLOSSARY OF ROMAN PLACES
AND WELSH AND LATIN WORDS

Atrium Large open area in a Roman house, from which rooms led off

Britannia Britain

Blaenafon Celtic, meaning source of the river. A village near Eberacum

Cambria Wales

Century A unit of 10 contuburnia led by a centurion

Compluvium A hole in the roof of the atrium allowing rain to fall into the impluvium and letting in light.

Contuburnium Smallest unit of the Roman army, comprising 8 men.

Deva Chester

Domus A town house, owned by a prosperous person

Dubris Dover

Dumnonia Cornwall

Durocortum Rheims

Durovernum Canterbury

Durovigutum Godmanchester

Eberacum York

Eira Celtic. Snow, the name of a horse

Gesoriacum Boulogne-sur-Mer

Hispania Spain

Impluvium A rectangular area to collect rainwater from the compluvium which drained through pipes to a cistern for household use.

Insula An apartment. Cheaper housing than the domus.

Londinium London

Mare Balticum Baltic Sea

Mater Mother

Mogantiacum Mainz

Oceanus Britannicus English Channel

Pater Father

Pen Coed Celtic, Wooded Headland. The name of a town near Eberacum

Pharus Lighthouse

Portico Entrance to a domus or villa

Primus Pilus Senior Centurion of a Roman Legion.

Rhenus Rhine

Tablinium A room in a Roman domus that was open to both the atrium and peristylium. It contained family documents and was often used as an office by the dominus.

Tân Celtic, Fire, The name of a horse

Thamesis River Thames

Triclinium Dining Room in a Roman house

Vestibulum A long, narrow passage leading from the portico to the atrium.

AUTHOR'S NOTES

I have tried to be as historically accurate as possible in this novel, but I have found some aspects difficult to research. One example is about the bathing of slaves. I came across one source that said that slaves did bathe, but not how often, and I could find out little about the bathing in private houses, although some of the plans I looked at had baths in them so I assumed they did bathe at home on at least some occasions.

Most Romans used the public baths because it was a social and business event as much as a cleansing process.

In the country villas, though, I imagine that the domestic baths were used, as there was not usually a public bathhouse near enough to visit daily.

I wanted to have a new governor to ask for Avelina, so I took the liberty of moving Agricola's appointment as Governor of Britannia from 77AD to 80AD

For the names of the Britons, I have used Celtic names that I found on-line, in the main, Welsh, although the name taken by Adelbehrt--Ailbert, is Scottish. It was the nearest to Adelbehrt that I could find. The names of Adelbehrt and Avelina, as well as Odila, are ancient Germanic names, again found on-line.

Everyday life in the villages of the Britons was also difficult to find out about. There is plenty of information about the Romans in Britain and about the Romanised Britons, but not much about the Britons who were not Romanised: how they lived, what they thought about the new crops the Romans had brought with them and what crafts they plied. There is also some confusion about whether or not the Britons used bows and arrows. Some sources said they did not, but others that they did. I have assumed that they did use them.

When talking about the building of the houses, I have used familiar measurements rather than the measurements that would have been used by the Celts as this will give people a clearer idea of the size of the things used.

Thanks to the You Tube video of the building of a Celtic round house at Llynnon Mill on Anglesey, and to Wikipedia for many other things about Roman history.

It is important for authors that they get reviews of their work. There are so many books being published nowadays that to get word out about any one book is extremely difficult.

I would therefore be extremely delighted if you could spare a couple of minutes to review Vengeance of a Slave.

It needn't be an arduous task. Just a few words as to whether you enjoyed the book and what you found particularly enjoyable.

Thank you for your time.

If you want to read some of my thoughts, background to this and other novels and more of my writing, you can visit my blog.

http://aspholessaria.wordpress.com/

ABOUT THE AUTHOR

V.M.Sang was born in Northwich in Cheshire, UK. and grew up in an idyllic place for children. With her friends she used to go out to play in the woodlands around the area. Of course, people were less anxious about what might happen to their children in those days. Not that they cared less, it was just that there seemed to be less to worry about.

While she was growing up she was a tomboy. She climbed trees, played hide and seek in the woods, dammed the streams, searched for caterpillars and butterflies, learned about the birds and wild animals and picked wild flowers. (That was not illegal then, of course.)

She always loved being with animals, especially dogs. She had a border collie and a corgie while she was growing up. Not at the same time, though.

When she grew up she went to teacher training college where she studied science with maths and English as subsidiary subjects. Here she joined the Hiking Club and on a hike to Kinder Scout in Derbyshire, she met her future husband.

During the time she brought up her children,she took up painting and a variety of crafts. She still does them when not writing. One of her favourites is tatting, a craft that not many people seem to do these days, which is a pity as it's quite easy and makes many very pretty things.

She now lives in East Sussex with her husband and enjoys the company of her grandchldren.

You might also like:
Stone and Steel by David Blixt

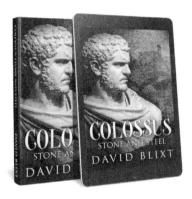

To read the first chapter for free, head to:
https://www.nextchapter.pub/books/stone-and-steel-
historical-fiction

Printed in Great Britain
by Amazon

81640281R00161